Women Like Us

Dan
Happy Reading!

Women Like Us

JASON POMERANCE

Published by Quill, an imprint of Inkshares, Inc.,
San Francisco, California
www.inkshares.com

Cover design by Marcia Parlow
Cover photograph "A Hint of Blue" © Claudia Domenig

ISBN: 9781942645108
e-ISBN: 9781942645252

Library of Congress Control Number: 2016935239

First edition

Printed in the United States of America

For C.J.R.P. and N.P.
and
For Sam Destro

I.

A revelation hit Susan Jones at the height of the barely controlled hysteria known in the restaurant business as dinner service. This thought—kind of a bombshell, the more she considered it—was crisp and clear, like the blast of bracing cold air that would slash at her face when she moved from the searing burners on the line to the giant walk-in refrigerator a few steps away. One more order of seared ahi, she thought, just one more, and I will cut open my wrists. I will walk out of this kitchen, right to the skinny girl in the miniskirt and stilettos who ordered it—because it always seemed to be the skinny girls in stilettos who ordered the ahi (their dates went with Wagyu steaks)—and I will spill blood all over the table.

Of course, the next words out of the mouth of the executive chef, also expediting that night, shouted at the top of his lungs, though he was only a few feet away, were to fire two more ahis, both rare, s'il vous plaît. And Susan didn't make a big scene or open up any veins, even though his use of French constantly annoyed her, because he wasn't French at all but had grown up in Illinois. "Oui, chef!" she answered brightly. She splashed olive oil into a screaming-hot pan. She grabbed a large pinch of coarse salt and let the grains rain down on the two slabs of fish, then gave them a few healthy grinds of fresh pepper. She laid them in the pan and let them sizzle while she prepped the plates, setting a few steamed haricots verts down one side next to a neat bundle of julienned carrots that had been simmered then tossed with sea salt and the giant globs of sweet butter that make restaurant food taste so delicious. She added a small cone-shaped mold of quinoa in the middle. She flipped the ahi and poked at it with a finger to assess its progress.

"It's not like I've done anything awesome with my life, have I?" she said to Bobby, the runner, who was standing at the ready to whisk off the order.

"What? What?" he answered in a panicked voice. He was a newbie, already addled and sweaty by the chaos of a kitchen at the peak of being slammed.

"Nothing. Forget it," said Susan.

She slid a spatula under the ahi, eased the pieces from the pan, and set them on the plates, the edges of which she wiped clean with the towel that she always kept tucked precisely into the apron string at her waist.

Bobby disappeared through the double doors, back to the hushed conversation and tinkling stemware of the dining room. And back went Susan—in between racing through three steak frites, one chicken special, and more and more ahi, between near collisions with her fellow cook on the line, between surly sneers of Beth at the salad station, who for some reason, when not artfully composing finicky plates of baby kale, didn't like her, between dodging the purposeful jostling of Jose, the horny dishwasher who never failed to make sure Susan could feel the hard-on in his pants—back went Susan to morbid thoughts about other ways of offing herself: Bullet to the brain? Overdose of sleeping pills? Carbon monoxide?

Because the truth was nothing had turned out the way she planned.

"I'm thirty-seven, I screwed up my marriage, and my son hates me," she said out loud to nobody in particular, but there was Bobby again with a look of terror on his face. Susan couldn't help it: she smiled. "Dude, if you want to make it in this business you really need to chill," she said.

He scurried off again, still terrorized, it seemed, and she even laughed a little. For a moment she forgot her troubles. Then the dark thoughts returned. She was supposed to have opened her own restaurant by now, but that hadn't happened. Guys she'd done stages with in bistros, grills, diners, cafés, and dives all up and down the East Coast were popping up on TV or with cookbooks of their own. One even had her own iPhone app, for God's sake. All Susan could manage was hopscotching from one line job to the next. She couldn't even work up the energy to blog. She hadn't bought that little house in the country she'd always fantasized about, the one with the weathered grey shingles, the garden, and the views of rolling green hills. All she had was her tiny one-bedroom rental in a ramshackle building filled with people either on their way up or down, and mostly down. Not that she blamed anybody for her misery, really. She had made choices in her life; they just turned out to be the wrong ones, now that she could look back on them. These bad decisions and missteps gnawed at Susan, keeping her awake at night long after flopping into bed at the end of her shift. In fact, sometimes all she could see down the road was poverty, decrepitude, and loneliness. She figured it made sense to just end it here and now.

And so later that night, at home in Brookline, Susan again started to formulate a plan. She sat down at her kitchen table, kicked off her shoes, and propped her achy feet up on a chair. She grabbed a pad and pen, having decided to make a list of the details that needed attending to before completing the deed. It occurred to her that number one on that list might be cleaning the place up so that when they found her corpse it wouldn't be too embarrassing. Because right now the apartment was a mess. The two potted ferns she had recently spotted at the market looking cheery and hopeful, the very ones she'd lugged home to brighten things up, were dead, dried foliage in sad, brown mounds on the floor. There was dust everywhere, unwashed laundry in a basket in the corner, piles of unopened mail, and a stack of cookbooks she'd ordered but still hadn't read, which now sat there in an almost reproachful way. The idea of setting everything right was exhausting. A drink might help, she thought.

She opened the cabinet over the stove and surveyed her inventory. There was a bottle of good vodka, but barely an ounce left. There was some pricey aged scotch an old boyfriend had left behind, but just the label gave her a headache. She tried to remember the man it came with, but all she could come up with was a vague musky smell and the flash of a dangerous grin. Behind the scotch was a nearly full bottle of Bacardi. In the refrigerator, she found simple syrup and a couple of decent limes. Daiquiri time. Into her cocktail shaker went a fistful of ice, followed by a couple of slugs of the rum. She reamed in the juice of a lime, added a little of the syrup, slapped on the cap, and started to shake, a process that made her think of her ex-mother-in-law, which brought to mind her ex-husband, and finally led to thoughts of Henry. Sometimes it troubled Susan that, occasionally, like when she was tired or distracted, she couldn't conjure up the face of her son, that she really had to think about what he looked like the last time she saw him. Then, when she did finally manage to picture his face, it was mostly simmering with disappointment. Part of her couldn't blame him. It's not that she didn't love him. She did. In spades.

It's not like she gave him up willingly. She didn't. It's just that she came up against a force she was unequipped to deal with when Andrew's mother, Edith Vale, decided that Susan, having given up on her marriage, was an unfit mother too. Fifteen years ago Susan wasn't sure the lady didn't have a point.

The daiquiri worked, the alcohol coursing its way almost instantly through her veins, calming her jangled nerves. Suddenly she wanted a cigarette to go with it. Susan wasn't a regular smoker—often, during a grueling stint manning the line, a cigarette was a nice way to break up the routine, an excuse to escape the scorching heat and blasting steam of the stoves. Now she rooted through kitchen drawers in search of a stray, and when she didn't find one, she decided to head down the hall and bum one from Mike. Near the door, though, a glimpse of her reflection in the mirror stopped her cold. The T-shirt she had thrown on at the end of work had unidentifiable stains, and the gym shorts weren't much better.

In the bathroom, Susan crammed the dirty clothes into an already overflowing hamper and then did something she found herself doing less and less because it was becoming somewhat alarming. She stood before the full-length mirror with nothing on at all and took a good, long appraising look at herself. She always wore her long hair the same way, pulled back tight, slicked down, and tied into a neat ponytail. It made her look competent and efficient, she thought, like a person to be trusted. Her hair had always been a pure deep ink-black, but lately silver strands were sneaking in at an ever-increasing rate. Her skin had a rosy flush to it, but that, she figured, was mostly due to heat and steam from the kitchen. Puffiness under her eyes made her frown until she remembered reading somewhere that frowning could deepen lines around the mouth. But it was recent developments further south that distressed Susan most. Her belly, always flat no matter what she ate, was beginning to expand into something she could almost call a roll. She grabbed at it and squeezed. Where did this come from, she wondered? And how was she going to get rid of it? Worse were the stretch marks staking claim to her breasts, once a source of pride, now cause for anxiety as gravity began to take a toll.

"All downhill from here," Susan said to her reflection. "Yes, I do have to kill myself."

Then she caught sight of something that always lightened her mood, her two tattoos, both the result of numerous Jäger bombs after long nights on the line. Every time she looked at them, she could recall that crazy morning-after feeling, the "what the fuck did I do?" sense of bewilderment. At her ankle was a tiny place setting—fork, knife, and plate. On a shoulder blade was a small, jaunty chef's hat. These were emblems (along with various cuts on her hands and burns on her arms) of the one thing she truly did love, despite her frequent complaining, the line cook's lament, really, of having to bang out the same dish perfectly hundreds of times. She loved to feed people, loved creating a delicious dish from raw ingredients, and the instant gratification of watching a person devour it.

A few minutes later, in a clean shirt and clean sweats, Susan headed down the hall and knocked on Mike's door. He opened it in plaid boxers and nothing else. Mike Finley once told Susan all about how he was a jock in high school—football in the fall, baseball in the spring—but he'd grown soft and paunchy. Still, his standing there nearly naked made Susan a little weak-kneed and fluttery.

"Can you spare a smoke?" she asked.

"Do you have company?"

"Why do you ask that?"

"I heard rattling around in your apartment. I heard ice shaking. That always sounds like a party to me."

"My, what big ears you have, Mr. Finley."

Mike smiled.

"I made a daiquiri. For me. And not one of those frozen ones. A classic daiquiri."

"Ah. What year is this, 1963?"

Susan smiled. "They're really good. Would you like to come and join me? I'll trade you one for a cigarette."

Back in Susan's kitchen, she poured Mike a drink, and they both sat at the table smoking. Mike Finley was an air traffic controller at Logan, which meant he was constantly under enormous amounts of stress. His shift was similar to Susan's, but when Mike would come home, unlike Susan, who often went comatose the instant her head hit the pillow, he would crack open a Budweiser, plant himself in front of his giant flat-screen, and watch all the sports he'd recorded from the week. Susan could sometimes hear cheering, razzing, and occasional belching all the way down the hall, but it didn't annoy her. It made her smile.

"Bad night?" he asked as Susan exhaled a huge cloud of smoke.

"Is it that obvious?"

"I had a bad night too," Mike said. "I nearly lost track of an Airbus inbound from Rome. I mean, one minute there it was, and the next, the dang thing had vanished from the radar screen. With two hundred and sixty-six souls on board."

"That would be a problem, wouldn't it?"

"You have no idea," said Mike. He took a really deep drag off his cigarette and tapped the ash into the empty soda can Susan dug from the trash.

"So my moaning about how many orders of ahi I had to plate seems pretty insignificant, huh?"

"I didn't say that. Anyway, turns out it was just some computer glitch again."

Susan nodded. "So," she said as she poured more daiquiri into both their glasses, "do you sometimes just hate your life?"

"Nope. Can't say that I do," Mike said.

"You don't have regrets? Things you did one way when you could have done them differently and everything would have turned out differently too?"

Mike cocked his head at Susan. "Are you ovulating, sweetheart?"

Susan attempted to burn Mike's hand with the end of the cigarette, but he swatted it away. "Maybe I'm just going through a phase," Susan said. "It just feels like everything these days gets on my nerves. The smallest annoyance can set me off, like if I run out of dental floss or a lightbulb burns out just when I happen to need it. Things like that just make me mad."

"Maybe we should get married," Mike said.

Susan rolled her eyes.

"What? I've shown you all my right-swipes on Tinder, haven't I? Lots of women would want me for a husband."

"Like the one who did have you as a husband and left without so much as a goodbye. She was a real winner."

"Now that was a mistake," said Mike and then thrust out his lower lip in a pout.

"I'm sorry," said Susan. "I shouldn't have brought it up."

"No, you shouldn't have. I mean, do I bring up the string of boneheads I've seen you hooking up with?"

"You're nice that way. No, you don't."

"Don't we have fun together?'

"Don't you think it's because we're keeping it casual?"

"Babe, that's always been your idea, not mine."

Indeed, Mike did pursue Susan more aggressively for a while. He'd be there casually checking his mail when she'd let herself into the lobby, or he'd take out his trash when she did. A couple of times, he even came into the restaurant. He wore a neatly ironed oxford shirt with a button-down collar and nicely pressed slacks instead of his usual jeans and a T-shirt. He had shaved, combed his hair, and slapped on cologne. He took a seat alone at a deuce by the kitchen. She'd catch quick glimpses of him as runners came in and out, and each time he seemed to be eyeing the food on his fork with suspicion. But he'd wink at her and pretend to like anything she sent out, even fancier plates, like foie gras she seared and served with a warm apple compote, or the little barbecued pork belly sliders she'd convinced the chef to add to the menu, slabs of rich braised belly that were crisped on the flattop, then slipped into warm, soft brioche buns and topped with slaw, followed by drizzles of a tart, vinegary sauce.

"Well, still," said Susan, "casual seems to work."

"Fine. You want to get naked? Because if you don't, I'm going to hit the sack. That casual enough for you?"

Susan considered her options. Then she reached out for Mike's hand.

***

Later, Susan let Mike spoon up against her, which was nice for five or so minutes before it got too hot and clammy. When he started to snore, she shoved him onto his back and poked at his chest. He still didn't stir, so she poked at him again and said, loud, "Hey, you sleeping?"

"Wha . . . huh?" he grumbled.

"You were snoring, actually."

Mike knew the drill. Without another word, he climbed out of her bed, grabbed his phone and keys, and lumbered drowsily toward the door.

"Hey!" Susan said.

He turned, looked at her hopefully, and made a move to hop back into bed. But Susan pointed at the floor, where his boxers had landed on the way in. He swiped them up and headed out.

Alone again, Susan pulled the covers up to her chin. She shut her eyes and tried to sleep, but her mind kept drifting back to ways of offing herself. Pills of some kind might work, she thought. Downers? What exactly are they, she wondered, and where do you get them? Then she worried she wouldn't keep the downers down and would wake up in some emergency room embarrassed or, worse, she wouldn't wake up at all, at least not completely; she'd hover in some vegetative state forever. She'd use a gun if she owned one, but getting her hands on a pistol seemed far too complicated. She was too strong a swimmer to drown herself unless she tied a weight or a large stone to her leg. That might work, but then she'd most likely need a boat.

She was racking her brain for more options when she caught herself staring at the one picture of herself and Henry she kept on the nightstand by the bed. It was taken shortly after his birth. He was swaddled in a huge fuzzy blue blanket, and all that was visible, aside from a portion of Edith Vale's hand, which Susan identified from the perfect manicure and the glint off a piece of bling, was a wedge of Henry's face, all pinched, shriveled, and shockingly pink. He seemed to look up at her in an accusatory way. Susan studied the picture, wondering for the thousandth time what Edie was pointing at, searching her own face for clues as to why things unfolded the way they did. All she could see was a very young person with a stunned, confused, and somewhat panicked look, as if she had wandered into this scene by mistake and somebody had shoved another mother's baby into her arms. It was nothing like pictures Susan had seen of mothers and their newborns over the years, the ones where mother and infant gazed lovingly into each other's eyes. In fact, it dawned on her now that perhaps this photograph should have tipped her off that there was trouble coming. Also, she wondered, deep down, if Henry would miss her if she was gone. She decided, before doing anything else, she needed to find out.

II.

One of Henry Entrekin's earliest memories was of his grand-mother throwing him into the pool at her house in Pasadena. Edith Vale did not like complainers or whining or indecision. She had no patience for people, no matter how small, who didn't behave the way she thought they should behave. Henry figured he must have been barely four years old. He could still recall the scent of jasmine wafting from the dense hedge at the rear of the yard, and he could still hear the frantic barking of her two Cavalier King Charles spaniels as she whisked him into her arms. It was a blazingly hot day, and Edie was saying to Andrew, his father, that it was about time that Henry learned to swim, and Andrew was answering that he was going to get around to it when Edie set down a glass with tinkling ice—a sound Henry would forever associate with her—bent close to Henry, and said, "You want to know how to swim, don't you, sweet pea?"

"No," Henry had answered emphatically. "I don't like the water."

"Oh, pooh," said Edie. "Everybody in this family swims and everybody finds the water simply divine."

Henry, already cranky from the heat, and hungry too because it always seemed like there wasn't enough to eat at Edie's house except the mayonnaise slathered on bread the maid would slip him, stamped his foot, burst into tears, and screamed that he'd rather die than get in the water.

Before he knew it, he was in her arms. He thought there might be soothing and comfort coming. He was wrong. He felt himself being raised up high, higher than what he always thought of as a large lamp shade, Edie's blond bouffant helmet of hair. Then he was sailing through air. Finally, there was the cool splash, a decided relief from the scorching heat. It felt good, actually. Until Henry opened his mouth and in came lungs full of stinging chlorinated water. He instantly began to choke and flail. Rescue came in the arms of his dad, who dragged him to the stairs of the pool and deposited him back on dry ground.

"You'll regret mollycoddling him," Edie said through the smoke of a Parliament as she marched back inside the house, yapping spaniels at her heels.

Although he eventually grew to love the water and even to surf somewhat decently at his grandmother's house at the beach, Henry sometimes wondered if all his insecurities and fears stemmed from that one moment. Certainly, he felt, it could be the root of some trust issues. Certainly it could explain a keen sense of caution, which is why he now found himself deep in the New Hampshire woods, his best friend, Zach Julian, at his side, the illicit stash seeming to burn a hole deep in the pocket of his regulation prep school blue blazer. Henry had just turned seventeen. So had Zach. Everybody else in the dorm had long started experimenting or, worse, were already stoners or borderline alcoholics, some might argue, but Henry and Zach, not a part of the popular or the cool set, watched from the sidelines until they finally worked up the courage to approach the upperclassman who was the rumored supplier for what seemed like the whole town and asked if they could buy a joint. At first, he suspected them of spying for the administration. Henry could understand the reaction. He looked like he could be a narc, he figured. Diagnosed at age six with an acute astigmatism, he had to ever since wear thick glasses that made him look like a dork. A large nose and ears that he felt stuck out too far didn't help. In fact, Henry always felt like an outsider, the lame kid whose mother was mostly absent, who lived with his dad at his grandmother's house.

The good news was he was largely left to his own devices at Mrs. Vale's; the bad news was the house was full of its own rules and rituals. Like the cocktail hour, a sacred time to his grandmother, it seemed. Henry was required to make appearances, trotted out in pressed slacks, a pressed oxford shirt and, if company was expected, a tie, and a dark blue blazer with gold buttons. He was taught to politely but firmly shake the hands of Edie's friends while looking him or her in the eye—directly in the eye—and these friends were allowed to fuss and coo over him for a few minutes, and then he would be marched back to his room with a stern warning to not make too much noise. If a gift came his way, Edie would sit him down and make him write out a thank-you note almost instantly, so fast, in fact, he almost expected her to hand-deliver it. He had to sit next to her at church on Sundays, sit still and not fidget, and remember all his pleases and thank-yous and yes-ma'ams and no-sirs. He had to remember to chew with his mouth closed, never ever talk with food in his mouth, and for heaven's sakes stop gulping his juice or slurping his soup. He always had to mind his p's and q's. Whatever the fuck that meant, Henry would think whenever his grandmother said it. Once, he pressed her on what exactly she meant by a p or a q.

She scolded him with a stern "Don't you take that tone with me, Mister Man."

He took most of his meals at the small table in the breakfast nook. Often, his father would still be at the office when he had dinner, but Mrs. Vale would sit with him, holding what she called a dressing drink, and she would quiz him about his day. She'd ask about the book he was reading, or she'd fire questions at him about current events as if he might have any clue about the news.

"What do you think about what the president said today, Henry?" or, "How about that situation overseas? Isn't it absolutely frightful?"

He learned that most of his answers had to jibe with Edie's views, that, apparently, there was Mrs. Vale's way of doing just about anything and then there was the wrong way. Also, his room had to be kept tidy and his closet organized. Certain drawers were for socks, and certain drawers were for briefs and T-shirts, and that was that.

Being sent away to boarding school was actually something of a relief. Indeed, Henry figured maybe he could make a fresh start. Gone would be the strange, reserved, and frequently uncoordinated goober who lived at Grandma's, the boy who was often the butt of cruel jokes or was bullied or taunted as gay, even though nobody would say that, Henry would think, if they knew the feelings he harbored in secret about Luz Guttierez. At a new school, he could reinvent himself altogether with a whole new background and personality that had no relation at all to reality, because who would know? Of course it didn't work. He couldn't truly escape or instantly turn himself into a star athlete or somebody witty. Then there were the letters from Edith Vale, weekly missives in her trademark slanted scrawl on her trademark engraved robin's-egg-blue stationery, encouraging him to study hard, mind his manners, keep his hair neatly combed, his nails clean, and never talk back to his professors. There was also this about Henry: he was always basically a loner, happy with a book or in front of the computer or playing a video game. He always had trouble making new friends. Though Zach Julian came from a more traditional background—he had two parents, heterosexuals, who were still married to each other—he occasionally stuttered, had an unruly cowlick, and generally felt as dorky as Henry, so the two had bonded long before they finally convinced the dealer they weren't miniature spies or narcs in training, and he sold them one measly little joint.

"You think we've gone far enough now?" Zach asked as they continued to slog down a narrow, muddy path. Henry could see he was beginning to sweat profusely and was in danger of breaking out in a rash.

Henry looked around. There was nothing but more woods as far as he could see. They had gone miles from campus, it seemed. "A little farther," Henry said. "Just to be on the safe side."

"Okay," said Zach, "but what if one of us has a bad reaction and needs an ambulance?"

"What kind of a bad reaction?"

"I don't know. Shortness of breath? Vomiting? Convulsions? Cardiac arrest?"

"You're such a hypochondriac," Henry said, but inside his nerves were beginning to gnaw at him too. He could feel it in the pit of his stomach. "Anyway, we'll just call 9-1-1. Or Snapchat somebody. Or shoot out a text."

"And tell them what?"

"I don't know."

"And what if we can't get reception out here?" Indeed, Zach held up his phone, then started moving it this way and that through the air. "See, no bars. Man, we're just screwed out here. Totally on our own."

"Look, do you want to just forget it?"

"Do you?" Zach asked.

"No," said Henry. "We've come this far. Let's just do it. I mean, I'm curious, aren't you?"

"Yeah. I guess."

Henry dug the joint out of his pocket. "You brought matches, right?"

"What?" Zach's eyes bulged like saucers. He started to stammer. Henry grinned and held up a lighter.

"Dude, I was kidding. Jeez, get a grip already."

Henry took a long look around to make certain they weren't followed. It was autumn, and while some trees were bare—blackish, spindly, and skeleton-like against a stark slate sky—orange and red leaves still clung to others. A breeze stirred up crisp whispers and eerie rustles. Satisfied they were alone, Henry lit the thing. He pulled smoke into his lungs and began to gag and cough like a maniac. "I think you have to hold the smoke in," Zach said.

"Duh," said Henry. "It's not that easy. You try."

Zach took a puff, then started hacking too, so hard that Henry started to fear he might bring up an intestine. When he could talk again, he said, "Maybe we should just call this off."

Henry insisted they try again. Soon they were like pros, passing the joint back and forth between them until, halfway down, they let it extinguish and lay back, staring up at the sky.

"So," said Zach, "are we high?"

"I don't know," said Henry. "I feel kind of funny. Light-headed, maybe?"

"Me too. Should we finish it? Can you overdose on this stuff?"

"I don't think so," Henry said. "Didn't your parents ever talk to you about it?"

"All they said was if anybody ever offers you booze or pot or any other kind of drug, all I have to do is refuse and keep in mind that I'm smarter than they are and don't need mood-altering drugs of any kind."

"And what did you say?"

"I said, why did you put me on Ritalin when I was five if I'm supposed to stay away from any mood-altering drugs?"

"And what did they say?"

"Nothing. My mom went downstairs to cook dinner and my dad turned on the TV and that was that. What did your dad tell you?"

"Nothing. It was my grandmother."

"What did she say?"

"Right before I left to come east, I was up in my room, just minding my own business, you know, and I hear her shrieking, 'Henry Andrew!' and I'm like, 'What?' and she pulls me into the library, which is where all the serious shit goes down, and she goes, 'Dear, one day some juvenile delinquent will approach you with drugs, because that's what juvenile delinquents do when they're not vandalizing property or robbing convenience stores or being loud and rude. When and if that happens, I want you to just say no, because drugs are for thugs and losers.' Of course, you have to keep in mind she had a big old cocktail in her hand. I'm fairly sure she was half-tanked at the time."

Zach nodded. Henry watched a large black hawk lift off from a branch above them. It circled overhead, crowing its disapproval, it seemed, before soaring off out of sight. He relit the joint and passed it back to Zach. They began to crack up over how they thought they might get caught and how insane that idea was when they were startled into near heart attacks by a booming voice from behind.

"What are you boys doing?"

Both exhaled huge plumes of smoke and turned around to see that the voice was coming from the associate dean of students and he was closing in on them fast.

"What do we do?" Zach whispered urgently.

At first Henry simply froze. All he could think was that he would always be this dumb loser. Finally, he said, "You know what we should do?"

"What?"

"Run."

III.

When Ronald Reagan was elected president of the United States for the first time, Edith Vale and her husband Anderson celebrated by purchasing a tank-like gunmetal-grey Mercedes with a turbocharged diesel engine. The Vales were part of a group of staunch California Republicans who banded together to raise the money needed to achieve victory, and after all those lunches and teas and dinner dances and golf tournaments, they felt they deserved a reward. Anderson Vale was long dead, but Edie still drove the Mercedes and still wore the three flame-red Galanos suits she bought that year in honor of Mrs. Reagan's installation as First Lady. The suits were still in pristine condition; Edith Vale knew all about acid-free tissue paper, padded hangers, and how to properly store couture. But the Mercedes, serviced for years by a silver-haired, increasingly deaf and cranky German named Hans, was loud enough to hear from blocks away, and despite Hans's loving care, had developed the tendency to belch black smoke like some clattery old-time locomotive. Which it was doing now, Edie noted after a glance in the rearview gave her a clear view of a dark cloud that seemed to be in pursuit as she drove west from Pasadena toward the coast.

Edie herself was in perfect shape. Although she would insist to anybody who might have the temerity—or the poor taste—to broach the subject that she was somewhere in her sixties ("Sixty-something!" she'd chirp jauntily and then quickly nudge the conversation to a new topic), the truth was she had passed seventy more than two years earlier. In fact, Edith Vale could scarcely wrap her mind around the real number. So she simply denied it. It didn't seem possible, even when sometimes she'd look in the mirror, especially early in the morning, and just like the cliché, she'd see the face of her mother. Then the thought would hit her—when her mother was Edie's age, she looked like an old lady, all stooped, knobby-boned and hunched, unable, it seemed, to move at anything faster than a worrisome, unsteady shuffle. Worse, she acted ancient, complaining constantly, for instance. Her soup was too hot or her tea too cold or the house was stifling or the damn mailman was late. That's what Edie remembered most, when her mother got old. It was the "damn" this and the "damn" that, the "Where are my damn glasses?" and "Turn up the damn TV." At the time, she wondered why her mother was so angry. Now Edie was starting to comprehend it. And then there was her sister Evangeline, younger than Edie, already losing her mind.

Meanwhile, although she'd never admit it, Edie's eyesight was getting weaker, and sometimes she could barely hear the voices on the other end of a phone call, so every other word out of her mouth seemed to be "What?" or there would be the occasional "Say that again." Sometimes these words came out in a thin, reedy, old-lady voice that startled her too. She had developed a sort of phobia of running into acquaintances or friends she had lost touch with, because the "How are you and so-and-so?" would inevitably turn into a litany of ailments—this one had back surgery or that one blew out a knee. Or that one was scheduled for a bypass while this one had the bad prostate, and yet another took the dreaded, inevitable fall. And of course, there was the morning dose of bad news that came with the obituaries: contemporaries or, worse, people younger than Edie dropping, sometimes it seemed, like proverbial flies. Edie's eyes would zero in on the causes: respiratory failure here, diabetes there. Cancer of this. Cancer of that. Cancer of some organ she'd never even heard of. She'd occasionally swear she'd stop looking at that section of the paper, just skip over the bad news altogether, and then she'd sneak a peek anyway.

But despite the issues with her eyes and ears, Edie's health was remarkably sound. She knew she should quit smoking, but wasn't her best and dearest old friend Oatsie O'Shea still puffing away after her bout with breast cancer? And then there was the cocktail hour, as Edie and her friends—the girls, as they referred to themselves, even though nearly all of them had passed the seventy mark—liked to call it, though often that hour would extend until bedtime. She felt physically formidable, strong, and steady from daily vigorous walks or the laps she'd swim in her pool. Well, she was robust and sound except for certain mornings when she wasn't, when various aches and pains plagued her, or she'd feel so tired she'd have to drag herself out of bed, or she'd have to take massive amounts of ibuprofen before she could even think of moving. Luckily days like that were still rare. Also, she was as fastidious as ever about her appearance. She wouldn't dare leave her house looking careless or sloppy. Like right now, just driving up to the house at the beach to rescue her son from yet another crisis, she was all decked out in a beige Carolina Herrera cashmere sweater set paired with slim, tailored Herrera slacks in black. She wore a strand of kicky Kenneth Jay Lane faux pearls around her neck.

Her blond hair was teased and shellacked into a bouffant, perhaps just slightly smaller than the one Andrew would remember from his childhood.

"What day is today?" This came from Evangeline, strapped into the passenger seat.

"It's still Tuesday, dear. For the third time in under an hour."

Asking the same question repeatedly as she was doing now or waving indiscriminately at other drivers or pedestrians on street corners and then sticking her tongue out at them, a new habit, were minor annoyances Edie tried to take in stride.

"You're going to get us in trouble," Edie said, as one particularly nasty looking driver responded to the waving by giving them the finger. Then Edie noticed a tiny bubble of drool at the corner of Evangeline's mouth. She handed over a Kleenex from her bag. "And please wipe your lips."

It wasn't always like this. When they were growing up, Edith and Evangeline Lee were known for their knockout good looks and the whispery voices with which they shared their secrets. Their great-grandfather, Henry Phillips Lee, was born in a remote corner of the Scottish Highlands. He left because home was a stark and miserable place, and early on, he was infused with the spirit of adventure. That was one version of the story, anyway, a hearty, pleasant one told around a crowded dinner table or fireside in the library with cocktails. Another version had to do with rumors that he was a rogue, a crook, some even said, and that he fled because he was on the verge of being tossed in jail. Edie stuck to the first version of the story if anybody asked, stuck to it so stubbornly and for so long that she had come to believe it was true. Not that it was anybody's business, mind you, Edie would think when people might pry, and they always did. In fact, the loss of privacy—the lack of boundaries really—in this day and age was appalling to Edith Vale.

One recent afternoon, Henry, eyes glued to his computer, yelled out, "Mrs. Vale, why do the next-door neighbors pay three times the property taxes you do when their house is smaller?" and Edie was astonished to discover that right there, for all of Pasadena to see, were real estate records going back decades. She had no use for all this technology; indeed, she was dragged kicking and screaming to computer use, only giving in sometime after having taken over the care of Henry and having to communicate with other mothers via e-mail to coordinate schedules and carpool.

"Really," Edie would tell anybody who would listen, "everything was so much nicer when people took the time to write notes," and the other mothers would look at her like she was mad.

Of course, e-mail (and the occasional text if she had her glasses on and the light was just right) did seem more immediate and convenient at times, and Edie secretly felt somehow more current, plugged in, capable, and yes, younger than most of her friends because she actually knew more than just how to turn on the machine and no longer approached the thing like it might explode if she touched the wrong key. But when she ordered Henry to find a way to expunge all public records of the family, she found it was impossible.

And Henry, for a middle school class project, had even dug up facts Edie didn't know. Like the exact year that his great-great-grandfather arrived in America or obscure records on his purchase of a piece of land in the Nebraska Territory almost as stark as the one he had left. Henry Phillips Lee next surfaced in those old records in California, in the northern part of the state during the gold rush. Family lore had it that Lee didn't strike gold in the mines of the northern part of the state, and so he turned south, landing in Pasadena on a hot, dry, crystal-clear day in January, marveling that he could take in the sun in his backyard—which he liked to do naked and slathered in oil and to hell with what the neighbors might think—and at the same time could see the snow-capped San Gabriels, could almost reach out, it seemed, to touch their tips. Henry Phillips saw the future in this place, saw the future in the horseless carriages that were quickly becoming the rage. Slowly, he began to amass a fortune, opening the first in a string of auto dealerships that ultimately spiderwebbed across the San Gabriel Valley.

Their grandfather, Henry Andrew Lee, grew the business all through the early half of the twentieth century until he dropped dead while teeing up at Brookside, and so the business passed on to their father, H. A. Lee Jr. Junior appreciated the money the dealerships threw off month after month but had a problem with actual work. One by one the businesses slipped through his fingers into the hands of men with far greater ambition, one of whom also took his wife, who tossed her husband out when Edith and Evangeline were barely in their teens, which is something most mothers just didn't do in those days in a small, conservative town like Pasadena. So while people rarely said anything to their faces, Edith and Evangeline felt a sting, something that set them apart from their friends and brought them closer. Their father's one saving grace had been a nose for real estate; over the years he had managed to acquire some prime holdings, the best of which were cherry-picked by Edie's mother—the family compound in Pasadena, the cottage on the beach at Trancas, and assorted other commercial buildings and well-situated lots. But by the time their mother died, Pasadena and Trancas were the only two parcels left, the rest long ago sold off to pay back taxes or raise much-needed capital, and the lot in Pasadena was slowly, over the years, reduced in size, from seven acres to six, to four, to two, to one, and finally to one-half acre plus pool. When Evangeline married, she and her husband bought their own home in neighboring

San Marino, but Edie stayed on in the house they grew up in through her first and then her second marriage.

Now, all these years later, she was sharing the place with her widowed sister again, Evangeline moving in once Edie had to face the signs that all was not well, that Evangeline could no longer live alone. Edie would go over to Evangeline's house and find jewelry in the refrigerator and empty soup cans in the dryer. Paint was peeling from exterior walls, and the gardens had gone to seed. Once, Edie brought her spaniels to the house; they got into the basement and were sprayed by the family of skunks that had nested down there. Bills went unpaid. Groceries rotted in cupboards. For somebody as organized and, well, anal about things as Edie, this was all like a form of torture. She ran her own house like a tight ship. Everything had its proper place. For a time, she tried to make things right at Evangeline's, but it was a losing battle, Edie knew. Then came the morning Evangeline left for her walk wearing no pants and, worse, no panties, waving gaily to passing motorists, wondering at all the shrill honking and irritating screech of brakes. Edie was called by the Pasadena police to come and fetch her. She had, that day, a scheduled luncheon with her girlfriends. As always she had taken great care in dressing, selecting a fine black-and-white herringbone Chanel suit that was almost as old as her son. Edith was proud that her figure still hadn't changed in all those years. So when she saw her sister sitting in the police precinct looking so small, confused, and messy in an officer's well-worn sweatpants and sweatshirt—Like some crazy old bag lady, was the thought that flashed, shockingly, through Edie's head—she nearly passed out.

When these symptoms first began to appear, Edie simply got mad because that was the way she dealt with things that got on her nerves or were annoying or unpleasant. Or they'd laugh about what they thought were the tiny indignities of growing old—"Ha ha ha, Evie, you wet your pants again!" or, "Ho ho ho, dear, what fun burning the house down would be because you took a nap after putting the kettle on to boil!" As things grew steadily worse, Edie summoned Evangeline's daughter from her home near Scottsdale, but Gigi's idea was to simply park her mother in a convalescent hospital and be done with it. Edith Vale might be many things—vain, egotistical, slightly demented after a few too many Manhattans in the evening hours, but she couldn't imagine her sister in one of those places, and so she decided they would live together with Blanca, Edie's loyal Salvadoran housekeeper, quiet as a breeze but built like a fireplug, helping with the bathing and dressing and feeding. They installed Evangeline in her old room, and while Edie was sometimes comforted by the presence of her sister, at other times she felt ten years old again, that her life was on some curious loop from which she couldn't figure out how to escape.

Now as Edie pulled off the Coast Highway and onto the rutty narrow road, she could see Andrew waiting at the gate to the cottage. "Do you think this has something to do with cheating?" Edie asked as they approached.

"Oh, Gigi doesn't cheat at golf."

"No, dear. Focus. We've driven out here because Andrew said that Linda left and took the twins, remember?"

"I remember once taking a ride on a spaceship."

Edie let out a snort of frustration and wondered, for what felt like the thousandth time, why she bothered. She maneuvered the Mercedes into a parking place near the cottage built by her father in the 1930s, with its weathered grey shingles, pale green shutters, and its riot of red bougainvillea growing like crazy over a fence. When she and Evangeline were children, the street was just a string of small cottages—little beach shacks, everybody used to call them. Now, all but hers were gone. On one side of Edie's sat a huge two-story modern, all sharp angles and shiny corrugated metal, designed, she was told, by some architect whose name she could never pronounce, and on the other was an enormous boxy beige rectangle that resembled a bunker and was about as inviting. Her own little house looked under siege. Indeed, both neighbors constantly harassed her with outlandish offers to buy her place, only so they could expand their own, but Edie was having none of it.

Andrew approached to help her from the car. Her son, though nearing forty, was still handsome and lanky. His sandy hair was thinning in spots, but his features were sharp, his eyes the same liquid blue she remembered from when he was a toddler. She noted he wore a somewhat startled expression, as if he'd been slapped, and Andrew, a trusts and estates lawyer like his father once was, rarely seemed to get rattled by anything.

"Out of nowhere, I get a call about Henry possibly being expelled, and then, while I'm on the phone with the dean, I find this tacked to the fridge," he said as Edie took a breath of the bracing salty air she still adored.

It was a note, scribbled hastily, it seemed. *Dear Andrew,* she read, *I have to leave. I'm taking the twins.*

"Did you give her a reason?" Edie asked, not certain if she even wanted to hear the answer. In fact, she realized he was nearly the age his father, her first husband, Frank, was when he had his own midlife crisis and walked out on her. But the less she thought about Frank the better. He could still cause her blood to boil, even all these years later. "I mean, did you do something to upset her?"

"No, of course not," said Andrew, more than a little on the defensive.

"Well, didn't I warn you marrying that girl would be a mistake?"

"You really have to lecture me now, Mother? I mean, seriously?"

"No, I came to help you pack. You'll come home to Pasadena." She leaned back into the car and called to her sister. "Let's get a move on, dear."

Evangeline's eyes were closed. She seemed to be snoring. Edie turned back to Andrew. "We can leave her here. We won't be long."

Inside was a simple house, built for function, with the ever-present, somewhat musty smell of the ocean and stray bits of sand always in corners, no matter how often the place was cleaned. A large open room with scuffed oak floors and a stone hearth on one end was used for living and dining. Here and there were well-worn slip-covered sofas and chairs. French doors opened to a rather ramshackle deck that ran the length of the house and had steps down to the sand. There was a small, old-fashioned kitchen with dinged Formica counter-tops and cabinets that had sticky doors that never quite closed. Upstairs was always referred to as the dorm, an open space under the roof beams Edith's father had filled with sagging, squeaky cots for the various guests who would often overstay their welcome. Two other bedrooms and a bathroom and that was it. Now Edie marched into the living area, pausing only to pick up the rocking chair Linda had moved from where it had sat for the past few decades and put it back in what she considered its proper spot.

She plopped herself onto the sofa, fished in her pocket-book for a Parliament, and said, "Now what is this about Henry and . . ." But she broke off midsentence, narrowing her eyes at a small, nearly infinitesimal spot in a corner of the ceiling. "What," she said, "is that?"

"I don't know," said Andrew. "It looks like we might have a little leak in the roof, I guess."

Edie shot out of the sofa for a closer inspection. Indeed, she could see not just the small rust-colored stain but the paint bubbling and puckering around it. The fact that the house was coming apart at the seams, no matter how many things she fixed, annoyed Edie to no end. "Oh, for goodness' sake, Andrew, when did you notice this?"

"I'm not sure. A while ago?"

"What do I always say about moisture? Moisture is *not* our friend, especially out here at the beach. We're going to have to get Mr. Ritter out here immediately to fix that." She pulled a small weathered Hermès notepad from her pocketbook, along with a tiny silver pen and immediately set the thought down on paper before it flew out of her head, and then later, she'd lie in bed racking her brain, trying to come up with what it was that had bothered her. "Now where are your suitcases?"

"I don't know if I should go home with you."

"But your house is under renovation."

"Yeah, well . . ." Now it was Andrew's turn to break off.

"What now?" Edie asked, tapping a foot, growing impatient, glancing at her watch just to see how long it was until she could safely pour a cocktail.

Andrew pointed to the window. She could see Evangeline, now apparently awake, wobbling down the stairs to the sand, then bobbing and weaving dangerously close to the surf.

"Oh, she'll be the death of me yet," Edie practically shrieked as she and Andrew headed for the door.

By the time they made it outside, Evangeline was knee-deep and wading farther out to sea. Edie started yelling at her sister to come back, to no avail. Suddenly she had to step back to avoid getting her flats wet. Andrew shot her a disapproving glance.

"Well, these are Ferragamo, Henry Andrew," Edie said, using his full name to indicate she didn't want any back talk.

"Why isn't she home now anyway?" he asked, as Evangeline was now in almost up to her neck.

"Blanca's day off," Edie said.

"Well, clearly leaving her unsupervised in the car is not a good idea."

"I do the best I can," Edie said, exasperated. Then she called out to her sister. "Evie, you come back here this instant!"

Evangeline looked back and stuck her tongue out at her.

"You see what I have to put up with?"

"Don't play the martyr, Mother darling, it was your idea to move her in."

He was right. Still, Edie clucked, fussed, and said, "Go get her already."

She watched as Andrew took long, strong strides into the surf. He was always such a good athlete, and she felt somehow proud of that, unlike Henry, who seemed like an awful klutz. Andrew gently took Evangeline by the arm and started to lead her back to dry sand. For just a brief moment, the thought crossed Edie's mind that they should just let her go, just let her drift further out into the murky depths until there was no return. Just as quickly she banished the thought and scolded herself for allowing it to surface.

"What were you thinking, Evangeline?" Edie said as they got closer. "Now you're soaking wet."

"It was so hot in the car," said Evangeline. "I thought it might explode."

"I can find her some dry things in Linda's closet," Andrew said. "That is . . . um . . . if she left anything. I haven't checked yet."

"That won't be necessary," Edie said. "I've learned to carry extra sets of clothing in the trunk." She took her sister's hand. "Come along now. We'll get you changed and then head home."

When Edie said "home," a look of utter confusion washed over her sister's face, a total blankness she had seen before. It was scary, she thought, how a person could be there but seem like just a shell, the spirit vanishing in an instant without a trace. She wondered if she'd suffer a similar fate one day. She was about to ask Andrew if he'd take care of her if that came to be. But before she could get the words out, he said something about the water being so nice he was going for a surf. She watched him head down to the storage room below the house where they kept all the gear and realized she'd be on her own.

IV.

Of course, Susan's first thought when she threw on some clothes, called the restaurant to request a long-overdue vacation day, and hit the road was that she should text or e-mail or call ahead and tell Henry she was coming for a visit. But it occurred to her that he would ignore her as he often did. Sometimes he would get back to her a few days after her initial attempt at contact. This would mean she would have to try a second time, or even a third, and therefore always sounded peevish and exasperated, which would elicit a just as put-upon and weary-sounding "What did I do now?" from Henry or, worse, a "Jesus, Susan, just get over yourself already." So she decided she'd simply surprise him, although she now wondered at the soundness of that plan. Raised mostly by his grandmother under the strictest of schedules, Henry never seemed to appreciate the element of surprise. On the other hand, she thought as she drove north and into New Hampshire, maybe Henry would be happy to see her. After all, she reasoned, he was a full-on teenager now, subject to sudden, abrupt, and random changes in mood. It was certainly possible. Sometimes it would seem Henry couldn't stand the sight of her, but other times, he seemed to tolerate her presence. You just never knew. Anyway, the more she thought of her son, the more her mind kept wandering back to that summer when she met his father and unexpectedly wound up pregnant. She wasn't even looking for a boyfriend when she came upon him fighting a wicked riptide in the roiling surf off Lighthouse Beach, but there he suddenly appeared before her, arms and legs flailing, panic setting in, startling her at first.

"You know," she said after she realized it was a person and not some large, strange fish, "if you swim parallel to the shore instead of toward it, you'll get past the undertow."

"I know that," Andrew sputtered, relieved to find her next to him so that he wouldn't, in fact, die alone, he told her later, "but I never actually had to test it. Are we sure it works?"

"It does," Susan said. "Follow me."

She swam and he followed until she could feel the undercurrent no more. Together they hit the beach and flopped down on the sand, Andrew all sheepish and more than a little embarrassed, explaining that normally he could swim through just about anything but that he had a crashing hangover and was therefore a bit foggy in the head. She thought his mortification was a little sweet, and while she toweled her hair, she looked him over. He was tall, lanky, with large ears and a big nose. He had deep blue eyes she figured she could get lost in and long light brown shaggy hair. He reminded her a little bit of the clumsy puppy that had once belonged to the next-door neighbor of the aunt who had raised her after her parents died.

Somehow, while she wasn't paying attention, they became a couple, just sort of fell into a rhythm of being together without a whole lot of analysis or discussion, which was just fine with Susan, actually. Unlike other girls she knew, she didn't want to cuddle and didn't need to talk, sometimes endlessly, about issues with men or dating or sex. Occasionally she'd wonder if she was missing some chromosome, but even that much self-analysis would irritate her, and she'd put it out of her mind. Anyway, she and Andrew just seemed to enjoy each other's company. They went to movies. They scarfed down greasy cheeseburgers. They chugged shots of Jäger with beer chasers. They got stoned and had sex in the laundry-strewn, vaguely moldy, crumbling old saltbox with slanted floors he shared with five other guys who had gone to college with him and now were all in law school. Quickly they progressed to that stage where they could poke fun at each other. Like when Andrew would imitate what she always considered her mild Boston accent, the flattening out of vowels or dropping her r's. She would throw it right back when, for instance, he might refer to her as "dude," a result of growing up in California, clearly. Soon they had little nicknames for each other. Andrew called her Snarf, which had somehow progressed from "enough," because he had discovered that she loved when he nuzzled at her neck, even when his scruff caused a rash. She'd laugh and scream, "Enough!" "It's enough!" But once, after too many beers, it came out funny, like "Snuff!" which somehow morphed into Snurf and then Snarf, which stuck. She started calling him Bard, because once he tried to impress her by insisting he was big on Shakespeare, which was bogus, it turned out, but Bard somehow remained. Before Susan knew it, she had practically moved in with Andrew and was cooking him and his roommates breakfast too. It turned out she didn't mind that particular chore. Fresh from her junior year at Tufts with an eye toward becoming a veterinarian, Susan began the summer working as a waitress in an old dive of a bar and grill in Chilmark, but one day the boozy cook failed to appear and the owner ordered Susan into the kitchen to make the chowder.

"You mean, like, open the cans, and pour them into a pot, right?" Susan had asked.

"No, I mean make the chowder, dear."

"I don't know how," Susan protested.

"Recipe's taped to the wall," came the reply. "Any moron could do it."

Susan headed into the kitchen and there it was, printed in fading blocky letters on a yellowing slip of paper that said "Vineyard Notion and Drug" across the top. She read it with some trepidation, but the recipe seemed straightforward enough: salt pork, diced onions, crumbled pilot biscuits, cubed potatoes, milk, cream, and chopped clams. Susan assumed the clams would at least come in a can. She was wrong again. There on the floor sat a fat sack of quahogs. She reached in and picked up one clam that was partially open. It snapped shut in her hand. She marched back out to the owner. "I'm sorry," she said, "but those clams are alive."

"Yeah?"

"Listen, I go to Tufts, as you saw from my application. And I was figuring I wanted to be a vet, you know, and they have this really great school for veterinarians? But I have to be honest with you. I've been thinking of changing course altogether because next year I have to take a class in dissection, and I'm not sure I really want to do that."

"You eat chowder, hon?" asked the owner.

"Oh yes. Only the New England kind, though. I don't like the red. Or the Rhode Island."

"And you understand the clams that are in the chowder are dead, right?"

"Well, yes."

"I'm only saying because you can try asking, politely as punch, but you know them clams don't jump into the pot on their own."

So Susan followed him back into the kitchen, and he walked her through steaming open the clams, sieving the broth, and then using it as the base for the soup. She mastered the process and was promoted to full-time chowder maker. When it turned out the bar's regular cook hadn't shown up because he'd actually been dead for days in his bed, she took over the grill and the flattop. The place didn't serve anything complicated: hamburgers, hot dogs, chowder, lobster rolls, crisp skinny fries, and onion rings, and Susan found she liked being in the kitchen, a tight little space to be sure, but a space of her own safely removed from the drunk patrons trying to grab at her ass. She learned to know when to flip a burger just by looking at it, at the little beads of moisture that formed on top and meant it was nicely browned and crusted on the bottom, and soon she could tell with just a quick poke if it was rare, medium, or well-done. She learned that timing was everything in a restaurant kitchen. One minute there would be no orders. Then she would get slammed. She'd be pulling potatoes from the deep fryer and sprinkling them with salt while topping one burger with cheese and another with onions; meanwhile, there was that hot dog on the grill next to a buttered bun waiting to get stuffed with lobster salad, all of this happening in the same instant.

Still, she found the time to get creative; she started experimenting with different cheeses and toppings on the burgers, for instance, and though some old-timers grumbled from their stools at the bar, Susan found cooking a satisfying outlet unlike almost any other she'd experienced so far. She'd finish off a plate, watch the newly hired waiter whisk it off, and continue to watch as the customer happily dug in. She liked the camaraderie of the kitchen, the lively, though often just plain filthy, banter between her and the small Portuguese man who washed the dishes and pots and pans. Of course, there was a downside. After her first night manning the kitchen, banging out order after order, she thought her feet might actually fall off. Constant heat and steam turned her face the color of the lobsters she would pull from their vat after twelve or so minutes of vigorous boiling. Andrew would tease her about it. He would come to the bar, sometimes alone and sometimes with his buddies, one of whom hooked up with Susan's roommate at the guesthouse they were sharing. Part of her resisted the growing relationship, and part of her longed to have Andrew rubbing her back after a long night or massaging those aching feet. And so they stayed a couple until Susan woke up one morning to find it was the end of August and the summer had somehow slipped away. She assumed she and Andrew would break up too; it was a summer fling, she figured, casual and easy.

While they brushed their teeth side by side—a somewhat disturbingly familiar act, Susan was thinking—he said, "You have a couple of weeks before classes start, right?"

"Yeah," Susan said.

"Come to California with me."

"What?"

"I'm going to spend about a week at my mother and stepfather's. I may drive up to see my dad in Sonoma. It'll be fun. Like a road trip. Except, of course, we'll fly from Boston to LA."

Susan rinsed her mouth, then briefly debated what flossing together meant.

"We haven't even been off the island. You think we're ready for a big trip together like that?" she asked.

"Why not? I've already stopped feeling embarrassed about passing gas or burping in front of you, so I'd say we're good."

Susan took another moment to silently deliberate on what that all meant and still couldn't come up with a reason not to go. She did have free time before reporting back to school. She didn't have any plans. "I've never been to California," she said.

Andrew just grinned. "You will so love my mother," he said.

Soon she found herself on a plane west. When they landed, she realized something wasn't right. It was that moment when the plane lurched to a stop at the gate and two hundred bodies rose at once and packed into the aisle, each one apparently determined to be the first person off, as if some prize was to be awarded. Susan found herself wedged between a heavyset man who somehow leapfrogged past Andrew and a stooped, smiling elderly woman who wore too much of a scent heavy with lavender. Susan started to gag and felt like she might faint. The sensation passed and was forgotten the minute they stepped out of the terminal at LAX. When they took off from Logan it was sticky and humid, the air thick as molasses, but here, at twilight, it was refreshingly cool, dry, and breezy. The setting sun cast an orange glow that filtered through swaying palms. Susan was already somewhat disoriented—ten minutes from touchdown, she had peered out the window and they were over mountains, followed by what seemed like an endless sea of houses, many with little blue dots behind them that Susan realized were pools, then the plane banked and gave her a first glimpse of a shimmery Pacific. Now she slowly took in the palms and the setting sun as if she'd set foot on a different planet.

"Are you okay?" Andrew asked.

"Yeah," she said. "It just feels different here. The air feels different."

"That's because it is."

She couldn't see much on the way to Pasadena, as it had grown dark, so she sat back, let Andrew take her hand, and felt strangely safe and protected, as if the car his mother had sent was their own little cocoon. Soon the car exited the freeway. It cruised down a busy main road and then a small quiet street lined with stately old oaks, their spreading limbs forming an impenetrable canopy overhead. The car turned into a long gravel driveway, which curved up a small hill lined with dense green cypress and ended in a small circle before the front door of the house, a sprawling Monterey Colonial that had caught the attention of Andrew's grandfather all those years ago. One of the few in Pasadena designed by Paul Williams, it was a classically proportioned structure with thick white walls, hidden balconies, and a second-story veranda that ran the length of the house.

"Wow," said Susan as they stepped out of the car, and she thought back to her aunt's tidy little row house in Brookline where she spent most of her childhood. "I should have known you were a rich kid."

"Really? How should you have known that?"

"Well, you drive a crappy car, and you never have any cash," Susan said.

Andrew smiled and led her through the front door into the center hall, which was lined with black-and-white marble and featured a staircase that wound gracefully up to the second floor. The first thing to hit Susan was the smell, a curious but somehow pleasing combination, she would later learn, of beeswax furniture polish, Murphy's Oil Soap, and Windex, all of which were used daily to keep the house spotless. They could hear hushed conversation, the tinkling of glasses, and the clacking of cutlery coming from the dining room, a gracious space candlelit for a small dinner, a fund-raiser, it turned out, for some Republican candidate for governor. Edith Vale sat at the head of the table in a smart houndstooth suit, a triple strand of pearls, real ones, at her neck. At the foot of the table sat Anderson, her husband, blissfully unaware he didn't have long to live. Edie's sister, Evangeline, was there, along with another couple whose names flew right out of Susan's head, although it would take a while for her to forget the woman's highly shellacked bouffant, even loftier than Mrs. Vale's, and to her right, the silver comb-over on the husband so precise it looked like it might shatter.

"So, this is the girl we've been hearing so much of," said Edie through a smile that, to Susan, seemed clenched awfully tight. "Her name is Susan, and she goes to Tufts, where she's studying to be a vegetarian."

"Veterinarian, mother," said Andrew.

"Well, please join us," said Anderson Vale, who stood, then looked around, befuddled.

"Blanca!" Edie trilled, and out from the kitchen marched a short, powerfully built woman with jet-black hair in a starched grey uniform so stiff Susan could hear the material rustle. She carried a tray with two plates.

Susan was seated opposite Andrew and looked down at rare roast beef, creamed spinach, boiled carrots, and mashed potatoes, and when she poked at the meat, it was so rare and bloody a wave of nausea washed over her again. This time it didn't pass, and as she listened to the second bouffant say what a shame it was that as a vegetarian she couldn't eat such delicious beef, she realized she had to act fast. She leapt from the table only to realize she had no idea where to go, and by the time she spotted the open door to a powder room off that center hall, it was too late. A half-digested airline meal made a second appearance all over that gleaming black-and-white marble. Susan could distinctly make out a chunk of the roll she had struggled so hard to butter only to snap the plastic knife in half and wondered whether or not it could be digested at all. She would have laughed had she not been so mortified, as out of the dining room came Edie, Anderson, Evangeline, Andrew, the second clucking bouffant, the silver comb-over, and two frantically yapping King Charles spaniels, one of whom snapped up the chunk of roll and ran in a sort of fancy prance of triumph. All of them were trailed by Blanca toting a bucket and a mop. Susan simply ran up the stairs, then into the first room she came to and slammed the door. She rolled onto the bed and she started to laugh because the situation seemed so absurd and she could imagine how insane she looked. Just as suddenly, she began to sob. Then slowly the idea hit that maybe, just maybe, she might be pregnant.

"Holy crap!" Susan said out loud and sat bolt upright because it also dawned on her that not only was she indeed late, but the reason she buttered that roll so hard was that sudden ravenous hungers had been appearing out of nowhere, that she had felt somehow off-kilter hormonally for days, if not longer. "Holy crap!" she said again.

"What?" Andrew had chosen that moment to poke his head in to check on her.

"Um," Susan managed, "what?"

"Are you okay? I mean, I didn't think it would be so nerve-racking for you to come here. Try to chill out a little. Anyway, Mummy said not to worry. Freddie threw up on that same spot this morning too."

"Freddie?"

"One of the dogs. She's got them so wound up one of them is always barfing or has diarrhea."

"It may not be nerves," Susan said.

"Oh. Flu?"

"I don't know. Yeah, maybe. Or that food on the plane."

Andrew sat next to her and softly stroked her hand.

It was a kind and generous gesture, considering, Susan thought, and suddenly she felt the need to confess. "Or . . . well, there's a slight chance that—now don't panic, I'm far from positive—but I guess I could be pregnant."

Andrew looked like he was trying to conjure up some sort of response. His mouth formed an almost perfect little O and stayed that way. There was a sound from him, like air deflating from a burst balloon, and somewhere the loud ticking of a clock. "We were careful. Weren't we? We took precautions," he finally said.

"Except that one night on the beach when . . ." Her voice trailed off. Better not go there, she thought.

Andrew nodded, then said, "Maybe it's fate."

"Fate?" said Susan.

"You know, like, destiny. Maybe we were meant to be together, um, forever."

"Or we were just careless, drunk, and stupid," said Susan.

Actually, had she been paying closer attention, she might have realized right then and there that they were totally unsuited to each other. Susan was a realist. She saw life in more pragmatic terms. She could be independent and smart about things, but she could also be impulsive. Andrew, on the other hand, was methodical, a little stodgy, she'd later learn, and, well, something of a mama's boy. Still, he was cool and collected about the whole mess while she felt frazzled and scattered. She debated telling him that she'd take care of everything, that she'd handle it, but before she could get the words out, his mother's head poked into the room.

"Everybody feels absolutely awful, dear," said Edie. "Shall I ask Blanca to bring up some consommé? I keep scads of it in the freezer at all times because Mr. Vale has a very sensitive stomach too. Do you know that Julia Child herself—who by the way grew up two blocks from here and in grade school was quite chummy with my mother—Julia gave us the recipe when she came to town for a high school reunion!"

Susan was still trying to process the idea of scads of consommé as Edie sat down on the bed, bringing with her the competing scents of Parliaments and her perfume of choice, Joy. Susan started to gag again.

"Oh, she is looking green, Andrew."

"She might be pregnant."

Susan pulled a pillow over her head. "Oh my God," she said, but it came out muffled.

"What did you just say?" Edie asked Andrew.

"She thinks she's going to have a baby. Or, well, we're going to have a baby, I should say."

Susan removed the pillow. "You know what? It is probably something I ate on the plane. I'm sure of it. That . . . um . . . chicken I think it was . . . it was way past room temperature . . . a breeding ground for bacteria. So, yeah. Food poisoning. I think."

"Do your nipples feel tender, dear?" Edie asked.

Susan's silence was confirmation enough, although she wasn't sure whether it was because of what it all meant, or that here was this perfect stranger asking about something that seemed so intimate. Edie didn't wait for confirmation anyway. She rose briskly and headed out the door. There was the sound of her heels clickety-clacking against the hardwood floors of the hall, then down the stairs. Five minutes later, there came the clicking of heels again, and Edie returned, a Manhattan and a Parliament in one hand, her weathered Hermès pad and slim sterling silver pen in the other.

"I've sent those boring old toads home so we can have some good quiet time," she said. "After all, we have a wedding to plan."

This time it was Susan's mouth frozen in that O. "You want to . . . what?" she finally managed.

"Plan a wedding," said Edie. "After all, you are having my grandchild. Now give me your mother's number. She'll want to be in on this for sure."

Susan looked to Andrew for help, but he was now taking drags off his mother's Parliament and drinking her Manhattan. "My mother's dead," said Susan. "So is my father." Edie regarded her for a long moment now, and it was as if Susan could read her thoughts: Bad genes. Lousy DNA. So, for good measure, she added, "They died in a car wreck when I was a kid. It wasn't even their fault. It was a drunk driver."

"Oh, my," Edie said. "Well, there must be somebody I should call."

"My aunt Louisa raised me," she said. "My dad's older sister."

Edie smiled, put pen to paper.

"Unfortunately," Susan continued, "she passed away last year." Again Edie seemed to be looking at her critically. "She fell off a ladder," Susan felt it necessary to add, "while stapling Christmas lights to the eaves of her house. She leaned too far forward or something, and that was that. Although the coroner thought she might have had an aneurysm."

"Ah," Edie said. Although now, to Susan it was as if she was thinking, Ah. Silly, unlucky people. She watched as Edie wrote in her notepad, No family, and underlined it twice.

From that moment on, it seemed as if she and Andrew were travelers in some alien city who lost their way, who missed the train that made local stops and wound up on an express from which there was no exit. Not that Susan didn't seriously consider simply ending this unplanned pregnancy once she got to a drugstore, peed on a stick, and confirmed that there was, indeed, a baby. She snuck the local phone book from its nook in Edie's kitchen, located the nearest clinic, and set up an appointment. When Andrew left with his mother on an errand, she called a cab and asked to be driven there. She sat on a hard plastic chair and filled out the forms. She went through a counseling session and signed what seemed like endless amounts of even more disclaimers and forms. She flipped through an old magazine and tried to pretend it was nothing, like a teeth cleaning or a simple checkup. But she couldn't meet the gaze of anybody else in the room, and when a nurse called her name, she got up, bolted for the door, and didn't look back. It wasn't as if she felt life growing inside of her; it was too early for all that. It wasn't religious grounds. Susan had been raised a Methodist, which was a bit more liberal about these things, but Aunt Louisa was lax about churchgoing, and Susan had sort of let the whole thing fall by the wayside. It was something else altogether, something she didn't realize at the time—it was that a baby would never leave.

And so she went back to Pasadena. Andrew was waiting at the front door when she got out of the cab. It turned out he and his mother had driven to the house on the beach. He was wearing flip-flops, board shorts, and an old ratty T-shirt. His shaggy hair smelled like brine and sand, his skin like Coppertone.

"Where did you go?" he had asked.

"I have to be honest with you, Andrew," said Susan. "I was going to . . . you know . . . take care of things."

"Is that what you really want?"

"I guess not. I couldn't go through with it," Susan said. "But I sort of figured that's what you'd want."

"I don't. Not at all. In fact, the more I think about it, the more I can't wait to be a dad."

"But this is crazy. I'm not even done with college. You aren't finished with law school."

"I have one more year. We can deal with it."

"Then there's the fact that we don't even live in the same city."

"You could transfer."

"Actually, I may not have mentioned it, but my grades kind of suck. Transferring probably isn't an option."

"I could transfer then. Or we can commute. New Haven to Boston isn't all that far."

"There's always adoption, I guess," Susan said, although even the words left a funny taste in her mouth, like she had bitten into something sour.

"You want to have a baby and then give it to some strangers?"

"No," said Susan. "But do you seriously want to get married? Because when you think about it, we don't really know each other all that well. We've spent one summer together. I mean, sure, we did practically live together toward the end, but still . . ."

"Here's the thing. I know enough to say I love you. I think I have since you saved me from drowning. There, I said it. I love you."

The words hung there in the air, it seemed. But he just looked right at her, his piercing blue eyes like bottomless liquid pools, and at that very moment, Susan felt like she truly did love him too. She saw them becoming a unit, something solid and unbreakable—she, Andrew, and the baby—they'd battle their way through the world together.

And so she found herself saying yes, yes she loved Andrew back. She agreed to everything about the wedding Edie put together in what seemed like record time, to the dress she picked out at Nordstrom, to the service at the old stone Episcopal church across from city hall where the family worshiped, to the food prepared by the caterers Edie hired, to the reception in her garden. Susan met Andrew's father, Frank, for the first time at the wedding, an older, softer version of Andrew, with wild greying hair and a discernible paunch. His khakis weren't pressed, and his blue blazer seemed a bit frayed, but there was a mischievous twinkle in Frank's eyes that Susan later looked for, and didn't quite find, in his son's. Back in the 1970s, after a Saturday morning tennis game, Frank Entrekin announced that he no longer had any interest in trusts and estates law and wanted to move north to Sonoma County to raise goats and make cheese. This didn't sit well with Edie, who promptly filed for divorce. Susan noticed Edie alternating between staring daggers at Frank and ignoring him.

They flew back east after the wedding, Susan still astonished to find how almost instantly her life had been transformed, as if some crazy wand had been waved over her head. Gone was the carefree college girl with no obligations, and here was a whole new person, married and pregnant. She suddenly lost all interest in classes, finding herself daydreaming or, worse, reluctant to even show up. She opted for a leave of absence, certain she would return and finish school at some point. With help from Andrew's parents, they rented an apartment in New Haven, a tiny walk-up with creaky floors that sat over a bagel store, and it was during these first few months that she developed a growing obsession with food. She had no morning sickness, no queasy feelings at all, except when she'd look in the mirror, see what was happening to her belly and her hips, and then want to cry. She did have cravings—sloppy cheeseburgers at Louis' Lunch one day, a clam pizza from Pepe's the next, and sometimes, even in the same day, a couple of pigs in blankets from the Yankee Doodle Sandwich shop. She began planning lunches at breakfast and dinners at lunch. Shortly after they moved into their apartment, Edie sent cookbooks, classics like The Joy of Cooking and The Gourmet Cookbook, but also—with the inscription, "Just for kicks, dear!"—Julia Child's Mastering the Art of French Cooking, volumes one and two. Susan first read them as if they were novels and then began cooking her way through the recipes. She tackled soups and soufflés, braises and roasts of all kinds. She found she loved not just the cooking, but the planning and shopping for their meals, making out the lists, pushing her cart through the aisles, and picking just the right eggplant or the perfectly ripe tomato. She'd present the results to Andrew, never an adventurous eater by his own admission, and he'd smile gamely and dig in, even if it might be sweetbreads or kidneys. Susan could judge the results by the requests for seconds or if there were remnants still on the plate he'd tried to hide.

When a part-time job opened up in the kitchen at the little bistro down the street from the apartment, she thought about taking it; she had been watching too much daytime TV when she wasn't shopping or cooking. She was starting to feel fat, lazy, and somewhat useless. Andrew worried about it being too much, but the more Susan thought about the job, the more intrigued she became. This was a more ambitious kitchen than the one on the Vineyard. Susan was hired as a part-time prep cook, and Jean-Paul, the owner, demonstrated almost everything she needed to know about knife skills one morning before her shift began, first showing her proper dices in small, medium, and large, then juliennes of different sizes, and finally the brunoise. Some days he'd drop a twenty-five-pound sack of potatoes at her feet and she would plop herself onto a stool and spend hours peeling and running them over a mandolin for the creamy, cheesy, superrich gratins that would be served at dinner. Jean-Paul saw a quick study in Susan, an eager student, and so he decided to promote her to omelet-making during lunch service.

"Watch close," said Jean-Paul.

"Yes, chef," Susan answered.

With one hand, he cracked three eggs into a bowl, added a dash of salt, a few grinds of pepper, and whisked vigorously, while with the other hand he ladled a small amount of clarified butter into his pan, letting it bubble and foam over high heat. When the foam subsided, in went the beaten eggs, and then it was all flick-flick-flicks of his wrist, moving the pan left, right, up, and down until the eggs set. With a couple more expert moves of the hand and wrist, he rolled the omelet into a neat cylinder onto a plate. He dusted it with finely chopped herbs.

"*Et voilà*," he said. "You do it now."

It took practice. Her first omelets stuck to the pan. Some were too runny; others nearly burned on the bottom. She rolled several right out of the pan onto the floor. Jean-Paul made her practice, over and over, rejects going to the rest of the staff for their midday meal, until finally she mastered the technique. Then he taught her variations: the *omelet aux duxelles*, filled with fragrant, finely minced, sautéed mushrooms, or *aux fromage*, this one oozing a thin layer of nutty melted Gruyère. When she wasn't working, she was watching Jean-Paul's wife, Ariel, making pastry or Jean-Paul himself breaking down chickens or filleting a whole fish. She was eager to learn more, but Christmas arrived, and she and Andrew flew back to Pasadena, where the following morning, Susan, who so far was finding pregnancy a breeze, woke up to terrible cramps and, even more frightening, bloodstains on the bed. With four months yet to go, she was in preterm labor, and while drugs stopped the contractions, strict bed rest was ordered for the duration.

"Well," Andrew said, "I won't go back to school."

"Nonsense. Of course you will," said Edie, who was with them in the emergency room.

"I have a wife now, Mother. She needs me."

"Susan will be fine with me, won't you, dear?"

Susan nodded because Edie was smiling in that somewhat frightful way, teeth clenched a little too hard.

So a picture-perfect Christmas unfolded with a towering noble fir dragged into the living room and placed before the oil portrait of Edith and Evangeline as willowy teenagers in draped

Mainbocher gowns, leaning into each other, their heads seeming to blur together, looking always to Susan as if they might be one person and not two. The tinsel-covered tree sparkled, there were crackling fires in all three of the house's hearths—living room, dining room, library—and on Christmas Day an open house brimming with guests who looked like they stepped from the pages of some magazine touting the kind of lifestyle Susan never thought she'd have. Several of the guests traipsed up the stairs to meet bedridden Susan, including Edie's best friend, Oatsie O'Shea, her husband, Patrick, and their coltish daughter, Cis, whom Andrew had dated all through high school. Oatsie was a virtual carbon copy of Edie, pencil thin, smoking furiously, and impeccably dressed. She and Cis cooed over Susan and were effusive in their congratulations over the coming baby. Also passing through were others Edie referred to as "girls"—Evelyn Brookby, high-strung and giggly with a bouffant the color of copper, and the most elegant creature Susan had ever seen, Tish Van Buren, her patrician features barely touched by makeup, the only one whose hair, a natural chestnut flecked with actual grey, was pulled back and knotted in a simple chignon and not rolled, teased, back-combed, and shellacked into submission.

The festivities continued with something taken very seriously in this neighborhood, the Rose Parade on New Year's Day, which, it turned out, ran practically right past Andrew's house. Edie, Oatsie, Evelyn, and Tish, charter members of the Alta Arroyo Women's Club, sponsored a float, another excuse for an open house, this time with lots of Bloody Marys and a breakfast buffet of pancakes, sausages, and perfect soft scrambled eggs, rich with tons of cream and butter. Andrew seemed to take all this holiday merriment in stride, but Susan's Christmas vacations with her aunt had been far more austere, and so all through the season, Susan found herself feeling lucky to have married him after all.

When he left in January to finish up in New Haven, she missed him. By then, she had settled in to his childhood bedroom, complete with its high school baseball trophies and Wonder Woman posters still on the wall. Anderson Vale would pad into the room every morning in his robe and black velvet slippers to bring her the papers. Behind him came Blanca, who would carry in a tray, and Freddie, one of the two King Charles spaniels. On the tray was the breakfast Edie decided Susan should eat. There was buttered white toast with honey, two eggs poached for exactly six minutes, two strips of crisp bacon, and piping hot chamomile tea, all served on delicate, flowery bone china that had been in Edie's family for generations. Susan loved everything about the morning breakfast in bed, and she was desperate to please her new mother-in-law, at least at first. Edie would make an appearance around ten, always immaculately turned out in either one of her tailored suits if it was a luncheon day or tennis whites or golf shorts or even, on occasion, jodhpurs.

"Is there anything you need?" she'd invariably ask and then be distracted by some detail that annoyed her, like an infinitesimal dust mite in the corner or a windowpane showing streaks. Out would come the Hermès pad and a tiny silver pen. Edie would scribble a note to herself and pin it to her blouse. Occasionally, she'd have so many notes and reminders pinned there, she'd run out of room and pin them on Blanca, who sometimes would dart into a closet or scoot under a bed to avoid her.

"You know your mother's insane," she would say to Andrew on his nightly calls. He would laugh and tell her his mother just liked things a certain way, and once Susan learned how not to annoy her, all would be fine.

So Susan got to work making mental notes. Her short list of Edith Vale's dislikes included dust, clothes dryers (all linens were hung on a line behind the pool and air dried), mildew, windows that didn't simply sparkle, arrangements of flowers in different colors, and the failure to write thank-you notes. Meanwhile, Susan began a tally of the things that made Edie smile, which included the color robin's-egg blue, chintz, any piece of clothing by Galanos or Chanel, fun kicky brooches pinned to her lapel, anything by Kenneth Jay Lane, Manhattans at five sharp, and beach picnics with sandwiches wrapped tight in Cut-Rite Wax Paper (and yes, she could tell the difference between Cut-Rite and some other lesser brand).

Still, no matter how hard she tried, she somehow would wind up on Edie's nerves. Like on the days when she was allowed out of bed to make doctor visits. None of her clothes fit anymore, so Susan would struggle into sweats, grab one of Andrew's button-down shirts, and join Edie in her big grey Mercedes, and she could feel the disapproval coming off Edie in waves. They tried talking but had nothing in common. Eventually Susan gave up on trying to please Edie, and since she grew more and more bored by the day and needed diversions, she began finding ways to annoy her. She tested Edie's hawklike attention to detail by making slight, nearly imperceptible moves of the knickknacks on side tables or on the mantel in the living room. She learned Edie could spot these imperfections from forty feet away. On future doctor visits she'd take her time showering just so she could look out the window to see Edie waiting behind the wheel of the Mercedes, leaning on the horn, and craning her neck so she could see through the sunroof to Susan's window, an exasperated look on her face.

On one of those trips to the doctor, Susan finally said, "You just don't like me, do you, Edie?"

"Since we're being honest, dear," said Edie, "you're right. I don't."

"Why? What did I do?"

"Do you want the truth?" Edie asked.

"Yes."

"The truth is I think you've gone and absolutely ruined my son's life."

"You were the one who pushed us to get married," Susan protested.

"Times have changed, dear. I know that all too well," Edie said. "Gone forever, it seems, are manners, good taste, and discretion, Lord knows. But let's face facts: a bastard's a bastard, and that's all there is to it."

Susan had asked for the truth. She wasn't expecting Edie's words to hit her like cold hard slaps in the face. She was still brooding on it barely an hour later—especially over the fact that Edie seemed to gloss over her son's part in the mess they found themselves in—when she saw her baby for the first time. She didn't want to know if it was a boy or girl. But this was the sonogram where what was inside her wasn't some vague, indistinct pulsing blob. It looked human, with a discernible head, feet, and tiny little hands that seemed to be waving hello from some far-off land. That image, and later ones, are what sustained Susan through the next weeks of gas, constipation, boredom with bed rest, and Edie's not always silent disapproval.

"She means well," Andrew would say over the phone.

"How do we know that for sure?" Susan would ask, and he would laugh it off, while in the background she could hear what she was missing, the sounds of school. Somebody would ask for the freaking bong already, or there would be wild gales of laughter, a chant like "Chug! Chug! Chug!" or screams that the pizza was here. Susan would look down at her swollen belly, trace a finger over the stretch marks, feel like a beached whale, and want to cry.

And then came Henry.

Andrew had graduated and come home. He tried hard to be a calm and soothing presence. He went out in the middle of the night for Fosselman's Ice Cream for Susan or to In-N-Out Burger for double-doubles, animal-style. He would bring her back barbecue from Gus's or drive clear across town for chili dogs from Pink's. But Susan, by this time, was endlessly uncomfortable, hot, and cranky, craving the chili dog one minute, sick over the whole idea by the time Andrew came back. The night Henry was born, she had insisted he go with Edie and Anderson to the O'Sheas', who were giving a party in the garden of their San Marino home for Cis, who was graduating that week from USC. Susan was half asleep, lazily leafing through a back issue of Edie's *Town and Country*, when her contractions began and her water broke.

"Blanca! *Por favor!*" she screamed into the intercom speaker next to the bed.

"*Si?*" came crackling back at her, along with the chatter of the Spanish-language TV station that was ever present in Blanca's tidy white square of a room off the kitchen.

"*Necesito ayuda.* Help!" Struggling with high school and some restaurant kitchen Spanish, Susan wondered whether or not she was making sense, but several minutes later, she was loaded into the huge old Pontiac wagon Edie had given to Blanca when she bought her Mercedes. Susan twisted in pain and screamed with each contraction.

Blanca drove calmly, smiled a gap-toothed smile, and said, "Oh, baby come soon."

At the hospital, Susan was wheeled into delivery, and Blanca managed to get the O'Sheas' housekeeper on the phone. The news sent Edie, Anderson, and Andrew scurrying to Edie's Mercedes, Edie still clutching the icy cold Manhattan the bartender had just placed in her hand. They arrived in the stark, harshly lit hospital corridor still in festive cocktail party attire, and so they huddled close, looking like refugees from some alien land of perpetual happy times. They found Susan when the doctor was asking whether or not she wanted something for the pain.

"Do not even think of not having an epidural," Edie said, and when Susan's eyes met hers, for the first time, Susan recognized something that appeared to be warmth and affection and not criticism and judgment.

And so when they placed the squirming, wrinkly, frighteningly dark-red creature in Susan's arms a short time later, she agreed to call him Henry, as was the tradition on Edie's side, partly as a thank-you to her mother-in-law but also, Susan later figured, because she was too exhausted to put up a fight.

Susan looked down at her son. "Hello, Henry," she said, still woozy and somewhat dazed but also in awe that this tiny little person came out of her. She checked to make sure there were ten fingers, ten toes, and of course, a pulse, and then, terrified that he had stopped breathing, felt for a pulse again.

He looked up at Susan and at Andrew. He started to wail. They cooed at him. They waggled their fingers in his direction. They made funny faces and funny sounds; they tried just about anything but standing on their heads or juggling, but nothing the new parents did seemed to calm him. It wasn't until Susan passed Henry into the arms of Mrs. Vale that he instantly stopped and fell into a deep slumber.

**

The ringing phone jolted Susan awake. She had fallen asleep in her car, which made her feel dangerously careless and sloppy.

She was parked on campus just off the quad, where she had been waiting to spot Henry.

"Yeah?" she managed, but her voice sounded like gravel. She scoured the floor for a bottle of water or a mint, but she must have slept in a funny position because a sharp ache shot through one shoulder.

"Where did you disappear to?" It was Mike Finley, who then directed an Airbus heavy to maintain five thousand feet.

"What?" said Susan, still a bit groggy.

"I saw you slip out this morning. You never leave your place that early."

"I decided to drive out to New Hampshire to see Henry," Susan said. "But what? Are you spying on me now? We're just casual and easy, remember?"

"Yeah, yeah," said Mike. "When are you coming back?"

"That is so not a casual, easy question."

She flipped down the visor and checked her appearance. Her ponytail had come loose and looked disheveled. She had the impression of the seam of her seat etched into one cheek and a piece of crud in the corner of an eye. She flicked it away and started to tie her hair back up while wondering where the nearest bathroom was and if she'd have to pee outdoors. Clearly this was not a plan that was thought through.

"Okay. How about this. What are you wearing?"

"Oh, please," Susan said, even though the image of that goofy naughty little boy grin he'd get when he wanted to take her to bed flashed into her head, "now is not a good time. Plus, should you really be making a somewhat lame attempt to get me hot and bothered when you have a plane to keep track of?"

"Oh shit," Mike gasped, "where'd it go?"

"Oh my God," said Susan.

"Really? That joke worked again? Seriously?"

"Okay, not funny."

But Mike was still laughing when Susan said she had to go and quickly ended the call because Henry was headed her way. Susan spotted his protruding ears, the large nose, and the glasses that she thought lent a funky, offbeat look but deep down she knew must cause him all sorts of psychic pain. He had that strange-looking kid with the cowlick at his side, and when they were practically next to the car, Susan almost lost her nerve and ducked for cover.

Instead, she got out, stepped right in front of him, and said, "Hi, honey!"

Henry saw Susan but pretended he didn't and kept walking.

Zach Julian said, "Dude, isn't that your mom?"

Henry didn't miss a beat. "I have no idea who that lady is."

They walked off fast. Susan stood frozen to the spot, her mouth open, searching her brain for a response that never came.

V.

Andrew couldn't recall the last time the house at the beach was so still and silent. Linda and the twins—Serenity and her brother, Alexander, born three minutes later—just created a lot of noise. He did track down his wife at the home of her father, but she refused to come to the phone. He figured he'd give her some space, so he ate his microwaved dinner alone and again tried to figure out where he had gone wrong. If anybody asked, Andrew did accept the blame for the breakup of his marriage to Susan Jones. Well, most of it anyway. She wasn't entirely innocent either, although Andrew always admitted he was the one who strayed. She just seemed to lose interest. It wasn't that he didn't love her. Or that he wasn't looking forward to becoming a father. Andrew loved the idea of the baby, but by that ninth month, Susan had become perpetually irritable; she recoiled when he tried to touch her. He couldn't be certain if she even liked him anymore. It was a difficult time, his mother always on his back too about how he should have been more responsible and how he should have been thinking with his brain and not another body part she didn't care to mention.

So after a few too many beers the night of the graduation party at the O'Sheas', actually the night Susan went into labor, he poured his heart out to Cis, who'd been there for him all through high school. In fact, Andrew and Cis surrendered their virginity to each other, a curiously businesslike arrangement where they discussed the matter at length, decided they should have reached this milestone by the age of seventeen, made a date to do something about it, and then, again after a few too many Heinekens and half a joint, got the whole somewhat messy business out of the way. They remained a couple because it was easy, because their families both approved—indeed, Edie and Oatsie were over the moon—because they knew each other inside and out, and they would probably would have stayed together through college and then gotten married had Cis had been accepted at an East Coast school. But sometime in their senior year, Cis rebelled. She fought constantly with her parents over every little thing. She started wearing nothing but black. She pierced her nose. She cut off most of her hair and dyed what remained a dark shade of purple, mortifying her mother. Most days she ditched school. She was lucky to squeak past the admissions board at USC, and only because numerous family members were graduates and her father coughed up a generous donation to some building fund.

So Cis and Andrew split, and Andrew spent his college years with a variety of hookups and the occasional longer term girlfriend. He didn't seem to have a type. There were bespectacled and, to be honest, annoying, intellectuals, a pothead or two, a vehement and radical vegan, one suburban girl who turned out to be addicted to crystal meth and vanished after half a semester, and several horsey athletic ones like Cis, sunny fair-skinned girls with freckles, who came from good families. If he'd stopped to look for a pattern in his relationships, he would find none. What Andrew did notice was a tendency to get in too deep too fast. He decided maybe it was because he just liked to be around women more than men. Had he really thought about it, he might have figured it had to do with his father leaving the family and his mother playing the dominant role in his upbringing.

Anyway, he fell fast that summer with Susan. He had seen her before she rescued him from nearly drowning, but he hadn't yet worked up the nerve to say anything. She wasn't one of the horsey girls. She didn't seem the overly intellectual brainy sort either. She seemed cool and efficient, her dark, straight hair pulled back and tied in a precise ponytail most days, her stride purposeful and direct. He knew where she worked and sometimes would go in for a beer or a bowl of chowder. He'd catch glimpses of her in the kitchen. He loved to see her smile, a sly slip of a grin peeking up from under the Red Sox cap she sometimes wore while at the stove. He saw her at the beach, tan skin against a formfitting suit, that ponytail draped over a shoulder, laughing at something a friend had said, and it was settled in his mind that somehow they'd be together. So later, when they had become a couple and when Susan told him she was pregnant, Andrew didn't feel trapped or panicked. What he did feel most was a mild amusement that they actually made a baby.

When Henry was born, Andrew crawled into the bed with Susan in the hospital. With the baby finally sleeping between them, he swore he'd love him forever, swore he would try to never let him down, even though technically he had already done so by having sex with Cis at the party behind the O'Sheas' pool earlier that very night after he had poured his heart out to her. Still, he tried to make it all work with Susan. Because of the baby, Andrew transferred from New Haven to finish law school at UCLA. They moved in with his mother and Anderson to save money. It all went south in a hurry, beginning with the day that Anderson Vale left for his weekly golf game. Doddering Emerson Brookby, Evelyn's much older husband, was behind the wheel of his new Lincoln Continental, and little did Anderson and his other golf buddies know Emerson had failed two driving tests. But they weren't even on the road when the accident happened. It was after nine holes, after a lunch of club sandwiches fortified by strong martinis, and after a long steam in the gym. The men were preparing to head home, ostensibly to tend to investments or catch up on the papers, but truthfully, every last one of them would fall into a coma-like slumber until it was time for cocktails or to dress for dinner. Anderson, done loading his golf gear into the Continental's trunk, noticed a shoelace had come untied and stooped to take care of it. Emerson, assuming everybody was on board and safely belted in, threw the big sedan into reverse and backed right over him.

"I had told him over and over again not to get in a car with Evelyn or Emerson behind the wheel," Edie had told Andrew after a shrieking, hysterical Evelyn Brookby called to deliver the horrible news. "If he had paid attention, he'd still be alive."

"Well, he wasn't actually in the car, Mother," Andrew had said.

"He never listened to me anyway. Always going off and doing whatever he wanted to do."

"That's insane," said Andrew. "You had him on a tighter leash than any of us."

Edie dismissed that, lit a Parliament, and there was silence as they got through the grim tasks of the rest of that afternoon, Andrew even accompanying her as she went down to the morgue to identify the body. He watched his mother mourn for a few solid days. Then she summoned Blanca, and together they boxed up all of Anderson's clothes and accessories. They packed them into the trunk of Edie's Mercedes and she drove them down to the Salvation Army. Then it seemed his mother was determined to move on—now a divorcée and a widow, she told Andrew she was all done with men. But clearly she missed having somebody to boss around. So she turned her attentions first on Evangeline, and when her sister fled Pasadena altogether for temporary exile with her daughter in Santa Fe, Edie zeroed in on Susan. Nothing she did was right, it seemed. The words "No you're not," or, "You're not wearing that," or, "That's just not the way it's done in this family" would fly out of Edie's mouth, often before Susan actually did or said anything, Andrew noticed. He would try to intervene, but commuting between Pasadena and Westwood, not to mention law school itself, was time consuming, and he wasn't around nearly enough. When he was home, Susan would complain. Between Edie and the baby and the feedings and the baths and the changings and the strapping him into a stroller and the taking him for walks and all the other little things he needed from her every single second of the day, she told Andrew she felt as if she was disappearing.

"You should maybe go back to school," Andrew said one night after they had put Henry down.

"I should what?" Susan asked.

"Finish school. You'd get in to UCLA easily. Then I'd have somebody to drive to campus with."

"Your mother won't let me. She thinks babies need their mothers around. All the time."

"You don't have to listen to her," Andrew had said.

"I don't? Are you sure? Because the truth is she really scares me. Like these thank-you cards for the baby gifts all her friends sent. You have no idea."

"Just don't tell me you bought cards without showing her."

"I did."

"Oh no . . ."

"There was this neat little shop down on Colorado I wandered into with Henry. They were on sale."

"Oh my God . . ."

"She wouldn't even look at them. I had no idea she had already ordered cards. From some place in New York, it turns out. Yeah, they're pretty, but they weigh a ton, and those envelopes—the edges are so sharp they could draw blood."

"Did she actually let you write the notes?"

"She told me my handwriting was atrocious and she did it herself. Can you believe that?"

"Just don't let her get under your skin. That's what I do. Tune it out."

"How?"

"You know what Anderson used to do? He'd turn his hearing aid all the way down. I don't think he took in half of what she said. Just pretend you have one and it's turned all the way to zero. Nod politely when she talks. And smile a lot. She likes happy faces. She hates mopers."

"Right."

That seemed to work for a while. Then, one evening when Andrew arrived at home after a late torts class, Susan was gone.

"I have no idea where she is," Edie said as she gave Henry a bottle.

"When did she leave?" Andrew asked. "I mean, should we be worried? Should I call the police?"

"I hadn't thought of that," Edie said.

"Well, what happened? Did you fight? Did you say something to upset her?"

"What could I say that would possibly upset her?"

"Just tell me what happened, then."

"We had just sat down to lunch. It was chilly today. And so grey. I asked Blanca for grilled cheese sandwiches and a cup of tomato soup, and I thought we'd eat them on trays in the library by the fire. Doesn't that sound cozy?"

Andrew just stared at his mother blankly.

"Anyway," Edie soldiered on, "I mentioned that maybe she might want to look into attending a meeting of my women's club or the local junior league. They do really marvelous things, you know. In my day, I was chairman of several committees. Did I ever tell you about the time we held a charity bazaar at—"

"Mother, where is my wife?"

"Well, the next thing I knew, she got up, right in the middle of a spoonful of soup, and before we knew it, she was gone."

She didn't come home until long after dinner. "I got a job," she had told him as she flopped down on the bed. "God, my feet are killing me." Andrew watched as she kicked off her shoes, then walked over to Henry's crib. She lifted him up, unbuttoned her blouse, and he contentedly attached himself to her nipple.

"A job?" Andrew asked.

"Yeah. It dawned on me today I can't sit around this house and do nothing forever."

"Being a mom isn't nothing."

"I didn't mean it that way. I know it's not. I just need to do something else too."

"I thought we talked about you going back to school."

"You know what?" Susan said. "Honestly, I never really liked college all that much. I went because that's what everybody expected me to do and I think I was just going through the motions. But you know what I loved? I loved working in restaurant kitchens. So I figured maybe I should see if there's a career for me there."

"In the restaurant business?" said Andrew, as if it was something mildly distasteful.

"What? Is it beneath me?"

"No."

"Is it beneath you, then? Would you be embarrassed to say your wife works in a restaurant?"

"Why are you so defensive?" Andrew said.

"I just think people should find what they love and do it, don't you?"

"I guess."

"I mean, do you love the law, Andrew?"

"I . . . hmmmmm . . ."

He couldn't finish the thought because the truth was he didn't have an answer. Most of the men in his family, both on Edie's side and on Frank's, went to law school. That's what was done. So he was plodding his way through, the way his father and grandfather had.

"Where did you get a job?" he finally asked.

She had answered an ad at an expense-account steak joint in downtown Los Angeles. It was entry-level, an assistant at the station where cold appetizers and salads were assembled, an easy job, she told Andrew, because mostly customers ordered huge hunks of iceberg lettuce drowning in thick blue cheese dressing, or big slices of tomato with crumbled blue cheese and bacon scattered over the top, or more iceberg wedges bathed in Caesar. She worked the lunch shift and had to be at her post by eight. She'd finish by three.

Most days Andrew didn't have class until later in the morning, so after Susan nursed Henry, he would bathe him and get him dressed. He'd throw on sweats or gym shorts and then strap Henry into his stroller and take him and Edie's dogs, Freddie and Min, for a jog. Sometimes he would bump into Cis, who liked to run in the mornings too, or she would pass by in her convertible and they'd grab coffee together. Since the night of the graduation party, he had tried to avoid Cis and stay faithful to his wife. But Susan's disinterest in sex, which started somewhere midpregnancy, seemed to intensify after Henry's birth. Once she started working, she fell into deep coma-like slumbers the minute she'd get home and be too groggy in the mornings. Andrew felt lonely. Also, he had to admit it, with Susan not interested, suddenly he was horny constantly. But Cis was right there and available, comfortable, like a cozy old sweater, and totally unencumbered like he was with all the baby paraphernalia and strollers, and lists of dos and do nots from Edie, and dog leashes and whatnot, and there was something appealing about that too. So they fell into an affair, easily and casually. They'd find someplace secluded in the park, or they'd do it, fast and urgent, in Cis's car, until one day they were nearly caught behind the restrooms in the park by a Pasadena cop.

"This has to stop," Andrew said after they were left with a warning and a stern, disapproving look.

"You know, Drew, sweetheart," said Cis, "if it's not me, it's going to be somebody else."

"It doesn't have to be. I am married."

"Uh-huh. You are so clueless."

"About what?"

"Please. A guy alone with a baby? With the dogs sometimes? Total catnip to certain women."

The truth was Andrew never understood what women saw in him. He was ignored mostly through adolescence, when his ears protruded too much and his nose seemed too big, and he was forever saying the wrong thing or tripping and falling, just overall feeling like a fool, and that's how he figured it would always be. But he was fairly athletic, although he hated working out. He'd swim or he'd ski. He could surf pretty well on gentle waves. He'd wipe out on the bigger ones. In college, he played on a softball team. He supposed he was in decent shape. He had a full head of hair. Still, inside somewhere, he always felt like a big dork.

"My mother actually thinks running with the baby is going to cause some sort of physical damage," he told Cis. "She says I might rattle something loose. She gives me dirty looks every time I leave the house with him strapped to my back."

"Face it: our moms are both insane. You know what Oatsie says to me every day? She goes, 'Nobody loves an old maid, dear,' and I go, 'Jesus, Mother, I just turned twenty-three,' and she says, 'Time flies. Before you know it, you'll be thirty and alone.' Oatsie O'Shea and Edith Vale should be sharing a padded cell somewhere if you ask me."

"Right."

Still, Andrew did his best to end things with Cis for good. Then she broke up with him because she said she didn't want to sneak around anymore. Andrew wasn't sure she hadn't just grown bored, which was another thing he always worried about—that he wasn't exciting enough a partner, was too staid and, well, dull. Anyway, he tried to take his marriage vows seriously. He wanted to keep this little family together. Then Susan got promoted at the restaurant, up from salads and apps to working as a line cook. A new semester began, with all of Andrew's classes in the morning just as Susan began working all night and sleeping until noon. One night, he stopped by the restaurant to surprise her. It had an open kitchen. She didn't know he was there, and as he watched, it seemed Susan had found her niche. She bantered back and forth with other line cooks and moved around her tight place at the grill as if she'd been doing this highly choreographed dance forever. He felt a little like an intruder. Also, he had to admit, he felt a little jealous, a little left out of this part of her life. He went home that night, and she never knew he had been there. Soon, they barely saw each other at all, and when they did, they seemed to be bickering, over what, Andrew could rarely remember.

His mother, meanwhile, liked nothing better than taking even more charge of Henry. She put him on a strict schedule, monitored his diet like a hawk, and regulated his almost every waking minute, and if she was unavailable—at the hairdresser, say, for her weekly wash, color, set, back-comb, and shellacking, or luncheon with the girls sans Evelyn Brookby, who, since the accident, had rented out her house and fled with Emerson to their condo in Rancho Mirage—there were strict instructions for Blanca, who mostly ignored them and did things her own way. Then, one afternoon, Andrew would learn later, a pipe just above the restaurant broke and flooded the kitchen. Susan and the rest of the crew were sent home. Edie was at one of her club functions, and Susan had found Blanca in her room, methodically ironing creases into Edie's sheets while nodding along with a telenovela.

"Mr. Andrew took him to the park," she said when Susan asked about the baby.

And that's where Susan found him. Henry was strapped in his harness on Andrew's back while Andrew was making out with a girl Susan recognized from a party he had taken her to a few weeks earlier, where members of his moot court team had gathered to celebrate a birthday.

First, in a surprisingly swift maneuver, Susan snatched Henry out of the harness. Then she screamed, "Oh, I should have let you drown. Asshole."

Her voice had a harshness he hadn't heard before. Her words rang in Andrew's ears, long after she turned and ran back toward the house. For the longest time, Andrew had stood rooted to the spot, the girl, mortified, having fled, abandoning him too, he thought at first, and then felt like even more of a shit. His father had left his mother, had cheated on her too, he suspected, and so Andrew figured maybe he was simply living out his destiny, that being dishonest, being a heel, was a rite of passage, at least in this family.

He made his way home slowly, a little afraid of what he'd find; despite all the problems he and Susan were having, he hated confrontation. But Susan had locked herself in their room with Henry. In a way, that was a relief. His mother managed to get in later that night with a cup of bouillon on a tray she urged Susan to sip. Andrew slipped into the hall to eavesdrop on their conversation. Peeking through a crack in the door, he saw Edie perched on the bed, Manhattan in one hand, Parliament in the other. They seemed suddenly closer, as if they shared some new bond and he was excluded.

"Men cheat, dear. It's unfortunate, but that's what they do," he heard her say.

"And we're supposed to just sit back and take it? What century are you living in, Edith?"

"The century is immaterial, Susan. Some things just don't ever change. What you need to learn is how to not see things that are unpleasant. Trust me, you will be far happier if you do. So, starting bright and early tomorrow, here's what I suggest: You begin the day with a good, vigorous walk. Then you march yourself down to Nordstrom's, and you charge something unnecessary and ridiculously expensive to Andrew's account. I'll end up paying the bill, of course, but don't worry about that. Finish your morning with a bowl of the macaroni and cheese from that little coffee shop on Lake Street. Just don't make eye contact with any of the other customers, and wash your hands thoroughly when you leave that place. But take my word for it, you'll feel worlds better."

It looked to Andrew, from the little sliver of Susan's face he could make out anyway, that she was wavering between wanting to scream and wanting to laugh.

Edith seemed to pick up on it. "You may just think I'm some silly ninny," he heard her say, "but one day, Susan, you might realize that I'm wiser than I look."

Susan appeared to debate that. But by the time Andrew tiptoed back down the hall to sleep in the guest room, Blanca was happily spooning down the bouillon, and Susan was fishing the maraschino cherry from Edie's Manhattan and taking drags from her cigarette, a very determined look on her face. Before he knew it, she had filed for divorce and found an apartment. Before he knew it, Susan and Henry were gone.

Now, as he dumped the remnants of his dinner into the trash at the house at the beach, Andrew wasn't sure what his next move should be. This time, with Linda, he was sure he hadn't done anything wrong, nothing he could pinpoint anyway, nothing he could promise to fix. Which made coming up with a solution to the problem far more perplexing.

VI.

Henry was pressed so hard against the passenger side door of the car that Susan was afraid he might fall out. "You know," she said, trying to lighten the mood, "I don't bite."

He didn't crack a smile.

"Okay. You're mad at me. That's fine. It's good. In fact, I think I understand the reason."

"Oh yeah?" said Henry. "Tell me, then. Why am I mad?"

"Because I promised you I would come up for Thanksgiving, and I didn't make it. That's it, isn't it?"

"Well, I will say it was such a joy spending the holiday with the dean of students, his wife, and their cats. Did I mention they have eleven? Eleven cats. Did I mention there was hair everywhere? Did I tell you how I was scratching flea bites for days? Until they bled, Susan. Bled."

"I explained about work, didn't I? How the guy who was covering for me flaked on us. A drug problem, if you ask me. So there we were, the restaurant fully booked with folks expecting turkey and dressing and gravy and something pumpkin of course for dessert—the whole shebang really—but nobody in charge of the kitchen?"

Henry didn't look sympathetic. But the truth was the holiday had been hell for Susan, a blur really, with two seatings at lunch and two seatings at dinner. There was an endless stream of anxious guests, families mostly, so naturally, tension was through the roof. All of them seemed fiercely determined to enjoy their meal no matter what, and therefore, they were all extremely difficult to please. By the end of it all, Susan was so exhausted she barely moved from her bed for days.

"Maybe we should address the larger issue," said Henry.

"The larger issue?"

"The one about why you abandoned me."

"I never abandoned you, Henry. You know that. You make it sound like I dropped you on some doorstep in the middle of the night. I left you in the care of your father and your grandmother."

"Mrs. Vale is crazy. I shouldn't have to remind you of that. She and all her friends. Mrs. O'Shea. Mrs. Van Buren. Mrs. Brookby. Nutjobs, every last one of them."

"I thought Mrs. Brookby got banished to the desert after her husband ran over Mr. Vale."

"She came back," said Henry, "after the husband croaked."

"He died?"

"Yeah. Hello?" Henry said, glaring, sending one of those looks that seemed to suggest she was the stupidest person on the planet.

"Anyway," Susan said, "you still call your grandmother Mrs. Vale?"

"Most of the time, yes," said Henry.

That all had to do with Henry's first word. It was *abuela*, "grandma" in Spanish. When Edie heard it, she promptly fired Blanca. This meant that barely hours later, a mildly panicked

Edie had to jump into her Mercedes, drive to the midcity area of Los Angeles where Blanca's daughters lived with an assortment of family members of all ages, climb four flights of stairs to the apartment, and hire Blanca back with a profusion of apologies and a small raise, of course. Still, there was the issue of what Henry should call Edie. They tried an assortment. In short order Edie vetoed Gran, Gramma, Grammie, Gam-Gam, Nana, and any permutation of any of those words. She settled on Grand Edith, which Henry had trouble pronouncing, so it came out as "Grainith" or "Granitith." So Edie decided that Mrs. Vale would have to do.

"All right. Well," Susan began again. "The point is you were always in good hands when I went away. Not just Mrs. Vale. Your father too. And there was always Blanca. By the way, how is her granddaughter Luz?"

"How the fuck should I know?"

"You don't really need to use that kind of language, Henry."

"I've seen you at work, Susan. You drop f-bombs right and left. In English and Spanish. Like a drunken sailor, some might say."

"Right. Anyway," Susan said, aiming for brighter in tone to try and lighten the mood, "Luz is good?"

"Why do you keeping asking me about Luz?"

"I don't know. I saw something on your Facebook page. Some posting or some picture, I think, and . . ."

"Oh, my God. I have told you over and over again. Do not follow me on Facebook. Stop with trying to Snapchat. Just stop."

"I wasn't actually following you. And I . . ."

Now it was Henry's turn to change the subject. "Anyway, yeah, you left me with Dad, but he's basically clueless too. If you ask me, the issue is abandonment."

Susan suddenly wondered whether the idea she threw out had been a mistake. She made the offer on the spur of the moment because Henry was refusing to talk to or barely even acknowledge her, even when she followed him right back to his dorm and straight up to his room on the second floor, sending half-dressed boys darting into their rooms. He said her visit was bad timing, that he was flying back home the next morning after one last final exam. The idea came out of her mouth without her even thinking it through, but there it hung, suspended in the air, a suggestion that did seem to get Henry's attention.

"I could drive you" is what Susan said.

"What? To California?" said Henry, the confused look on his face seeming to indicate she had offered to rocket them both to the moon.

"Yeah. I could. You know," Susan said, "road trip!" She tried to make it all sound upbeat, a little crazy, and, well, awesome! But it may have come out needy and pathetic, she worried. "We could have some really good quality time together. We could really talk," Susan continued, "bond even, sort of."

"Don't you have to work?"

"I have a ton of vacation time banked up. I haven't had a break in ages, as a matter of fact. I can't remember my last vacation. So there's no reason not to take one now." She was just making this up as she went along, but it was too late to take it back because it seemed as if Henry was actually considering the idea. And that made her happy, that he might actually want to spend time with her. Feeling encouraged, she said, "I'll even let you drive part of the time if you want. How about that?"

"I don't know. My playlists on the sound system too? Because, frankly, Susan, your music always kind of sucks."

"Whatever you want."

Henry considered that.

"Of course, if you decide to come with me," she added, "you'll have to call your father and clear it with him."

"Right." He pulled out his phone right there and placed the call. Susan watched as he negotiated with his dad, and she could tell by the pained expression on Henry's face that things weren't going well. But then he smiled and ended the call. "We're good to go," said Henry.

"Really?" said Susan, suddenly wondering what in the world she might have done. "Great. When can you leave?"

"Right after lunch was when I was supposed to head to Logan," Henry said.

Indeed, she suddenly noticed packed suitcases and boxes full of books. She scanned the room and also noted there was not one picture of her or any of the two of them together.

Meanwhile, it almost seemed as if Henry sensed impending panic on her part and decided to use it to his advantage by making her even more uncomfortable. "You know, maybe this is a good idea after all. We have so many issues to hash out."

"Great," she said again, smile frozen in place, now also realizing she had maybe one change of clothes crammed into a knapsack and no other real supplies, or even a map she could look at to chart a possible route, and how could she even consider taking a child on such an absurd journey? What kind of a lousy mother would even consider it? Would her own mother have, Susan wondered? She had such vague memories of both parents that she wasn't sure about the answer to that question.

But when Henry went off to take his last exam, Susan figured she'd use the time to prepare. She drove back into town, found the nearest big-box store, grabbed a basket, and headed inside, tense already, because these places always gave her a headache. Inside the store, with all the aisles packed to the rafters with whatever on earth anybody could possibly need for just about any situation, she stood there, disoriented and daunted by it all, other shoppers swarming around her, all of them seeming to know exactly what they were after. She'd never actually taken a trip like this, so spur-of-the-moment, without so much as a tiny bit of planning or at least a list. The only thing that made her smile is she knew the idea would make Edie apoplectic. Okay, she told herself, focus. Clothes first. Luckily Susan mostly wore the same thing, almost like a uniform: jeans and T-shirts under her apron and sometimes a chef's jacket, with clogs or Crocs if she was behind the stoves or boots in winter if she wasn't or some kind of sandal in warmer weather. She picked up the clothes she'd need and a small duffel bag to pack them all in. She grabbed toothpaste, a toothbrush, and dental floss. She bought travel-sized packages of soap, shampoo, and moisturizer. The makeup in her purse would have to do as the selection was too dizzying. She didn't wear that much of it anyway. Her final purchase, in electronics, was some nifty GPS gadget that, according to the salesman, would tell her exactly where to go.

She toted her purchases back to the car, and then another thought struck her—would her dented old Volvo wagon actually make it? This was already a used car when Susan purchased it because it seemed solid and sturdy. Suddenly, though, she couldn't recall how many years ago that was or when the last time was that a mechanic looked it over. So she found the nearest full-service gas station and had everything checked out. While she waited, she texted Mike Finley and asked him to pick up her mail. She called the restaurant to request some of the vacation she had banked but never used. When the owner gave her a hard time, she quit. Another one bites the dust, she thought when she ended the call, and then it started to bother her that she always seemed to be leaving something behind, like a job or a boyfriend or, well, her son.

Now, a few hours later, as she and Henry sped along a twisty back road toward the interstate, she again tried to steer conversation back to why she left him in the care of his father and grandmother. "It was very complicated. But maybe it's time we really did put our cards on the table. The truth of the matter," Susan said, "was that I always had your best interests at heart."

"Whatever," he said. He plugged his phone in to the car's sound system, cranked up the volume, and turned to look out the window at a muddy field dotted with sturdy black-and-white cows that watched with casual indifference as they passed. Susan wanted to continue the conversation and turned the volume down, earning another icy look of disdain.

"I think we should try and talk through our differences. Don't you want to try to do that? Instead of always being at odds?" Susan asked.

"When's my turn?"

"Your . . . um . . . what?"

"I believe you mentioned that I could drive," said Henry.

"Oh. Well, all right then."

The GPS had led them to an intersection, still in rural territory, the narrow road lined on either side with thick copses of dense evergreens, all around them the sharp, heady scent of pine. There was no traffic at all, so Susan threw the car into park, hopped out, and walked to the passenger side while Henry climbed over the console and took her place at the wheel. She settled back into her seat and looked over at him. He looked remarkably small for his age and somewhat fragile, it suddenly struck her, as he pushed his glasses back up from where they had slid down the bridge of his nose. He smiled for the first time since they left, gripped the wheel tight, and then stomped on the gas. The car rocketed forward, shockingly fast, sped right through the intersection, skittered up the embankment on the other side, just missing one of those trees, and came to rest in a ditch. When the dirt and dust the car kicked up settled, Susan asked the question she should have asked before letting him take the wheel.

"You don't know how to drive, do you?"

"Well, if you must know, I have the basics down."

"Do you have a license?"

"Hello? Have I been home long enough the past year to get one?"

"So you weren't planning on telling me?"

"Shouldn't mothers just know these things?"

Susan let out a sound, a sort of snort of frustration. "Trade places with me so I can get us out of here."

They switched seats again. She put the car into reverse, and gave it some gas, but all the wheels did was spin, which only seemed to make Henry smile.

"You know," she said, "it wouldn't be too funny if you had broadsided another car. You could have maimed somebody. Or killed them."

"You're going to lecture me about responsibility?"

"You know what? How about if I just drop you at Logan after all."

"Why would you do that?"

"You said your father had a flight booked for you. Maybe this isn't such a good idea. I'll come out and see you this summer. Or in September when you come back."

"I'm not sure I'm going to be here in September," Henry said.

"Really? Why is that?"

"Because I think I'm getting, like, kicked out."

Susan stopped trying to move the car. She turned and gave Henry a long look. He always seemed like such a serious child. She wondered sometimes whether or not he had mischief in him. She was glad to see maybe he did. "What did you do, Henry?" she asked.

"Well," said Henry, "me and Zach Julian bought a joint because we wanted to see what the big deal was. We took this long hike into the woods to smoke it. What we didn't realize is we actually hiked into one of our professors' backyards. He could see us from his kitchen. So like the freaking idiots that we are, we got caught. Red-handed."

Susan wasn't quite sure what to say because the image almost made her want to laugh.

"Anyway," Henry continued, "it's not like you can lecture me."

"Oh really? Why not?"

"Hello? Miss Pregnant at Twenty-One? That's only a few years older than I am now. And don't try to tell me you never smoked pot yourself. I mean, if you were sexually active . . ."

"First of all, yes, I was very young when I got pregnant, but do remember that your father and I got married. We thought we were in it for the long haul."

"Guess you were wrong. Are we going to sit in this ditch forever, by the way?"

Indeed, motorists in cars that occasionally passed were giving them odd looks. Susan again tried to get the car moving and had no luck. "Like I was trying to tell you before," she said, giving up once again, "I had your best interests in mind when I left. But I know what you're trying to do."

"Oh, and what's that?"

"You're trying to change the subject. It's not about you committing an illegal act and getting punished; it's about me."

"Well, what about you? You didn't answer my question. You going to tell me you never tried pot?"

"You know what, Henry? I won't lie to you. Of course I did. But to be completely honest, I never really liked it much. The occasional cigarette, yes. Mostly when I'm on a break at work. Which doesn't mean you should smoke, by the way."

"Uh-huh," said Henry. "That's what Mrs. Vale says every time she lights a Parliament."

Suddenly, there was an old man at Susan's window with a long grizzled beard and a stub of a cigar in his mouth. They hadn't noticed the tractor he rode, its slow, stately approach, or the aging golden retriever with the grey snout who sat behind him on the seat, gazing out regally at the scenery through watery eyes.

"You stuck or something?" he said, the words in that harsh, clipped New England accent that made a person sound mad, or at least very impatient.

"Apparently we are," said Susan.

"Well, I could tow you out of there, I guess. Better than sitting like a bump on a log, I'd figure."

"Thank you," said Susan. "That would be very nice."

She and Henry stepped out of the car. They watched as the man attached a line to the rear axle of the Volvo. He climbed back up onto the tractor and eased the car back to the road.

"That ought to get you folks moving again," he said. "Untie that line, sonny," he said to Henry, "and hand it back up to me."

Henry fiddled with the knot and delivered the rope back up to the old man, who turned the tractor and continued his slow journey.

"So you got expelled? Is that what you're saying?" Susan said as they got back into the car.

"I'm not sure," said Henry. "I know they called my father. It may just be we're, like, suspended or something. Or probation."

Susan revved the engine, shifted gears, turned the wheel to the left and the right. "Well, doesn't seem to be any damage," she said.

"I guess I should have told you I didn't have a license."

"We'll make sure to get you one when you get home."

"That'd be cool."

"Can I ask you one more question, Henry?"

"Shoot."

"Do you really want to do this? Because it's a long drive to California. I don't want to sit with you for all that time if you're just going to be mean and surly the whole way."

"I won't. Let's do it."

She tried not to let him see her smile as she hit the gas.

VII.

Andrew, strapped in the backseat of Edith Vale's Mercedes, stared down at the e-mails on his phone and tried to tune out the conversation that was taking place up front between his mother and his aunt, but he wasn't having much luck.

For the third time now, Evangeline said, "We've been past this point. I'm just absolutely certain of it."

"We've been past this point, dear, because we're circling. On purpose," said Edie for the third time.

Edie had driven them all to LAX to meet Henry's plane, each of them unaware as yet that he had defied his father's insistence that he be on it and by no means drive to California with his mother, but when they arrived too early for a flight that was, of course, late, Edie insisted they circle the terminal rather than pay some exorbitant amount of money to park. Then, while they were idling at a crosswalk, a young man with ratty dreadlocks, tattoos, and Birkenstocks approached Edie's window.

"You could run that thing on veggie oil, you know," he said. "I have a friend who converts them." He tried to shove a card in her hand.

Edie responded by stubbing out the Parliament she was smoking and raising the window. "What the devil? I swear I simply hate to leave Pasadena," she said and then hit the gas.

"You can do that," Andrew said. "It's called biodiesel. The firm did some consulting for a company that converts old Mercedes and VW diesels to run on vegetable oil. You get the used oil from restaurants. Which basically means you have free gas. Except I think you have to filter it or something. Plus, the exhaust can smell like French fries, I gather. But it's not a bad idea. Maybe you should think about it."

"Oh, Hans would never stand for us tinkering with this car like that," said Edie.

"Mother, when are you going to realize Hans could care less about this old car? It's you he's after."

"Don't be ridiculous," said Edie, suddenly all huffy and even blushing a little, Andrew could see.

"I used to buy vegetable oil to make croquettes," said Evangeline. "Gigi loved my croquettes."

"You never made a croquette in your life, and even if you did, your daughter with all her phobias about food would never eat one," said Edie.

Another inane back-and-forth between Edie and Evangeline began. Andrew tried to block out the noise until rescue came in a text that the flight had arrived. He jumped out of the Mercedes. He practically jogged toward the baggage claim, anxious to see his son. Henry had been gone for months, and it suddenly hit Andrew how much he missed him. But there was no sign of Henry in the baggage claim or, apparently, in the terminal once Andrew had him paged. He felt a sort of panic start to rise when Henry's phone went straight to voice mail, as did Susan's. Andrew finally asked at the airline counter and learned Henry never checked in or boarded the flight.

"Oh, that's fine, dear. That's wonderful. So we drove all the way out here for nothing?" Edie said when Andrew climbed back into his mother's car and told them the news that Henry was driving with Susan. This he had confirmed by a call to Zach Julian, who had watched them leave.

"I suppose."

"And so you've now lost track of not one child, but three? I'm sorry, sweetheart, but I have to say it: your life is going down the toilet."

Evangeline tittered and started playing with the window switch.

"And, old woman," Edie said, "if you keep monkeying with that switch and break it, I will put you on a slow bus to the convalescent home."

Andrew suppressed a grin, swiped one of his mother's Parliaments, and lit it up. "By the way," he said, "that hippie dude slapped a sticker on your back bumper. It's green, and it says 'French Fries for Freedom.'"

"Oh, for crying out loud," said Edie. "Do people have no respect anymore for a person's property? It better come off."

"And also," Andrew felt it necessary to add, "I haven't lost track of all my children. I know where the twins are, so two of three are accounted for."

"Well, perhaps it's time you paid them a visit."

"You're driving. You know where Linda's father lives."

Indeed, whenever Andrew visited Robbie Landesman's house at the top of Mulholland Drive he thought back to that first time they all had dinner there. It was shortly after he and Linda Landesman met, after he literally collided with her on Canon Drive in Beverly Hills. He was leaving a client's office, one of those meetings where a whole family was present to hash over an estate, so his head was filled with bickering, accusations, and tears, and as was often in these cases, somebody storming from the office and vowing to see everybody else in court. So he was distracted, as was Linda, walking up the street with her arms full of fabric swatches and carpet samples. They collided head-on in the middle of the sidewalk, creating something of a spectacle. Linda, the pampered daughter of a former child star turned TV producer, was trim and toned, so firm, she liked to say, she could bounce a quarter off her ass. She had streaky blond hair, a heart-shaped face, and eyes a mesmerizing greenish olive that Andrew got lost in. Single and wrapped up mostly in work and more than a little lonely, he fell for her immediately, which was his habit anyway, just as Linda, he learned, was in search of a man who was normal and stable after years of dating the sons of actors and the puffed-up scions of Hollywood moguls, kids her father liked to say had too much money and too much time on their hands. They'd only been seeing each other a few weeks or so when she invited Andrew, Henry, who was ten at the time, and Edith Vale to her father's house for a Seder. It was a singularly disastrous evening that should have stopped any relationship in its tracks, Andrew always thought. His sense of dread began when Edie came down the stairs in a strikingly red number from St. John Knits.

"I don't know, Mother," he had said. "Is that appropriate?"

"What," asked Edie, "could be more appropriate for spring than a light wool bouclé cut just below the knee?"

"I meant red at a Seder."

"Is there some law against it?"

Andrew didn't have an answer to that. "What about that brooch?"

She looked down at her lapel. Pinned there was a large faux emerald and ruby crab. "What's wrong with it? It's Kenneth Jay Lane, for goodness' sake."

"Crab? Shellfish? These people are Jewish, remember?"

Edie rolled her eyes, but went back upstairs and swapped out the crab for a butterfly.

So off they drove to Los Angeles, arriving at Robbie Landesman's house at the top of Mulholland Drive at dusk, and when they got out of the car, even his mother gasped at the vista that spread out at their feet. To their left, the San Gabriel Mountains, snow still capping their tips, framed the skyscrapers of downtown. To their right, beyond Century City, was the shimmering Pacific. Jetliners on final approach seemed to float in lazy arcs toward the runways at LAX. Crisscrossing it all were the boulevards, arteries, and byways of the city that seemed to have the heave and pulse of something alive.

Inside, they were introduced to Robbie Landesman, now portly in late middle age, with a receding hairline and a clipped beard flecked with grey, a far cry from the squeaky-clean tow-headed kid who had a twelve-year run on a popular TV western in the 1960s.

"And this is my partner, Steve," said Robbie of the husky ex-jock, twenty years younger, who materialized at his side.

"Oh," said Edie. "What business are you two in?"

"No, no," said Robbie. "I meant life partner."

"Oh," said Edie, at first not grasping the concept, but then noticing the matching gold bands they wore on ring fingers and nodding as it slowly sunk in. "Ohhhhhh," she said. Andrew wanted to disappear when Edie then asked if they knew Bruce, her hairdresser.

"Let's show Henry the pool," Linda had said, a way to break the moment. She took Henry's hand and Andrew followed them toward sliding doors that led to the backyard. "Your dad is gay?" said Andrew as they went.

"Well, obviously, he wasn't always. But I thought you knew," Linda said. "I mean, they've been together nearly thirty years. You should hear them bicker. If it's not like any old married couple, I don't know what is."

Andrew had to explain that in his and his mother's part of Pasadena, the goings-on of Hollywood romances could have been taking place on Mars, even though the two towns were barely twenty miles apart. But by the time they returned with Henry to the living room, Edie, Robbie, and Steve were on their second round of Manhattans, and Edie was laughing at Robbie's story of the grandmother, the beloved family matriarch, from his 1960s drama, played by the crusty old actress who had gotten a start in silent films and had been working like a horse ever since.

"You might remember," Robbie was saying, "that late in the life of the show she lost a leg. It was something to do with a circulation problem and diabetes in real life, but for the show, they wrote in an accident with the grain thresher, and then, for the next few seasons, they had to keep creating scenes where she didn't have to move around much."

"What a trouper. Bless her little heart," said Edie.

"Oh, she was a major pain in the ass," said Robbie. "The whole crew was terrified of her. And get out of the way if her pages weren't done by five sharp when she expected to have her scotch and soda in hand."

So tension seemed to have eased until they all moved into the dining room and Linda noticed the Seder plate missing from its place at the center of the table.

"You don't mean the one with the old dried-out bone and the broken eggshell?" Edie asked.

"Yes," said Linda. "That one."

"Every element represents a part of the Jewish faith," said Steve, himself a lapsed Catholic.

"Oh, dear," said Edie. "Well, I threw that out."

Apparently, while passing through on the way to the powder room, Edie spotted what she assumed, she later insisted to Andrew, was a housekeeping faux pas and dumped the whole thing into the trash. Robbie, a lapsed Jew—he only hosted these ceremonies for Linda, who went in and out of religious phases—couldn't stop laughing.

"Mrs. Vale," he finally managed, "this is your first Seder, isn't it?"

Then the readings began. Henry, sitting stiffly upright in his Brooks Brothers blazer and striped tie, stumbled and struggled over the passage read by the youngest at the table, only to be interrupted by the doorbell. Soon Blanca marched into the dining room with the one-pound box of See's Candies that Edie meant to bring as a hostess gift and had left on the table in the front hall of the house.

"You took the bus from Pasadena?" Steve asked, incredulous, when Blanca, looking somewhat winded from the hike up the long, gated driveway, agreed to accept a glass of water.

"*Si. Tres,*" said Blanca. "Three buses."

"You don't drive?" somebody asked.

"She did until the cataract surgery," Edie said gaily, then noticed everybody staring at her. "First of all, I gave her the car she used to drive, and second of all, I paid for that surgery."

Blanca refused all pleas to stay and wait for a lift home. She turned and hiked back down the hill toward the bus stop.

Still later that night, they all climbed back into Edie's Mercedes. "What's that smell?" Henry asked as they headed down the hill.

Edie opened her purse. Inside, it was lined with plastic—a dinner party trick cribbed from the ever resourceful Oatsie

O'Shea. Without being noticed, a smiling, genial, and chatty Edith had slipped into her purse two matzo balls and a hunk of gefilte fish.

"My God, Mother" was all Andrew could manage as he watched her pull over and dump the contents onto the street.

"Well, I ate the chicken and every last green bean," Edie said in her defense.

"And why did you ask for a second matzo ball if you hadn't eaten the first?"

"It is important to be polite," said Edie. "Always remember that, Henry," she added.

Andrew just groaned. He figured Linda would break up with him first thing the next morning. He was wrong. She told Andrew she wanted to get married, that she had fallen in love with him, and that she was falling in love with Henry too.

"He has a mother, you know," Andrew said.

"Who isn't around much, is she?" said Linda.

"That's not exactly by choice, if you want to know the truth."

"Still, I've been feeling very maternal lately. Like I want to nurture. You know, the other day I almost adopted a kitten, and I don't even like cats."

"Actually, if you must know," Andrew interjected, "I'm allergic to cats. I break out in terrible hives, and . . ."

"It's probably that body clock thing," Linda continued, "but I'd make a good stepmother, don't you think?"

He agreed that she would. He also felt it was time to make a home for Henry that wasn't his mother's. And so Andrew once again found himself rushing headlong into marriage, and Henry, at first skeptical of this somewhat neurotic but always determined woman, grew attached to her as well. He even served as ring bearer at the wedding. This time, Edith Vale was unhappily relegated to the backseat because Linda had a fantasy of what her wedding should be and wouldn't stand for any intrusions. And so Edie, in blue silk organdy from I. Magnin and a single strand of pearls, sat primly, knees together, in her mother-of-the-groom spot and kept her mouth clamped shut as a lavish ceremony and reception she found a bit vulgar and unnecessary unfolded at the Hotel Bel-Air.

They honeymooned at the Halekulani on Waikiki Beach, and when they got back, Linda—who had drifted from college to college, from career possibility to career possibility, and had finally found her niche as an interior designer because of the bedroom she redid in a friend's Malibu beach house and the photographs of it that landed in a magazine—set about to find them a home. She settled on a Brentwood grand dame, a sprawling old wreck with great bones that she gutted and rebuilt. This began a new career for her—rehabbing these drafty relics with their leaky pipes and downright dangerous wiring, with all the dry rot and termite damage—which meant a move every two years or so.

And when she wasn't focused on fixing up houses, she turned her attentions to her stepson. Even Andrew could see that Henry had inherited the most unfortunate attributes from both parents, from his side the prominent ears and nose, from Susan's the dreadful eyesight. Linda insisted he try contact lenses, but they never could get the prescriptions right, and he'd stumble into walls or trip over the furniture, so it was back to glasses. Linda tried trendier frames, but the results were always somewhat of a letdown. Henry was also, Andrew had to admit, slightly uncoordinated. So Linda tried to turn him into a better athlete. She'd throw baseballs with him in the afternoon and play one-on-one basketball after dinner. Henry never seemed to improve. Like his father, he could manage on skis and could hold his own on a surfboard in the waves off his grandmother's house, but when the twins came along, Linda's attention shifted to them. Before long Henry was packed up and sent east to boarding school.

Everything seemed to be fine, Andrew thought now, as he left Edie and Evangeline in the Mercedes and approached Robbie Landesman's front door. He wondered how he missed all the signals that Linda was unhappy.

"She hasn't stopped sobbing since she got here," said Steve when he opened the front door.

Behind him Robbie was holding Serenity and Alexander, two blond towheads, perpetually in motion, it seemed to Andrew, who generally felt he could never take his eyes off them or they'd get themselves into some kind of trouble. When they saw their father they jumped into his arms, forcing him to juggle all the slithery limbs that seemed to be going every which way all at once.

"Mommy's mad," said Serenity.

"We didn't do anything," said Alexander.

"Nobody said you did. Where is she?"

"Pool house," said Robbie, waving at Edith, who sat in the Mercedes puffing on a Parliament while gesticulating wildly at Evangeline, who was toying with the window switch again. "Do your mother and aunt want to come in?"

"They'll be fine. I'll go talk to Linda. Stay with your grandpas," said Andrew to the twins as he set them back on the floor.

He found an uncharacteristically disheveled and teary-eyed Linda sprawled on a couch in the pool house. She started crying harder when she saw him. Not a good sign, Andrew figured. He lowered himself down next to her and waited for the jag to subside.

"It just hit me the other day," Linda finally said, "how meaningless my life is."

"What are you talking about?" Andrew asked. "You have two beautiful children. And a great stepson. You have a husband who loves you. Your career is going great."

"You know what I did the other day?" she asked but then went on without waiting for an answer. "I had to come up with a plan for the Robson backyard . . . it's those clients who just bought that lot on Canyon View? Anyway, when my mom divorced my dad, for a while she rented this place in Studio City. It was a horrible house, but it had the most awesome backyard. A pool that looked like some tropical lagoon—you know, like in the opening credits of Gilligan's Island? And a separate play area for the kids and a more grown-up garden and patio area, and there was this one little detail of the layout I wanted to see because they're similar lots, and so I'm like, 'Oh, I'll Google it.' So I type in the address, and the street comes up on my screen, and I keep zooming in on it. And you know it's so weird because as you get closer you start to recognize things . . . houses that your friends lived in or the corner where we used to all meet on our bikes and even this big rock at the end of my friend Lisa's driveway with the house number painted on it. Anyway, I zoom in closer, and all of a sudden it hits me . . . the house is gone. Just absolutely gone. The rock in front of Lisa's house is still there, but our old house isn't!"

"What? They knocked it down?" said Andrew.

"Yep. And some monstrosity now takes up the whole lot."

"Well, you know that happens all the time. You do it yourself."

"Oh, no I do not, Andrew. There's a difference to what I do. I always look for houses with pedigrees and workable floor plans that just need updating. I have never completely erased what was there. In fact, I always try to leave some original details intact."

"But still . . ."

"You don't get it. It hit me. It's all so meaningless. It all gets bulldozed and there's no trace of your past. It's like I was never there in that house as a little girl. My little room that I loved. And my bathroom. It's like I never existed."

Here, she started sobbing again. Andrew couldn't find words that would comfort her, so he put his hand on the small of her back and started moving it in circles. "I spend all my time mulling over these choices—granite or soapstone or stainless steel for the kitchens, do we want bamboo floors or cork, or how can we move that wall, and don't get me started on the choices for the bathrooms—and in the end, none of it really matters."

"Did you take a Zoloft?" Andrew finally asked.

"Yeah."

"Have you eaten? Because you know how you get when your blood sugar gets low."

Linda just looked at Andrew and once again burst into tears.

***

When Andrew got back to the Mercedes, he had the twins with him. "Where is your wife?" asked Edie as Andrew belted each one into the backseat.

Evangeline turned around and started making faces at them.

"She wants me to take the kids for a while."

"While she does *what?*" said Edie. "What exactly is it with these women you find who keep pushing their children on other people!"

Suddenly Andrew felt exhausted. "I don't know, Mother. She needs some time to sort things out. You can drop us at the beach house."

"Well, I can't do that."

"Why not? That's where we've been staying."

"I told you . . . when I noticed a damp spot in the ceiling, I called Mr. Ritter."

Mr. Ritter, a handyman, had been doing odd jobs for the family at the beach for as long as Andrew could remember. He had seemed ancient when Andrew was a child, and like Hans, who fixed the Mercedes, seemed to have a soft spot for his mother.

"You may have told me, but it didn't register. Besides, he's still alive?"

"Of course he is. He has a little bit of the gout is all. Oh, and he's blind in one eye. Anyway, he looked it over. There is a leak, so I told him to go ahead and fix that section of roof and repaint the living room."

"So where are we supposed to go?"

***

Later, Andrew found himself seated at the little table with the twins and Evangeline in the breakfast room of his mother's house in Pasadena as Blanca served up dinner. This was the same table with the same slight wobble next to the same bay window that looked out over the rose garden where Andrew, as a child, took most of his meals. Sometimes, Edith would join him at the table with a Parliament and a dressing drink, or with some knitting in her lap, before she and his father, or later she and Anderson Vale, would go out for the evening. He loved these times together. He would regale his mother with stories about that very garden out the window, elaborate fantasies about the little forts he would construct under the shrubs or in one of the towering oaks, places where he was always a king and lorded over his realm. He hated when his parents went out, which they did constantly. Sometimes he would stay awake, alert for the sound of tires on gravel that signaled their return. Sometimes, if they were really late, he'd fear they'd never come back, so he would climb out of bed and sit by the window until he could see the twin pools of light creeping up the long drive-way. He'd wait until the door to his room cracked open and Edith padded in, heels in hand. She'd lean over and kiss his forehead, and—Andrew could still conjure up the oddly reas-suring smell, an intoxicating combination of cigarette smoke, alcohol, and her favorite perfume, Joy—that would mean it was safe for him to go to sleep.

Now Blanca served up one of Edie's favorite recipes, creamed chicken and peas on toast points with the crusts cut off, the same recipe that had been in the family forever, a bland concoction that was somehow comforting on the one hand to Andrew but on the other made him feel as if time was whir-ring in reverse and he was ten years old again, especially since Serenity and Alexander were both playing with their food exactly the way he used to. Andrew pushed his chair back, fished his phone from his pocket, and tried Henry's number again. Again he got voice mail. He left one more stern message and instructions for Henry to call him back on the double. He sent a text and an e-mail too, figuring at least one of those mes-sages would get through and make an impression.

When dinner was over, he took the twins upstairs, and through various squawks and protests managed to get them through their baths and into clean sets of pajamas. He made sure teeth were brushed and tucked them into the beds in his old room. He pulled one of the books from his childhood from the shelf—a well-worn and tattered edition of The Travels of Babar—and opened it to page one.

"Babar," Andrew began, "the King of the elephants, and his wife, Queen Celeste, have just left for their wedding trip in a—Oh, my God!" The outburst came midsentence and was practically shrieked.

The twins, their eyelids already growing heavy, sat up suddenly, as if an alarm had sounded and they might have to flee.

"It's nothing. Never mind," Andrew said, but in fact, he had, out of the blue, a vision of this same book being read to him in this very same room by his own father. Then he saw himself reading the book to a young Henry in this very same room after Susan had left.

These weren't warm and cozy images, but ones he found vaguely strange and disturbing, like something out of a recurring nightmare. Until he forced them out of his head altogether and started to read again, focusing on the words, until the twins grew quiet. He switched off the light, stood in the doorway until they began to sleep, and then headed downstairs.

In the library, Edie was seated at her bridge table like a queen at her throne, her King Charles spaniels at her feet. To her right was Oatsie O'Shea, and to her left was Evelyn Brookby, ladies in waiting. He noticed too late to turn and beat a hasty retreat that the seat across from Edie was empty as he crossed the room to pour himself a drink at the bar.

"Andrew, darling. Tish Van Buren is home with the flu. Come and be our fourth."

Actually, he felt like screaming; somewhere deep down inside was a rant about how he kept on making the same mistakes over and over again, and he would keep making them, over and over again, until he was dead. Instead, he poured himself two healthy slugs of a single-malt scotch and sat down while his mother smiled and began to deal the cards.

VIII.

After two days on the road, Susan and Henry had covered nearly a thousand miles. Susan tracked progress not by the little signs by the side of the road announcing miles or by the GPS, which they switched off because the voice had become somewhat annoying, but by regional foods they encountered. So when they passed through the northern portion of New York state, they ate buffalo wings, crisp celery sticks, and blue cheese dressing. ("Equal parts mayonnaise and sour cream, thin with buttermilk, add crumbled cheese, tons of cracked pepper, dash of hot sauce, and salt to taste," said the waitress at the joint when Susan asked for the recipe.) They bisected a corner of Pennsylvania and stopped for scrapple and eggs, Susan dodging Henry's questions about what exactly went into the little meat patty they were eating because she knew it would gross him out. She wasn't even sure herself of the ingredients. She just knew it was nose-to-tail eating of the most primitive kind. When they made a straight line through Ohio, they sampled belly-busting chili sizes (buttered spaghetti on the bottom, topped with meaty chili, and then giant mounds of grated sharp cheddar).

They were on the verge of crossing into Illinois when Susan, exhausted, beginning to see double, found them a motel. Henry fell into a deep slumber, but Susan found the air in the room stale and musty. She slept fitfully, finally getting up and stepping outside, where it was cool and damp. She checked her phone for e-mails and texts. Mike Finley wanted to know where she'd disappeared to and when she was coming back. Since she hadn't figured that out, she didn't return the text. Feeling restless, she walked a couple of fast circles around the parking lot. Back in the room, while Henry still slept, she inventoried the small kitchenette in the corner and decided to cook them breakfast. So she slipped out of the room again and headed down the street to the 7-Eleven.

A few minutes later, she was standing at the register with the makings of French toast, wondering why her heart seemed to be racing and her palms were beginning to sweat. Until it dawned on her that she was doing almost the same thing fourteen years ago, and that was the start of all the drama, and all the questions about who was going to raise her son.

Fourteen years earlier, Susan came home after a long night at work, said goodbye to Caridad, the Guatemalan nanny she had hired to sit with Henry while she was gone, and then realized she was out of Cheerios, practically the only thing Henry would put in his mouth without a fuss. It was winter. All day long, all she heard about was the impending arrival of some Pacific storm that had been gaining strength in the Gulf of Alaska and was now barreling south down the coast. All night long, as Susan threw stew steaks and chops on the grill and occasionally manned the flattop, reporters on the radio in the restaurant kitchen, tuned as it always was to one of the Latin stations, kept issuing urgent bulletins about *mucha lluvia* and *inundacion*, and *barro peligroso*, about the torrential rain and floods and mudslides that were on the way. Henry was asleep in his room, and Susan figured she'd be gone ten minutes max if she ran down to the Ralphs on the corner to pick up what she needed so she wouldn't have to go in the morning in the middle of a deluge.

Ten minutes was all it took for the building to catch fire. She could hear the sirens when she was in line to pay for the groceries, but at that moment, it was background noise, nothing to do with her life and unimportant. Then she turned the corner to their block; her building, a 1920s-era three-story Mediterranean complex with a red tile roof, was surrounded by fire trucks, their lights sending red and white slashes swirling in every direction. Still, panic didn't set in until Susan got closer and saw smoke pouring from the windows where Henry was sleeping, and then, suddenly, she was like one of those people she'd see on the news, all hysterical and being restrained by burly, uniformed firemen. They kept her from rushing into the building, and she could only breathe again when she saw Henry being carried out, an oxygen mask over his tiny face. They took him to the hospital, where he was treated for smoke inhalation. But he was lucky—there was no permanent damage, at least not the kind she could detect, Susan later thought. The fire, started deep inside a wall by old, faulty wiring, couldn't have been prevented either, but in the eyes of Edith Vale, the idea that she had left Henry alone and defenseless was strike number two against Susan.

The first strike was when she left Henry with Andrew while she went to France for an apprenticeship that was supposed to last four weeks but stretched to nearly twelve. She was still working at the downtown steak house. The executive chef, Istvan, a Hungarian with a thick accent and a mean temper, spent much of his time yelling at Susan and the rest of the kitchen crew, accusing them all of incompetence and laziness, but half the time, they couldn't understand what he was saying, so they'd wait until the tantrum passed and continue on with their work. One day he called Susan into his office and she figured he was firing her.

"You will want to go to Gascony," said Istvan. She wasn't sure if he meant it as a question or an order.

"I'm sorry," Susan had said. "What?"

"Relatives of my wife. They have a small restaurant and pensione. You will be their commis."

Susan sat there with a blank look on her face.

"*Commis! Commis!*" he said, louder, slapping a hand on his desk, and then, when Susan still looked clueless, practically shouted "Apprentice! You will be their apprentice. Understand? Yes?"

"Right," said Susan. "But . . . this Gascony . . . that's in France?"

Here Istvan exploded, an expletive-laden tirade, partly in English and partly in Hungarian, about a know-nothing generation of imbeciles. Eventually Susan pieced together that he felt she had talent, but that she needed to spend time abroad to learn about cooking and about food from people who really knew what they were doing. Susan said she had to think about it. The truth was she badly wanted to go. At barely twenty-three, already married, divorced, and the mother of a fussy two-year-old, she was feeling as if life was closing in around her, that she was hemmed in on all sides by poor judgment and bad choices.

Indeed, for a while after she took Henry and left Andrew, she regretted the decision. If she set aside his cheating—and maybe she did need to shoulder some of the blame, she reasoned—she could have done worse. Andrew was smart and stable. Okay, she did find him a little boring, she had to admit, but was that such a bad thing, really, in the long run? Didn't that also mean maybe he would be somebody solid, a person she could rely on to be there? There were times she feared no other man would love her. How many chances does a person get, she'd wonder, as she changed yet another horrifyingly poopy diaper or agonized through one of those anxious, sleepless nights when Henry came down with a cough or a cold or the croup or the flu and she was afraid he'd choke or stop breathing altogether if she wasn't paying attention. Not that she didn't date. She went out with a couple of men in the period after the divorce—restaurant guys mostly, scruffy hard drinkers with attitudes, bottomless appetites for bizarre late-night meals and tattoos. But then Susan would reveal she was a single mother, that there was a toddler at home, and mostly they'd bail. Which, admittedly, made Susan resent Henry, as if he was deliberately ruining any shot she might have at another relationship. So when the idea of going to Europe came up, she considered bringing Henry with her, but wouldn't he'd be better off in familiar surroundings? At least that's what she told herself when she dropped him at his grandmother's house and dared not look in the rearview mirror as she headed down the driveway.

So Susan flew alone to Paris. As she settled into her seat and the jet taxied down the runway, she had the sudden sensation that she was free, that here was a chance to make a clean getaway. She could start all over again and never go back. Then, as if on cue, came the memory of how Henry smelled after a bath, fresh like new rain and sweet, or how sometimes he would absently grab one of her fingers and hold it tight, and something else took over, a cloak of guilt that seemed to engulf her like a cloud. Again, she reasoned, the separation was temporary, and so she willed herself to put all these thoughts out of her mind as she spent the next few days exploring the streets of

Paris, staring slack-jawed at some beautiful sculpture in a garden that seemed to appear out of nowhere or at some intricate
carving of godlike creatures she'd spot over a door. There was
something beautiful—or a breathtaking vista—at almost every
turn, it seemed. She marveled at the imagination of the people
who built it all. She came armed with a list of suggestions from
fellow cooks, out-of-the-way bistros, dives, and brasseries to
try, but nothing stuck with her more than the little picnic she
put together for herself at the small shop just down the street
from her pensione. It was a ham sandwich, really, but it was
unlike any ham sandwich Susan had ever eaten, on a fresh
baguette that had a shatteringly crisp crust but a soft inside.
Sweet butter was spread down one side of the bread, a thin
layer of Dijon mustard down the other, and then came slices
of salty ham. Simple, but the finest ingredients, thought Susan,
as she sat on a bench in the Tuilleries and devoured the sandwich with a split of champagne and then a napoleon, and then,
because it looked so pretty with its dark chocolate glaze and
hint of pastry cream inside, the entire eclair she swore she'd
stash away for later.

After a couple of days of exploring the city, eating just about
anything she could get her hands on that looked or smelled
or tasted new, she took a train to Bordeaux. The restaurant
and hotel, run by Michel and his wife, Claudine, was a bit of
paradise, unlike anything Susan had ever experienced. A rect-
angular, deep beige chateau-like structure with long windows
framed by crisp white shutters sat amid a lush green vineyard
on one side and a garden overflowing with sunflowers and vegetables of all kinds on the other, zucchinis here, row after row
of tomatoes there, next to plump, deep purple eggplants. From
her room—a small, spartan, cramped space just under the eaves
on the third floor, the ceiling so low Susan spent the entire time
she was there stooped and with a mild backache—she could

see the tips of the Pyrenees in one direction and in the other the Atlantic. She figured she'd immediately start in the kitchen, but Michel and Claudine left her alone that first day, which she spent wandering the vineyards and gardens, which teemed with bees, butterflies, and hummingbirds. She watched as guests—mostly well-to-do Americans, it seemed, guidebooks in hand—noisily came and went.

She reported to the kitchen that second day, and even though she had some experience under her belt, Michel started her right back at the bottom, making stock. He showed her how to season the veal and beef bones with lots of sea salt and fresh cracked pepper, lay them out on old battered trays, and roast them until they were sizzling and golden. Then they'd go into towering pots, along with aromatics and water. She'd bring the pots to a simmer and stand guard, skimming off foam until the broth was clear. She had to be vigilant; Michel—short and stubby, a burning cigarette perpetually clamped between his lips—would threaten to throw out the stock and make her start from scratch if it turned out cloudy, although soon she figured that was an idle threat as he was also, she discovered, almost comically cheap and flinty. The liquids would continue to simmer over the very lowest flame, a portion of them all through the night, so by morning all that was left was syrupy and concentrated, the demi-glace that could instantly turn a sauce into something sublime. A crash course in those sauces came after she had mastered stock, from béchamel to beurre blanc, from béarnaise to mayonnaise. She graduated to making pâtés and sausages, but before she mastered those tasks, Michel drove her down the road in his rattling old truck and stopped at a farm, where sheep and goats grazed on a hillside and pigs lolled in a muddy sty. Susan looked at the livestock, and then at Michel, a sinking feeling in the pit of her stomach because she had an idea of what might be coming.

"Pick one," Michel said with a nod toward the pigs, "and once the deed is done you will learn to break him down."

"This may be a problem," Susan tried to explain.

She told him the story about how she thought of being a veterinarian, and when she started cooking, she had trouble just steaming open clams or plunging live lobsters into pots of boiling water. Through her various kitchen jobs, she learned the basics of butchery—she could, for instance, take apart a chicken in a matter of minutes and she could French a lamb chop like a professional, and she was proud of that—but so far she had managed to avoid the part of the game that brought the animal to the point of actually being broken down.

Michel would hear none of it. He insisted that what she would witness would teach her to respect the animal more, and though it was difficult and disturbing, in the end she realized he was right.

After charcuterie, she went on to braises and roasts, and then Claudine took over to teach pastries and desserts, starting with basic pâte brisée and continuing through all sorts of genoise and on to crème caramel and beyond. One day a week, the restaurant would close, and on those days Claudine and Michel would take Susan to nearby vineyards, where she was schooled in all things wine, from the care of the vines themselves through the harvest and crushing of the grapes, through the sampling of vintages as they aged.

All through this time, she picked up bits of French from her mentors, who spoke little snippets of broken English, and although she swore up and down she wouldn't go there when she first laid eyes on him because hadn't sex gotten her in enough trouble already, she slept with their tall, shaggy, heavy-lidded son, Jacques, when he'd come to visit from his apartment in Paris, where he worked at some Internet start-up. Slowly but surely she was developing a palate, really tasting things for the first time, it seemed, and realizing the importance of technique and quality ingredients. She nurtured a relationship with food that wasn't there before, with the rich foie gras and the stinky cheeses, with the breads baked daily in a woodburning hearth, the creamy sweet butter, and the vegetables plucked right from the garden. When she wasn't working, she'd simply watch. And every other day or so, she'd sit down and scribble notes and postcards to Henry, updating him on her progress and sending hugs and kisses his way, or she'd call, and after some awkward small talk with Mrs. Vale, who seemed solely concerned with whether or not she'd visited the bar at the Ritz and Maxim's in Paris as advised, she'd babble on to Henry about what she was doing and seeing, even though he was too young to comprehend or reply. She had, by this time, convinced herself that this separation was good for them, that it would make their bond stronger somehow.

But when she finally returned to California, nearly eight weeks late because she kept delaying her departure, it was as if some invisible cord had been severed. Andrew, busy clerking for a judge, had ceded most of the decisions regarding Henry to his mother. Edie, having given up control of her grandson once, when Susan and Andrew divorced, seemed more determined than ever this time to maintain it. Susan was no longer sure that Henry wasn't better off with her. Especially after the third strike against her, which occurred a short time after her return from France. She had gone back to work with Istvan, the Hungarian with the explosive temper, but he had opened his own place. He had hired her as sous chef, at higher pay than before but with even longer hours. Susan would return to the apartment exhausted, but she'd haul herself out of bed in the morning to give Henry breakfast.

One day, after a particularly long and grueling night, she took Henry to the park, plunked him into the sandbox, and promptly fell asleep on a nearby bench. When she woke up, he was gone. Susan ran frantically through the park, shouting his name so loud her throat felt raw and her voice went hoarse, certain he had vanished into thin air and would never been seen again. It would be all her fault. How would she live with it? She raced to the Pasadena police department, only to find he was already there, and only then did it feel like her heart might not beat right through her chest. He'd been found wandering Colorado Boulevard. The officer who picked him up managed to coax two words out of him: "Mrs. Vale." Not that it mattered, in the end, because Edith, years earlier, perhaps predicting just such an emergency, had Blanca painstakingly sew Henry's name, address, and phone number into the label of every last piece of his clothing. So Edie was already at the precinct when Susan arrived, impeccably turned out in one of her gaily patterned, finely tailored Bill Blass suits, having been summoned from a club function, she wasted no time telling Susan.

"I think I should take custody of Henry," Edie said as she drove them home.

"Oh, come on," said Susan. "He's my son."

"I'm aware of that. But let's be honest—you're doing a lousy job of taking care of him. I hate to say it, but Andrew isn't doing much better. It's clear to me now that both of you were just not ready for this. Small children need a sense of permanence. Routines and schedules are what's best. And right now, neither of you can really provide that."

She was right, Susan thought. Already Henry had nearly perished in a burning building. She left him behind so she could selfishly pursue her culinary education. It was an education, but Susan always felt Edie was thinking it was just an excuse for her to indulge in rich food, fine wine, and sex with a Frenchman while somebody else was taking care of her son. And now she had put him in danger of disappearing altogether.

She felt as if her mere presence was putting him in physical peril.

And so what began as a temporary experiment—Henry would stay with Edie for a month and they'd see how it worked out—turned into six months and then one year and beyond. Henry seemed to thrive under his grandmother's care. He was always neatly turned out in clothes that were pressed, his hair combed and shoelaces tied. Susan would take him overnight, and within hours, his clothes would be stained or his nose would be running or he'd fall and wind up with some bloody scrape that would inevitably become infected. He read beyond his grade level. His manners were impeccable. Whenever she'd ask if he was happy at his grandmother's, he'd either dodge the question and change the subject or say, curtly, he was fine, thank you for asking, ever polite. Susan didn't push him or dig deeper because she wasn't sure if she'd like what she heard. And so even though she'd see Henry whenever she could, she wound up feeling more like a distant aunt or a much older sister than his mother, a feeling that remained as the next years passed in what felt like a blur, until the day Edie and Andrew announced Henry was going to fly east to attend boarding school, just like his father and grandfather had before him.

"But, New Hampshire?" Susan said to Andrew, once the initial shock wore off that he was actually old enough to go away. "That's so far."

"It'll be good for him," he answered. "He'll learn to be independent. He'll make friends he'll keep for the rest of his life."

"Are you still friends with kids who went with you?"

"Well, no," Andrew had to admit.

Susan hung up the phone that day and decided to move east. She lied to herself and said she needed a change of scenery, that she missed Boston and its very distinct seasons. Well, she *did* sort of miss that, the leaves turning brilliant shades of orange and red in crisp autumn air, or the city, hushed and muted under a heavy blanket of fresh January snow. Until she'd recall scraping ice from her windshield in subzero temperatures after a long shift or having to abandon the car altogether after skidding into a drift. Still, the move seemed to make sense. The truth was she felt she was a terrible person who had abandoned her son, and it was time to try and make it up to him. Her plan was she'd find a job in the city and see Henry on weekends. What she didn't consider was the hostility and attitude that seemed to come off Henry in waves any time she made an attempt to bridge the gulf that had formed between them like some deep, unfathomable crevasse.

Now, though the trip started off well enough, she could sense the bad attitude returning, and it was starting to get on her nerves. So as she beat the eggs for the French toast and tended to the frying bacon in the motel kitchenette on the Ohio-Illinois border, she said aloud to a still-sleeping Henry, "It's not like I never made a sacrifice for you."

"What . . . ?"

He wasn't really asleep. She had bacon sizzling in a pan and was brewing fresh coffee, and Susan always figured those aromas could rouse the dead.

"I was on the verge of being offered my own restaurant when I moved to Boston, you know. I don't recall if I ever mentioned it," said Susan, now dropping pats of butter into another preheated pan. The truth was she had wanted her own place and didn't realize how much it meant when she decided to let it go. She longed to be the boss and not some underling.

"Yeah, yeah. There was a group of investors. They thought you were brilliant. They were scouting locations all over Los Angeles."

"All right, so I did mention it."

"About two hundred times at the very least."

"The point is I want you to try to stop being mad at me."

She dunked bread slices into the beaten eggs, let them soak, and then laid them into the pan.

"I'm here, aren't I?"

"Are you having fun? Or are you here just to humor me or because you didn't want to go home to face your father and stepmother and Mrs. Vale?"

"I'm having fun, all right? Jesus," he said. He climbed out of bed and padded over to the table, where Susan had set out orange juice. She put down a plate of hot French toast and bacon.

"Sorry about the syrup," she said.

"Why? What'd you do, spit in it?"

"Oh, that's funny, Henry. Hilarious. No, 7-Eleven doesn't stock the real stuff. There wasn't a maple tree or a drop of sap within a hundred miles of that shit. Stuff. Sorry."

"Mrs. Vale wouldn't serve that."

"Mrs. Vale will never know," said Susan as she joined Henry at the table with a plate of her own, and they both dug in.

***

"Do you think you could take our picture?" Susan asked the woman who was standing nearby. She was old, with pale, papery skin and she smelled of lilacs.

Earlier, Henry had gone online to chart roadside oddities along their route, and they had stopped at one he was curious about: Bellefontaine, Ohio, home to the first concrete street in the United States. The town had erected a statue to honor George Bartholomew who, they learned, brought concrete to the Midwest. A plaque read "Here Started the Better Roads Movement," and Susan felt it was appropriate to capture the moment.

"Come stand by me," she said. Henry walked over but stopped about three feet away from his mother.

"Closer," said the lady taking the picture.

Henry moved an inch, maybe.

"Oh, come on, honey," said the lady. "Give your mama a big old hug, why don't you?"

"That's not likely to happen," said Henry.

Here Susan took the initiative. She put an arm around him. At first Henry flinched, as if Susan's hand had some sort of electrical charge. Then he stiffened.

"Now smile, sonny," said the lady.

Susan looked slightly askance. Henry made an attempt to smile. Still, his teeth were clenched together, and his hands were balling into fists, but maybe, she reasoned, this was because suddenly the old lady became all tentative and fumbling with the phone, taking forever, it seemed, to be sure they were framed properly and asking, repeatedly, if she was pushing the right button. Susan was starting to get annoyed too.

A short while later, the thought flashed through Susan's mind, If we hadn't detoured, this wouldn't be happening now. They were back on the interstate, and Henry was showing her the picture. She barely took her eyes off the road, she'd remember later, although it was long enough to note how uncomfortable they seemed standing next to each other, as if really they were two strangers and not mother and son.

Then Henry said, "Dude, you planning on stopping?"

When she looked back at the road, traffic had suddenly come to a complete halt, but the Volvo was still hurtling forward and was about to slam into the rear end of a giant semi. She wasn't sure if she screamed. She wrenched the wheel to the right. This sent the car skittering to the shoulder, which might have been fine had the road not dropped off precipitously. The car banked sharply. It started to roll. Susan threw out her arm to protect Henry, an instinctive gesture, but an unfamiliar and powerful force pressed her back into her seat and the world turned upside down. She could see Henry brace himself against the dash. So this is how it will be, was the strange thought that flew through her head. And in that same instant, she wished there was a way of turning back time and starting the day all over again.

IX.

A caravan pulled up to a once pristine but now sad little Craftsman on the north fringe of Pasadena at nine sharp, first Edith Vale in her battleship-grey Mercedes, followed by Oatsie O'Shea in a purring Jaguar, then Evelyn Brookby in a boatlike Lincoln, and finally Tish Van Buren in a well-worn old Range Rover nearly as old as Edie's car. This latest project of the Alta Arroyo Women's Club Beautification Team was about to come to fruition after months of discussion and careful planning over luncheons, cocktails, and the club's annual chicken potpie fund-raising dinner. Every year, as each member of the team drove around town on errands and whatnot, she would note when she came upon some derelict property in need of sprucing up. Addresses would be recorded, pictures taken, e-mails exchanged, debate would take place, and all of this would be followed up by a visit to the owner of the property in question. Sometimes, the sight of these four women, with their hair back-combed and shellacked into place, with their tasteful strands of pearls and severely well-cut suits, would produce reactions similar to a visit from royalty, a general deference and obeisance that then allowed for the ladies to push through their agendas in a smooth and orderly fashion. Other times, doors would be slammed in their faces or not opened at all, in which case they'd move on to the backup property, because these ladies always had a backup.

The owner of this house, a stooped, wild-eyed man of nearly ninety who used a walker and badly needed a bath, admitted he'd let maintenance go since the passing of his wife. All the ladies clucked in sympathy and understanding until they heard that the poor woman died thirty-seven years earlier, and then Edie, at least, was thinking he was just lazy or flat-out insane because shouldn't he have been over it by now, shouldn't he just move on? His classic Craftsman, built in 1910, they had learned when they did a little research, was a wreck: wood was rotting, paint was peeling, and the yard was an overgrown tangle of weeds and hard-packed dirt. Workers the club hired had already restored the wood and given the house a fresh coat of paint. Now the ladies were tackling the yard under the direction of Tish, whose gardens in San Marino had been photographed for magazines and who had been winning awards on garden tours for decades. And each was dressed for the part, stiffly creased chinos tucked into Wellies, neatly pressed Oxford shirts, and cardigans thrown over their shoulders to ward off a September chill.

"Step lively, ladies," said Tish as she popped open the rear hatch of the Range Rover to reveal flats of plants and bags of soil amendments she'd picked up at the nursery.

"I think it's high time," said Oatsie O'Shea, "that we hired some strapping young boys to do the planting for us."

"Strapping young boys don't exist anymore," said Evelyn Brookby. "They're all big softies like my grandsons. They lay around all day tap-tapping on their computers or texting their friends or playing those video games."

"Exercise is good for you, dear. The brisker and more vigorous the better," Edie said as Tish doled out shovels and hoes.

"I happen to play tennis three times a week," said Oatsie. "Any more exercise and I'll keel over."

"That'll be the day," said Tish with a wink, and so began the slinging of barbs, which these ladies could get away with because they knew each other so well.

Edie and Oatsie, the former Odette Burnham, had the longest history. They, along with the now deceased Bunny Vale, the first wife of Edie's second husband, were classmates at Miss Dudley's, a Pasadena institution, a school not known for producing academic excellence, but one where young girls emerged with a smattering of French, a familiarity with all the right literature titles, and the knowledge of how to properly run a house. Edie knew Evelyn and Tish from the early days of her first marriage to Frank, over forty years, pushing fifty, if she really cared to do the math. They were all newly married, the men beginning careers, the women starting to have babies, the turbulence of the times—the antiwar protests, all the casual sex, and the rampant use of illegal drugs—seeming to be taking place on some planet that wasn't Pasadena as the couples gathered for golf, tennis, cocktails, and buffet suppers.

Not that young Edith Lee didn't have thoughts about rebelling or dropping out. She'd see those other girls, with their dirty, stringy hair and their frayed jeans and glazed looks in their eyes as they shook tambourines or strummed guitars on street corners, and she'd wonder what it might be like to not care about appearances, or hygiene in general, it seemed, which she was always a stickler for, or what her mother and estranged father thought. Anyway, Evangeline rebelled enough for both of them, still in high school when she ran off with a boyfriend to a commune in Idaho, becoming a vegetarian and wearing a lot of flowing batik, which Edie thought looked awful, just didn't flatter a figure at all. She'd thought, Well, what was the point of having a nice figure if you looked like a sack of potatoes? Evangeline and a whole group of her friends got hauled into jail after some antiwar protest turned violent, and that threw the Lee household in Pasadena into something of a tizzy. Edie found she liked being praised as the good girl, and so a good girl she stayed, as did her friends.

Now, after all these years, these ladies had seen each other through dramas and crises of every kind—Edith's divorce, remarriage, and widowhood, a stint at Betty Ford's for Evelyn Brookby after she developed an addiction to amphetamines, Oatsie's mastectomy—and now, as each was approaching—or had already passed—seventy, their bonds only seemed to strengthen, and while all the ladies had occasional aches and pains, now they worked like a well-oiled machine as they unloaded the Rover and began to tackle Tish's plan for the garden.

"Before we start digging," Edie said, "who wants refreshments?"

She was met with a chorus of "I do," and so she popped the trunk of the Mercedes and brought out the tray Blanca had prepared of tea sandwiches tightly wrapped in waxed paper—cucumber and sweet butter or egg salad with finely minced celery and tons of mayonnaise on nice white bread with the crusts removed and each sandwich cut into neat triangles—and the thermos of Bloody Marys Edie had mixed before she left, adding generous amounts of fresh-squeezed lemon juice, horseradish, and Tabasco, just the way she knew the ladies liked it.

Newly fortified, they turned their attention to the work at hand. Soon, the little house was transformed. At the gate leading into the yard, they'd installed an arch and planted wisteria. Along the path leading to the porch was a hedge of iceberg roses. Flats of sod that had been delivered earlier were laid over what had been dirt and weeds. In the backyard, they laid down more sod and put in citrus, a Meyer lemon on one side, a Valencia orange on the other, with jasmine to grow along the fence at the property line. Done, the ladies stepped back to admire their work. The sad little cottage had been reborn.

**

Later, as Edie steered the Mercedes through Old Town, she wished all the problems in her life could be resolved with just a few cans of paint and some new shrubbery. When she first heard the news about Henry, her first reaction was denial, for she had long ago learned if she didn't acknowledge something unpleasant, it didn't really exist or it would simply go away. In fact, she had taught herself—willed herself really—to not see things she didn't like. What did those doctors in what-the-hell-was-the-name-of-that-town know anyway, she said to Blanca, when she set down the phone after Andrew called. She lit up a Parliament, mixed herself a Manhattan, and settled into a favorite chair in the library by the fire she had just stoked. There, feeling better already, she had mused as bourbon sent warm surges through her veins.

There had been an accident somewhere near the Ohio–Illinois border. Susan was at the wheel—Well, no surprise there, Edie had thought, the woman was positively dangerous—and Henry in the passenger seat when the car apparently left the roadway and rolled over more than once, landing back on its wheels as if nothing had ever happened. At first, Edie was told, it seemed a miracle they were both unscathed. Until, Andrew reported, Susan saw a large welt forming on Henry's forehead that was quickly turning all shades of red and purple. Another motorist had called 911. Paramedics transported Henry to the emergency room. The doctor, concerned about a skull fracture, ordered up an MRI. There was no fracture; what the MRI did reveal was a small shadow near the base of his brain. The doctor suggested Henry see a neurologist, and though he didn't seem unduly alarmed, Susan drove like mad the rest of the way to California because Henry suddenly insisted they finish the trip they started.

When they arrived in Pasadena, Edie gathered the family to wait by the front door and greet them, so they were all there—Andrew, Linda (who when she heard the news decided to put her nervous breakdown on hold and return to her husband), the twins, Evangeline, Blanca, and Edie's King Charles spaniels. Henry's grandfather Frank was supposed to fly down from Sonoma, but he called Edie at the last minute with some long-winded excuse that had something to do with ailing goats or some such thing, and Edie got so annoyed she simply hung up on him.

Henry stepped out of the car and saw them all, with huge smiles plastered on their faces as Edie had ordered, and said, "Jesus, I'm not dead yet."

And so what might have been an awkward moment was broken and they all went inside for dinner. After dinner, though, the awkwardness returned when Susan got up from the table.

"Well, I guess I'll find a motel," she said.

Edie was about to offer up suggestions, but Andrew said, "No, you move into the guest room."

"I thought we were all staying in the guest room," said Linda.

"We'll take the twins and go back to the beach."

"You can't," said Edie. "Mr. Ritter is painting, remember?"

"He can work around us," said Andrew.

They all looked at Edie.

"Oh, fine, then. Whatever."

She was on her second Manhattan by this time and felt too warm and cozy and, well, partly looped to make a fuss. Plus, she didn't want to be the bad guy. I always have to be the villain, would often run through Edie's head whenever she tried to get anybody to adhere to her rules, which she herself never found so strict or intrusive. So after Andrew, Linda, and the twins left later that night, Edie escorted Susan upstairs.

"Gosh," Susan said as they headed down the hall toward the guest room, "nothing ever changes around here, does it?"

"Meaning what?" Edith asked, annoyance creeping into her voice.

"Oh, nothing bad. I just meant it all looks exactly how it did when I lived here."

"Well, my dear," Edie said, trying not to sound huffy, "I never understand this obsession young people have with redecorating."

Indeed, it was almost startling how much everything was precisely as it was when Susan left Andrew, Edie had to admit, the same pictures in the same frames in the same places on the tables, the same vases and little statues, the same books in the library. In Edith Vale's mind, decorating had been done once when she and Frank took over the house—by a charming young former actor from Los Angeles with very good taste—and it was done properly. Of course, she would freshen things up when needed. Walls would be repainted in the exact same shade. Chairs would be re-covered in the identical chintz. Drapes would be replaced with the same fabric. Only these days, of course, all of it had to be special ordered.

Now, Edie waited until Susan seemed to get situated in the guest room and then headed for the door. But at the last second, out of habit, she turned back. "All set, dear?" she asked.

"Well, actually . . . ," Susan started to say.

She couldn't possibly need anything. The guest room was perfect, from the carefully chosen linens to the correct light for reading to the bathroom, which was stocked with pain relievers and tummy medications and shampoos and soaps of every kind.

"All right, night-night, then," Edie chirped, suddenly feeling exhausted, cutting Susan off midsentence and closing the door.

She clapped for her spaniels and then rushed back down the hall to the sanctuary of her own room, which was, indeed, a sanctuary, a subtle and sophisticated space, light and airy, all in a soothing palette of cool, creamy blues. A curved-back chaise upholstered in blue tufted satin and set at a jaunty angle sat in one corner. An antique inlaid desk was placed just so in front of a sparkling clean bay window that overlooked pool and garden. Edie's canopied bed was made with neatly pressed sheets that had hung to dry in the morning sun. In her dressing room, she changed into nightgown and slippers. She removed her makeup and slathered cold cream all over her face and neck in tight little circles, as her mother had taught her and Evangeline. She brushed and flossed her teeth, and then, after pushing the dogs to the end of the bed, she slid between the sheets, stretching her legs, wiggling her toes, and for a brief second, all was well in the world.

Then thoughts of what might be wrong with her grandson crept into her head, and though she tried crowding them out by making lists of things that needed to be done and notes she had to write and birthdays that were coming up that needed remembering, she knew sleep wasn't going to come on its own. So she took an Ambien, and that, along with all the alcohol and, oh, she suddenly recalled, there was that half a tranquilizer she took earlier too, put her into a deep, dream-free, coma-like slumber.

In the morning, Edie was still in a bit of a fog as they all piled into her Mercedes and drove to the office of the neuro-surgeon. Dr. Sheila Yang was all crispness and efficiency, her dark hair cut short and blunt, her skin white as cotton, her mouth a small red O, one of the best doctors, Edie had learned from a friend on the hospital board.

She looked at Henry's MRIs and X-rays and said, "Of course we won't know for sure until we go in. But my guess is it's a pilocytic astrocytoma."

There was a long silence. Susan looked at Henry. Henry studied his shoes. Andrew looked at Edie.

"What exactly is that?" Edie finally asked when nobody else would.

"Listen," said the doctor. "I'm going to use a scary word, but it's no reason to be alarmed."

"It's a tumor, isn't it?" said Henry before she could get the word out.

"Well, yes."

Henry nodded, then went back to looking at his shoes. That silence again fell over the small office.

"So," Dr. Yang continued, "most likely, if it is a tumor, and it's malignant, we're going to have to remove it."

Henry looked up again. "Oh great," he said, "brain surgery." Then he added to nobody in particular, "Why does everything have to happen to me?"

"Anyway, we'll get that sucker out of there. And then, maybe—we'll know better after the surgery—a round of chemo."

"So, on top of everything else," said Henry, "my hair's going to fall out?"

"Um," said Dr. Yang, "that's a distinct possibility."

"Great," said Henry. "Big nose. Glasses and bald. Like I'm ever going to get laid."

"Henry!" said Edith. "Is that really appropriate?"

"Sorry, Mrs. Vale," said Henry.

"I mean, really," Edie continued, "there is a time and place for . . ."

She trailed off because she noticed Susan, who looked, on the one hand, horrified, and on the other, like she might laugh. She noticed Andrew also trying hard to stop his mouth from curling into a smile. Edie didn't find anything remotely amusing about what Henry said. Indeed, all she could think was that this bit of bad luck must have come from Susan's side of the family, because after all, weren't all her relatives dead at a young age?

Finally, Edith flat out asked the doctor another question that popped into her mind: "How can it be," she said, "that the boy seems perfectly fine one minute and has this thing in his head the next?"

"Henry, have you had any dizziness lately? Blurred vision? Headaches?" asked Dr. Yang.

"Well," Henry admitted. "I guess. Sometimes."

"And you didn't say anything?" said Andrew.

"Nobody asked," said Henry.

Here Edith had to protest: "I am constantly asking how you are. Once a week, young man, at the very least, I call you to check in. Not to mention the letters and cards and whatnot. And all you do is mumble your responses, so how is a person to know if you weren't feeling well?" Then she turned to Andrew and Susan. "How many times have I complained about his enunciation?"

"His vocabulary. Well, that I've heard you complain about. But enunciation? I don't think so," Andrew said.

Edie snorted, snapped open her purse, started to reach for a Parliament and her lighter, then remembered where she was and snapped the purse closed.

The surgery took place two days later. While Edie, Andrew, and Susan sat in hard, plastic waiting-room chairs, a tiny hole was drilled in Henry's skull, and then a miniature saw was used to slice through the bone. A tumor, about the size of a walnut, they later learned, was excised, Henry's skull was reassembled—like the jigsaw puzzles she loved as child, Edie imagined—and the wound was stitched closed. The oncologist was fairly certain all of the tumor was gone, but a course of chemo was advised, just to be on the safe side, and now, three weeks postsurgery, halfway through the treatments, Henry was pale, weak, nearly hairless, and unable to hold down anything but clear broth.

And so as Edie headed home from helping to transform the Craftsman's garden, she found herself making a detour. She was passing the big old stone Episcopal church across from city hall, the place where she was baptized, where she was confirmed, where her two weddings took place, and where she'd be eulogized. Indeed, she had her whole funeral planned, all the specifics written down and locked away in her safety deposit box, from the flowers—white lilies only, please, no mixed bouquets—to the psalms to be read to the hymns to be sung to the secular music she wanted. The service, she long ago decided, would open with Rodgers and Hammerstein's "You'll Never Walk Alone" because she always just adored the words.

At the end of the storm
Is a golden sky
And the sweet silver song of a lark.

And when it was over, mourners would follow the casket—simple and plain as can be—as it was rolled from the church to another favorite, a stirring version of "The Battle Hymn of the Republic."

In the beauty of the lilies
Christ was born across the sea
With a glory in His bosom
That transfigures you and me.

Whenever she thought about the service, how beautiful it was sure to be because of her careful planning, and of course how moving—there wouldn't be a dry eye in the house, she was sure—her only regret was she wouldn't be there to enjoy it. But lately she had become lax in her churchgoing. It wasn't that Edith Vale had lost faith. She hadn't lapsed in her belief in some higher power, but somewhere along the line, although she loved the rituals of the church, faith had gone out of her daily life. Now, feeling that events were starting to spiral out of her control, a feeling she detested, starting with her sister beginning to lose her mind and now Henry with his body turning against him, she felt a strong urge to pray once again.

Inside, the church was as comforting and familiar as a well-worn glove. Edie bowed before the altar, then slipped into a pew toward the rear. A few had gathered for the noonday service. She opened the Book of Common Prayer and followed the reading of the Psalms, and then she said aloud when it was over, "Glory to the Father and to the Son and to the Holy Spirit: as it was in the beginning, is now, and will be forever. Amen."

She closed the book, but a thought occurred to her. She used to repeat a passage when Andrew was small and in bed with one ailment or another. She leafed through the pages of the prayer book. They made a loud, crackling sound, and the few people in the church turned to look, but Edie didn't care. She found what she was searching for and said it softly: "Heavenly Father, watch with us over your child Henry, and grant that he may be restored to that perfect health, which is yours alone to give: through Jesus Christ our Lord. Amen."

Suddenly she realized she was reading through a blur of tears so hot her eyes began to sting. And then Edith Vale did something else she hadn't done in ages: she let herself cry.

***

Later, Edie checked in on Evangeline, who was propped up in a chair in her room, staring blankly at an afternoon talk show, and then she looked in on Henry, who surprised her by asking for chicken hash, a childhood favorite. She took it as a positive sign that hunger was returning. It was Blanca's afternoon off, so she marched down the hall, Freddie and Min at her heels, and knocked on the guest room door. When she got no answer, she pushed her way in. Susan was asleep, splayed on the bed in bra and panties, clothes scattered willy-nilly around the room.

"Oh, for heaven's sake," Edie said, loud, hoping it would jar Susan awake, but Susan continued to snore away. So Edie swiped up various items and walked up to the bed. She gave Susan a little shove. "Meet me in the kitchen in five minutes," she said when Susan's eyes cracked open. She dropped the items of clothes on Susan's head and walked briskly out of the room.

Edie headed downstairs to the kitchen, which was dominated by a hulking eight-burner Vulcan range that had been installed in the 1940s and, due to vigilant maintenance and regular checkups, still cooked like a dream. This was a purely functional kitchen, the way it had been originally designed, not some fancy showplace, like the ones her daughter-in-law Linda conjured up. Edie disapproved of those, with their endless amounts of granite and all that stainless steel machinery nobody ever seemed to know how to use. And don't get her started on all those great rooms Linda was always talking about. Edith saw nothing great about them at all, really. No, her kitchen floors were well-scrubbed linoleum, her countertops tile, most of it original, and her cabinets sturdy functional ones that gleamed with coat after coat of glossy white enamel paint. With reading glasses perched at the tip of her nose, Edie now sat at the table flipping through the small weathered wooden box she had taken from its spot on the shelf over the sink. She was still at it when Susan finally appeared, sleep in her eyes, and joined her at the table.

"Have I ever told you about my mother?"

"Um," said Susan, "well, bits and pieces. But for the most part, I don't believe you have."

"This file box has all the recipes that were handed down to my mother by her mother. But both women had a filing system that's just absolutely confounding. So my old chicken hash recipe, which Blanca knows by heart, is not under C or H. I'm trying to figure out where in this box it might be."

"Maybe B," Susan offered.

"Why in the world would it be under B?"

"Because maybe it was a beef hash recipe, but somebody along the line substituted chicken."

Edie regarded Susan for a long moment. Indeed, that made sense. She flipped through the recipe cards in the B section, but it wasn't there either.

"Would you happen to know who came up with the recipe?" Susan asked.

"Of course. It was Viola. My grandmother's cook. I adored Viola. She practically raised me."

"Try V."

There it was, filed under "Viola's Chicken Hash." Edie handed it to Susan. "Your son is hungry and has asked for this for dinner. As you know, I am perfectly hopeless in the kitchen."

"You want me to help you?" said Susan.

It seemed to pain Edith Vale to admit it. "Yes," she finally said.

Susan scanned the recipe, written in faded ink on a yellowing card. "You've been eating this for years?"

"Yes. Everybody adores it. Didn't we ever serve it when you were here?"

"I'd remember, I think. Anyway, it looks dry. There's no liquid. There's nothing in it to bind the ingredients together. Does it taste dry?"

"Well, dear," said Edith, "you're meant to absolutely *drown* it in ketchup."

"That sounds sort of revolting."

"Oh, no. You smoosh it all together and make a sort of mush."

"So it's like baby food?"

"Exactly."

"Listen," said Susan, "I have a great method for hash. It's an old New England recipe. I actually learned it at the bar I worked in the summer I met Andrew. What if I make that one?"

Edie felt unsure, as if she feared the world might stop turning on its axis if she allowed Susan to make the change. "I don't know, dear. We've always done it this way."

"You want good hash or bad hash?"

"All right. Let's be daring and try it. I'll fix us a Manhattan."

Susan gave her an odd look.

"What now?" Edie asked.

"Edith, it's barely four o'clock."

"So it is," said Edie.

She set the small wooden box back on the little shelf over the sink and then headed down the hall to the library. She poured a few slugs of bourbon into her shaker with several cubes of ice. She added a slug of sweet vermouth and a few dashes of bitters. She capped the shaker and shook it vigorously. She dropped a maraschino cherry into each glass, then poured. When she returned to the kitchen, icy cocktails in hand, she found Susan surveying the pantry, scanning neat rows of canned green beans, canned peas and creamed corn, a look of consternation on her face. Lined up next to the cans were boxes of Triscuits and Ritz Crackers. Then came tuna, deviled ham, jar after jar of mixed nuts, and bottles of chocolate syrup.

"Is something wrong?" Edie asked, feeling defensive for some reason she couldn't quite pinpoint.

"No, no. Nothing," said Susan. "It's just sort of like digging up a time capsule."

"Yes, well, I think you'll find whatever you'll need," she answered tersely.

Indeed, she watched as Susan gathered ingredients: chicken stock from the pantry, along with onions, potatoes, and flour, butter from the refrigerator, and chicken breasts from the freezer, which she popped into the microwave to defrost. She slapped a skillet down onto a burner and then set an onion down in front of Edie and handed her a knife.

"Why don't you dice that for me while I poach the chicken," she said.

"Oh, I'm not good at that," Edie said as she lit a Parliament and took a long sip from her drink. "I'll just watch, dear."

"Can you peel a potato?"

"I'm not an idiot, Susan," said Edie, but she set down her cigarette and inspected the peeler, and the potato, as if they might be alien life-forms of some kind.

"Do you need a demonstration?" Susan asked.

"I know how to do it," Edie said, now getting irritated.

She started tentatively, careful not to damage her recent manicure, but soon she got into a rhythm. Meanwhile, Susan dropped the defrosted chicken breasts into a pot, covered them with water, added a carrot, a stalk of celery, a few springs of parsley, a large piece of onion, generous amounts of salt, and some whole peppercorns. She set the pot on the stove to simmer. Edie hated to admit it, but Susan moved with a confidence that she found reassuring.

Susan took a long sip of her drink and smiled. "You may not know how to cook, Edie," she said, "but you sure make a mean Manhattan."

"Ah," said Edie, "that came from my father. He would come home by six sharp every night when he and my mother were still together. He'd kiss her on the cheek, and then he'd head into the library and make them both a drink. Evangeline and I would slip in and watch. Later, I'd make them for my husbands."

"I always thought you Waspy types drank daiquiris back in the day."

"Oh, we drank those too, naturally. Mostly during daytime hours. Like at lunch after a game of tennis. Now, that was the time for a nice cold, fresh daiquiri. How's this?" She held up the potato for approval.

"Good," said Susan. Then she added, "Geez, Edith, I wish I was an adult when people played tennis and drank daiquiris all day long."

"Well, I didn't say all day long. I mean, really," said Edie. "There was a good long break between lunch cocktails and those in the evening."

Susan laughed and went back to her cooking. Edie settled in to watch. She always found something comforting about being around when a person cooked. First Susan ran her knife through the onion and measured out flour, butter, and stock while keeping her eye on the chicken now bubbling away in the pot. She diced the potatoes Edie peeled into perfect little cubes, then dropped them into another pot of simmering water until they were just tender. When the chicken was done, she removed the skin, took the meat off the bones, and chopped it into a dice. She melted butter in the sauté pan, then slipped in the chopped onions, sprinkling them with salt and pepper. She did that chef's trick, flicked her wrist so the onions tossed and danced and flipped in the pan, a showy gesture, Edie thought, maybe to show Edie she was indeed good at something. She added a couple of tablespoons of flour, stirred for a couple of minutes more, then whisked in hot stock, which began to bubble and form a dense sauce. Into that she folded in the diced potatoes and the chicken. She covered the pan, cranked down the heat, and let the hash begin to cook. Through it all, they polished off one Manhattan and started in on a second.

As the aroma of dinner began to spread through the house, first came Evangeline, wearing a flannel nightgown and heels, and then Henry shuffled in, painfully thin, his T-shirt hanging on shoulders that poked out sharply. He had an unsteady gait and faint smile, and to Edie, it was as if some strange, elderly man had taken over his body. Susan, stirring the crust that was forming on the bottom of the hash, adding the shredded Jack cheese and stirring again, paused to watch his slow progress too, but like Edie, she seemed to be looking while pretending not to look.

"What?" said Henry, because even the two King Charles spaniels seemed to have stopped to hold their breath.

Edie racked her brain for something encouraging or at least upbeat to say and came up blank.

Finally, it was Susan who broke the silence. "We're just happy to see you out of bed," she said.

Henry made his way to the table and took a seat. Evangeline leaned toward her sister and said, "Who's Baldy?"

Edie closed her eyes and let out a long sigh. Again, Susan seemed to be stifling the urge to laugh in the face of horror.

"God, Aunt Evangeline," said Henry. "We've been over this. It's me, Henry. Your nephew? Hello? The big loser, the brain tumor?"

"You are not a loser," said Edie as Evangeline tried to take a sip of her cocktail. Edie slapped her hand away.

Susan slid the hash, now brown and crusty on the bottom, onto a plate. Then she inverted the skillet over the plate and flipped the hash, so the other side would brown. When it was done, she served it with gently poached eggs on top, the warm, creamy yolk providing the perfect contrast to the crisp and salty crust. As promised, it was delicious. Edie didn't even think to ask for the ketchup.

***

Much later, Edie was settling in for one of her coma-like slumbers when she heard noises coming from the little white square of a room off the kitchen. She heard Blanca put away her coat and her handbag. She actually heard two voices, speaking in a low murmur. Blanca must have her granddaughter Luz along, Edie thought, and into her mind sprang a picture of the shy, sweet girl with almond-shaped eyes and long, straight hair that had the intense color and deep shine of fresh black ink. Luz's mother, Blanca's youngest daughter, was always off with some man, it seemed, as was her older sister, and Blanca didn't like her granddaughter left alone in the apartment in the Westlake district of Los Angeles, which was up several flights of stairs and surrounded, Blanca always said, by gangbangers, drug pushers, and all sorts of bad influences on teenage girls. Edie then heard a grunt of disapproval as Blanca passed through the kitchen. She remembered they hadn't finished doing the dishes or tidying up. She listened as steps approached the library, where, after a couple of nightcaps, she, Susan, and Evangeline were all snoring away in chairs before a still-burning fire. At least she assumed it was Blanca and Luz in the house. For all she knew it could be a bunch of ax murderers. But the dogs would be barking, wouldn't they, Edie reasoned, still unable to muster up the energy to open her eyes or get up out of her chair, especially when she realized that one arm had fallen asleep too, which briefly made her wonder if she might have had a stroke.

Of course, it was Blanca, who stepped right up to Edie's chair and poked her. "*Despierta, vaca vieja,*" Blanca muttered under her breath. "Get up!"

Edie stirred. Feeling began to return to her arm too, itchy little tingles. "Who are you calling an old cow?" she asked, but there was that thin, reedy old-lady-just-waking-up voice again.

"If the shoe fits," said Blanca, amused sometimes at how much Spanish Mrs. Vale actually understood.

"You can go shit in your hat," said Edie.

Blanca smiled, went to wake Evangeline but turned back to Edie. "*Su hermana,*" she said, fingers pinching her nose, "*necesita limpiar.*"

"Oh God," Edie groaned and let Blanca help her out of the chair.

Her sister soiling herself was something new and disturbing, the indignities piling up one after another. Edie woke Evangeline as gently as she could, and together she and Blanca helped her up the stairs and into the bathroom, where Edie started to draw a bath as Blanca removed her clothes, cleaned up the mess, and then lifted her with surprising ease and deposited her in the tub. While Blanca headed downstairs with the laundry, Edie perched herself on the tub ledge, grabbed a bar of soap, and began to bathe her sister. At first, Evangeline was silent; her sense of embarrassment and shame were still sometimes surprisingly intact, but it wouldn't be long before she forgot how she got to this point or why.

"We used to have so much fun in the bath," she said to Edie. "Mumsie would come in, and we would laugh and laugh. What were we laughing about?"

"You know, I have no idea," said Edie.

In fact, Edie was thinking of the past, to a time when Andrew was young, younger than Henry was now, a child, and she was still married to Frank. It was one of those perfect moments, it seemed. It was a winter night. There was a terrible storm raging outside, wind and rain pelting angrily at the windowpanes, but Andrew was tucked securely in his bed, and Edie was spooned up against Frank, the spaniels she had at the time at her feet. Everybody was healthy. Everybody was happy, or so it seemed, and Edie recalled wishing she could freeze the moment forever. Now, with Henry's illness, and now, as she looked down at her little sister, who suddenly looked so helpless and frail and, honestly, so old, it was all Edie could do to not look away.

X.

An unexpected but welcome surprise was that, early on in this whole ordeal, Henry discovered he had a newfound power, like the superheroes in the stacks of comic books he devoured as a child. Well, he didn't have the X-ray vision he once so badly wanted. He couldn't soar up into the air on his own either or vanish into thin air at whim, but he found he could control those around him—Mrs. Vale or his father and Linda or even his mother, now that she seemed back on a permanent basis—by a well-timed comment or just the right word. For instance, there was the time they were all coming home from that first visit from the doctor, where surgery was discussed for the first time. Mrs. Vale was telling Susan it must be something she did to Henry, and Susan was blaming Andrew, and there was all kinds of squawking and yammering going back and forth until finally Henry told them they were giving him a headache, and they all instantly shut up, lapsing into penitent silence. It made him smile, this new sense of power and control he could wield like a sword. Another well-timed word and they'd become solicitous to no end. Did he need a sweater? Was he too hot?

Too cold? Would he like a cold drink? Hot tea? Often, Henry would ask for something he had no intention of putting on or of eating or drinking, just to watch whoever spring into action.

There were occasions, in fact, when Henry didn't feel all that sick, once the retching stopped anyway, not that the retching wasn't so awful he was sometimes fearful a vital internal organ might come up and that would finish him off. And yet, there might be a period in the day—sometimes a few minutes, sometimes an hour or two—when he would feel normal again, even without the pills that were supposed to decrease the nausea or the pills that were supposed to relieve anxiety or any of the other drugs he couldn't keep track of anyway. Sometimes he wouldn't even notice the funky metallic taste in his mouth, and his throat would stop throbbing. Sometimes he could hold down more than a few spoonfuls of broth. And in that time, it was as if this whole episode was like some really long and elaborate bad dream. The one sense that would overtake him, on occasion, was an overwhelming fatigue, as if his limbs were made of sand and he could move them only with a great concentrated effort, like sometimes in a nightmare, when he needed to escape from some unseen monster, but it was like his feet were mired in wet cement. Now he felt some of that weakness, but not enough that he couldn't tear himself away from simultaneously playing something on his Xbox or Snapchatting back and forth with Zach Julian. He climbed out of bed and headed into the hall, where from the top of the stairs he peeked at Luz, who had been left in a chair in the front hall with her nose in a book. He considered going downstairs. He'd throw a casual greeting in her direction as he passed into the kitchen. Then he recalled what he looked like now, a wreck, he felt, when he saw himself in the mirror, his skin unnaturally pale and almost ashy, all his hair gone, even his eyebrows and lashes, for God's sake, like some circus freak really is how he felt. He retreated back to his bed and tried to sleep.

But his mind started to race as it had been doing ever since this ordeal began, starting with that day his mother's car skidded off the road. He could remember feeling the start of a rollover. He could recall groping for something to hold on to, and then, in that blink of an eye, one dizzying three-sixty and then one more. He could remember the sound—or absence of sound because everything went suddenly silent, as if it were happening in some alternate universe or a vacuum, or it was some special effect in a movie. And then they were upright again and Susan was shouting about how they should get out of the car because maybe it was going to explode or something but forgetting about her seat belt and then screaming that they were trapped, until Henry reached over and set her free.

He didn't remember bumping his head at all. When he touched a certain spot, though, he could feel the swelling welt; that's when his knees started to shake and he had to sit down. But the ride in the ambulance was sort of a trip, Henry thought. Something like this had never happened to him before, being the center of attention, and he sort of liked that everybody— including his mother for a change—had an urgent stake in his well-being. So, honestly, he was enjoying it all—the sincere and earnest concern of the paramedics who asked all sorts of dumb questions, like what day it was or who was the president or how many fingers were they holding up. Also cool were the lights and sirens and the traffic moving out of the way to let them pass. Then Henry caught the look in the emergency room doctor's eyes when he glanced at the MRI. Just for a second, Henry could see there was genuine alarm, and in the pit of his stomach, he started to feel it too, as if he were standing on the edge of some steep hole where he couldn't see the bottom even though he was in danger of falling because the dirt beneath his feet was starting to crumble.

He tried to put that sense out of his mind on the rest of the drive back to California, but then his mother kept looking over at him too, a smile frozen on her face, her knuckles white she was gripping the wheel so hard, as if waiting for a time bomb to explode. And then there was Dr. Yang and all her annoying questions about headaches and double vision. Well, yes, he had been having headaches, and there were a couple of instances where he was seeing two of everything, but never did it cross Henry's mind that there was a tumor the size of a fucking walnut in his head. A walnut!

"You have a what?" Zach Julian had asked when Henry called to tell him the news.

"It's a tumor," said Henry. "Doesn't that suck?"

"So what do they do?"

"They're going to cut my head open and take it out."

"Oh, man," said Zach Julian. "Are you going to keep it?"

"Keep what?"

"Dude! Your tumor!"

"Oh my God," said Henry. "That is insane."

But then he thought about it, and it didn't seem like a horrible idea. He could have it bronzed or something and wear it like a charm around his neck, and it would become sort of a talisman, a symbol of strength and courage in the face of disaster. He could show it to girls, and they'd see how intrepid he was. In fact, Henry stayed brave through it all—the packing a bag, the ride to the hospital, the checking in, with a nervous, perspiring Andrew fumbling with his wallet and insurance cards, the settling into his room on a floor filled with other sick children—he remained cool and collected and, really, somewhat removed from it all, it felt like, until he noticed a chink open up in the armor of Mrs. Vale, who all along seemed to be pretending as if none of this were really happening. It was the afternoon after the surgery took place. His father and his mother had gone down to the cafeteria. Henry had been hovering in and out of sleep, and when he opened his eyes, a big white and blue blur was all he saw, and then when he was able to focus, he could see it was his grandmother, perfectly turned out in powder blue and a simple strand of pearls, her helmet of hair sprayed firmly in place.

"Is it over?" His mouth felt dry, like it was filled with sand, or cotton.

"Yes," said Edie, "and you did very well, Henry."

Henry nodded. "Thanks for coming, Mrs. Vale."

It was here he saw something he'd never seen in his grandmother before. It started as a sort of flinch. Then she started to blink rapidly. Her face looked all squinched up. It seemed as if she might actually start bawling, Henry was shocked to note. But she caught herself and instantly shut it down. Then Edie leaned forward and poked at him, shocking him again when she said, "You know, if you really want to, you could call me Grandma."

The problem was she nearly choked on the word, like the idea left a terrible taste in her mouth. "Oh. Okay, Grannie," he said, knowing it would get on her nerves.

"You know what?" said Edie. "Bad idea. Never mind."

They didn't talk about that moment again, and Mrs. Vale went back to pretending everything was fine. Even when the chemo started. His hair began to come out in clumps and he'd hold them up for her to see, but his grandmother refused to acknowledge what was happening right before her eyes. After a few days stressing over the loss of each strand, Henry asked Susan to drive him to the barber shop, and the guy shaved his head and so that took care of that. His mother offered to have her own head shaved.

"As a show of unity," she said, too brightly, and Henry could tell she didn't really want to do it.

"Right," he had told her. "Awesome. A bald mother. Just what I need when I already feel totally insecure."

Now his head was so smooth he wondered if hair would ever grow back, and then he wondered, if it did, would it look the same and be the same color, and would his eyes ever improve enough so he could ditch glasses, and would he still be around to care, and these were the thoughts that would keep him up.

He noticed a new text from Zach. "WTF. U do it?" it said.

Henry texted back that no, he didn't go downstairs and talk to Luz. Zach tried to convince him to man up already. But this thread was exhausting him, so Henry signed off and again tried to sleep, but once more his mind began to race. Finally, it occurred to him that indeed he should just go downstairs because who knew if he'd be around for much longer anyway, and then what would have been the big deal?

They had known each other since they were babies, Henry and Luz. Now nearly eighteen, she had long outgrown the pudgy, reserved phase that had lasted years, it seemed to Henry. At some point, he couldn't pinpoint when, she had turned slim and leggy, taller than Henry, but she moved with grace and ease, with an air of confidence. He never saw her tripping like an oaf over her own big feet or walking smack into walls like he was prone to do. Her skin was smooth and cocoa-colored, her olive-green eyes flecked with brown. She wore her long, straight, jet-black hair tied back in a ponytail, or sometimes she let it fall across her face in a casually rakish angle. She always smelled good, like she just stepped from a fresh shower.

Henry was determined to tell her how she made him feel, but he worried about how she might react; actually he worried about his whole family—Luz was, after all, the granddaughter of Mrs. Vale's housekeeper, and you never knew what Mrs. Vale might do or say, if you asked Henry. He wasn't sure what his father would think. His mother probably wouldn't care. Henry realized that he and Luz did actually come from two different worlds, separated by less than twenty miles, but still so, so different. Sometimes he wondered if that was part of the attraction. And he worried she'd blow him off for that reason alone or for one of the other ten thousand reasons he could imagine she'd have. Still, she was all he could think about these days. He had it all figured out, how to finally break the ice. He rehearsed it. He'd ask her to come with him down to the Starbucks or the Coffee Bean or wherever, and then he'd spill his guts. But as much as he kept telling himself, "So what if she throws you shade or turns you down or laughs in your face," he still kept chickening out.

This time felt different, as if he could tap on a reservoir of courage that previously wasn't there. But first he decided he needed a hat. He headed to his closet. He tried a baseball cap, but it just made his ears seem to stick out more. There was a top hat Mrs. Vale brought back from a trip to London she had taken with Mr. Vale. He thought it was the coolest thing, but he was a kid then, and now when he put it on, it looked clownish or like he had to tap-dance down the stairs or pull a rabbit from it. He finally yanked a black woolen ski cap down over his ears, and then, even though it was night, put on a pair of sunglasses. Then he took them off. He bared his teeth, searching for stray bits of food because how gross would that be? He checked his nose for stray boogers. He checked his breath, then went and brushed his teeth just to be sure. He changed into a clean T-shirt. He put on new socks. He stood before the mirror and rehearsed, because the last time he tried to talk to a girl he liked, he got all tongue-tied and bashful and felt like a total jackass. Sometimes he thought he was maybe unlovable anyway, that he'd be alone for the rest of his life.

He tried to adopt a casual pose as he said into the mirror, "Hey, what up?" No. Too ghetto, he thought. He tried, "Hey, what's shaking?" and then just "Hey."

He wondered if he shouldn't just crawl back into bed with his laptop, some porn site, and wouldn't that be easier all around. Even with the fatigue, even with the rotten taste in his mouth and everything smelling funny, he found that, just like before this all started, he was horny twenty-four seven. He wanted to bring it up with the doctor, find out if that could possibly be normal, but always his mother or, worse, Mrs. Vale was around and he'd be too mortified.

He strolled out of his room, the ski cap pulled low and actually starting to make his scalp itch, but he tried to pretend as if he didn't have a care in the world. He could see Luz was no longer in the chair in the front hall. He padded down the stairs and checked the library, but the only thing in there were the dregs of some cocktails on the coffee table, which he considered finishing but then decided that might be a bad idea. Nobody was in the living room either. He peered into the kitchen but there was no light under the door to Blanca's room. Most likely Luz was asleep, and even if she wasn't, what was he going to do? Barge into the room like some crazy person? She'd probably tell him to get lost anyway. He had no clue if she had a boyfriend or not, but maybe she did and then what? He headed back up the stairs, only to find his mother poking her head out her door.

"What's wrong?" Susan asked, that look of mild panic on her face that had been there since the day of the accident very much in evidence. Indeed, Henry had paused on the stairs as a wave of nausea suddenly hit.

"Nothing. All good," he said. But then it hit again, and he had to get to the bathroom fast, and as he made the mad dash, he knew his mother and his grandmother weren't far behind.

XI.

"Really?" was all Edith Vale said when Susan came out of the house and joined Evangeline and Henry in the clattering Mercedes.

Susan could tell from the up-and-down look her former mother-in-law gave her, and from her tone and inflection, that she had done something wrong, and it was like no years had passed and she was twenty-one and married to Andrew again.

"What?" Susan said.

"Well, it's just—we're going off to the beach, dear, not some dreary poetry reading."

It took her a minute to figure out Edie was referring to how she was dressed. She wore old jeans with rips at the knees, scuffed boots, a black T-shirt, and over that a large faded Oxford button-down shirt from some boyfriend. Her hair was pulled tight in a businesslike ponytail. Edie, on the other hand, wore a pink Lilly Pulitzer A-line shift with matching headband and matching frosty pink lipstick. On her feet were Jack Rogers sandals. A big beachy straw bag sat on the console next to her.

"We have more important things to worry about, don't we?" Susan said as she settled in and fastened her seat belt.

Edith clucked and hit the gas. Susan figured they could all be under nuclear attack and Edith Vale would insist on dressing properly—and maybe even sending the bombers handwritten thank-you notes—but they were on a sort of mission, and that's what really mattered, she thought. The pills Henry was taking to curb nausea, which actually had pot in them somewhere, Susan understood, weren't getting the job done. The idea of a prescription for actual marijuana was discussed, but Henry's doctor was cagey about recommending it to a minor and thought the pills should do the trick. Meanwhile, Henry was miserable and continued to lose weight.

Then, at the breakfast table that morning, Evangeline said, "Why don't we just buy him some ourselves?"

"Yes, but where?" Edie had asked. "We can't just lurk around some street corner."

"At the beach," said Evangeline. "You know those surfers are nine times out of ten stoned out of their gourds. You can smell it from a mile away. We could all use some fresh sea air anyway."

"Of course, hurrah!" Edie said. "You are right on all counts! It's nice to know, dear," she added to her sister, "that your brain hasn't entirely turned to mush."

Now as they drove west and then turned north, Henry said, "Susan, Zach Julian wants to fly out and visit."

"You mean, 'Mom, Zach Julian wants to come?'" She had been making an attempt to get Henry to think of her more as a mother, but it didn't seem to be taking.

"Whatever," said Henry.

"Who's Zach Julian?" came from Edie up front. "Is he that strange boy with the cowlick?"

"Yes, he has a cowlick. So what?" said Henry.

"Besides," Susan added, "it's your grandmother's house. You'll have to ask her."

"Okay. Mrs. Vale, can . . ."

"Yes, yes, I heard you," Edie snapped, "I'm not deaf. Is he a juvenile delinquent?"

"Um, not to my knowledge," Henry answered.

"What does that mean? Does he break laws behind your back?'

"No. Jesus."

"Well, I suppose it will be all right," Edie said.

"Just don't mention the cowlick," Henry added. "He's very sensitive about it."

"Why would I do that?" Edie asked, exasperation growing in her voice, Susan could tell.

"You tend to be critical that way." Here, he turned to Susan. "Isn't she?"

Susan opened her mouth, then closed it. It took her what seemed like a long minute to find the right words. "Your grandmother means well" is what she finally said.

"Just what are you implying by that?" Edie said.

Susan rolled her eyes. She looked over at Henry. He was smiling. He always seemed to enjoy watching her squirm. Susan managed to assuage Edie with a few words assuring her that she was never, ever overly critical.

They continued on in silence, Susan gazing out the window as they cruised up the Coast Highway toward Trancas. The sea was calm and glassy. Overhead a small plane cruised by trailing a banner, and every so often, an umbrella was propped jauntily in the sand. The silence was soothing, and for a while Susan did what she often found herself doing lately: staring off into space, thinking. For instance, she'd turn over and over in her mind whether what happened to Henry was her fault. Did leaving him at such a young age have something to do with it?

Did it somehow trip a wire in his brain? In the kitchen, behind a stove, she felt powerful; she had in her hands the ability to make something great, to make a person happy and satisfied. In the face of this, she felt utterly powerless, at the mercy of others. Sometimes she thought it would be too much to bear, would drive her mad, and she had to change the subject, literally will her mind to think positive thoughts.

When they arrived at Edie's house at the beach, all was pretty much as Susan remembered it, the cottage still charming and weathered. New to her were the two giant behemoths on either side.

Edie noticed her checking them out, but before Susan could comment, Edie said, "Don't even get me started."

Andrew was waiting outside to meet them, but as they all headed to the house, Susan noticed Edie's Mercedes continued to chug away and belch black smoke. "Um . . . Your car is still running, Edith," Susan said.

"Well, it does that sometimes," Edie said blithely. "I did turn it off, though." Indeed, she held up the keys and jangled them for everybody's inspection. Andrew stood there and looked at the car, a baffled expression on his face. "It's temperamental," Edie explained. "Eventually it turns off all by itself."

"Mother, that car is nearly forty years old. Don't you think it's time for something new?" Andrew finally asked.

"Nonsense," said Edie, "it's perfectly fine."

Andrew offered to call AAA, but Edie plucked her phone from her purse and insisted on calling Hans in Pasadena, who told her not to touch a thing until he got there.

A few minutes later, they were all inside when Edie announced the reason for their visit: "We need to buy some marijuana."

"Oh," said Andrew. "Huh?"

"For him," Susan said, pointing over at where Henry was being piled on by the twins. "You know it can help with the nausea and the appetite."

"Yeah, but aren't you supposed to get it from his doctor? With a prescription? From one of those clinics?"

"The laws about it are kind of dodgy. Especially with a minor, apparently," Susan said.

"Well, I'd do it," said Andrew. "But if I get caught, I might get disbarred."

"Oh, we didn't expect you to do it," said Edie. Here she pulled from her bag huge dark sunglasses, binoculars, and a hefty wad of cash.

"Okay," said Linda, who came out of the kitchen, drying her hands on a towel. "I understand the sunglasses. I get the cash. What's with the binoculars?"

"Well, we can watch from here until we spot one of those pot-smoking ne'er-do-wells, and then we pounce."

It was decided that Edith Vale would scare them all away. Susan took the cash, headed to the beach alone, and plunked herself down. She pulled off her boots and her socks and dug her toes into the warm sand. The sea was still calm, and the surfers who were out on the water were mostly prone on their boards, lazily paddling back and forth before her in a way that was almost mesmerizing. She looked up, squinting at the sun through the hazy blue sky. She always felt a deep connection to sand and sea. She never could figure out why, except maybe it was like an old roommate once told her, she was a water sign, an Aquarian. Now she closed her eyes and for a minute just absorbed the sounds of the beach, the soft whoosh of the waves, the gulls cawing overhead, the yapping retriever chasing a stick, and the "Where the devil is the darned sunblock?" from the harried mother with two toddlers who whacked at pails with little metal shovels.

Then there were the smells, the whiff of coconut-scented lotion and the seaweedy funk, and Susan was transported back to her own childhood. She had few memories of her mother and father, but what ones she did have seemed to always center around trips to the ocean they'd take to somewhere on the Cape or to the Connecticut shore. Mostly her parents were a blur, two heads in the front seat of the car, but she had one distinct memory of a day spent on the beach, complete with a thick vanilla milk shake and a gritty cheeseburger wrapped in greasy paper, when a wicked storm seemed to come out of nowhere. Wind whipped up whirling cyclones of sand, and dark clouds churned toward them, along with teeth-jangling booms of thunder Susan could feel rattle inside her chest while the sea was suddenly awash in angry foam. There was no time to make a mad dash for the car. Her father took the umbrella, laid it down, and planted it on the sand, the open end toward the approaching storm creating a barrier, and then he laid blankets all over and around to make a sort of fort, where they all huddled together, rain and then hail pelting the little shelter, until the bad weather passed. They managed to stay warm, cozy, and dry, and Susan could recall nestling in the crook of her mother's arm, could still smell her damp, briny skin, could still recall wishing the storm would never end.

A new sound roused her out of this reverie. Her eyes snapped open, but she had to squint against the glare because all she could make out were floaty funny spots. When those cleared she could see that a man had rammed a board into the sand and flopped down next to her. He was tall, thin, and sinewy with shaggy black hair down to his shoulders, a goatee, and a good couple of days of scruff. His eyes, startlingly blue, crinkled at the corners. His arms were a riot of color, intricate tattoos snaking up from his wrists. He wore a wetsuit unzipped and peeled down to the waist like a banana.

"What's up, pretty lady?" he said when he noticed she was looking at him.

"I . . . huh?" said Susan, suddenly flustered.

"What's shaking?"

"Oh, you know, um . . ." was all she could manage.

"Well, I'm Griffin. Griffin Barnekie."

"Susan. Susan Jones."

"Well, hey there, Susan Jones. Waves bite today, if you were wondering. Just real mushy. Do you surf?"

"Um. No. I swim. But . . . uh . . ." She broke off as she remembered why they had all come to the beach. Then she figured, why not just ask. "You got any pot, Griffin?"

"Whoa. You don't waste any time, do you, honey?" He smiled a snaggletooth smile.

She couldn't help it. She smiled back. "It's not for me."

"Oh, yeah. Uh-huh. I know this one. It's for a *friend*, right?"

"No, seriously. It's for my son."

Griffin squinted for a closer look at Susan. "You don't seem old enough to have a son who's old enough to party."

"Really? How old do you think I am?" Susan asked because she hadn't given much thought lately to her fading looks, and she was curious to hear what a stranger would say.

"Oh, I don't know. Twenty-eight?"

"You're sweet," she said. "Not a very good liar, though."

"Seriously, dude, you can't be more than twenty-nine."

"I'm almost thirty-eight, actually. In just a very short time, I will be forty. My son is sixteen, and he has a brain tumor."

"Get the fuck outta here," said Griffin. He looked truly stricken, almost as if it were his own kid she was talking about.

Then she almost did something that had been happening a lot lately. She almost burst into tears. Usually it was the result of some unexpected kindness, like when a nurse did something nice or thoughtful for Henry without her asking. For now, though, she managed to control her emotions.

"It's true about my son," Susan continued. "That's why I want the pot. He needs it for the nausea. From chemo. They gave him pills but they don't work. I will buy it from you." She pulled Edie's wad of cash from her pocket.

"Whoa, there. What do you want, a kilo?"

"We'll take whatever you've got."

"Wait. What if you're, like, a cop or a Fed or something?"

"Oh, yeah. Right," said Susan. "Look behind you. At the cottage between those two giant houses. What do you see?"

Griffin glanced over at the house. "Hmmmm. Okay. For starters, there's a lady in a white and pink helmet who's . . ."

Susan interrupted. "Wait, what?"

She turned to see what he was seeing. Edith Vale stood on the deck watching them through her binoculars. "That's not a helmet," said Susan. "It's a bouffant, the big white thing, and the pink is a headband. Which matches her lipstick. Don't ask."

"Okay," Griffin continued. "Anyway, she's with a really skinny brunette who's next to a guy who could be a cop, a couple of little towheads, and a bald guy. Who are those people?"

Suddenly, from a stranger's eyes again, it did seem like a very motley crew. "My ex-mother-in-law, my ex-husband, his current wife, their twins, and my son, the one with no hair," Susan said.

"That's some posse, lady."

"Yes."

"Well, they don't look like Federales. I'll give you that."

"So do you have any?"

"You know what I'd really dig right now?"

"What?" said Susan.

"Food. If you make me a sandwich, I'll score you some really excellent weed."

"I happen to make a really mean BLT," said Susan. Griffin smiled that snaggletooth smile and this seemed to seal the deal.

***

When Susan got back to the house, she found everybody had gathered to puzzle over Edie's Mercedes, which was still rumbling away, only now the engine was racing, like it was speeding full throttle down the freeway. Hans had just arrived from Pasadena in a gleaming Mercedes diesel even more ancient than Mrs. Vale's and was staring at the back of the car.

"First of all," he said in a thick accent, the lingering residue of his upbringing outside Stuttgart, "what is that?" He was pointing to the "French Fries for Freedom" sticker that was still attached to the back bumper. Actually, Susan had been wondering about it too.

"Some absolute kook accosted us at Los Angeles Airport," Edie said.

"But you can run your car on vegetable oil," said Linda. "I've read about it. You get it from restaurants and nothing goes to waste, and it doesn't pollute the air. Or it does, but it in some good way, apparently."

"Feh," said Hans, dismissing Linda with a wave. "Kerosene, okay, maybe good in a pinch, or home heating oil, but good old regular number two diesel is best, yes?" He turned back to Edith, smoothed down the sprightly wisps of cotton-colored hair he had left over the hearing aids in both ears, and smiled a toothy smile. "*Bitte*, Frau Vale. Pop the hood."

Hans found a frayed wire, replaced it, and the clattery old diesel went silent. A pleased Edie announced she'd treat them all to lunch at the fish shack up north, but Susan said, "I'll fix us lunch. Because I just made a deal to exchange a sandwich for the . . . you know . . . ," she said, eyeing Henry, hoping the others would get the hint. "I just need to go to pick up a few things, if I could use your car, Edith."

Here Hans shot Edie a look of apprehension. Andrew said, "I'll drive you."

A few minutes later, Susan was belted into a spanking new Prius with Andrew as they headed to the market.

"Well," she said, because she couldn't think of anything else. "This is a nice car. Very quiet. Maybe I should get one. Do you like it?"

"It makes me feel like I have no balls, if you must know," Andrew said. "Linda made me get it because she keeps insisting our carbon footprint isn't small enough yet. But I miss my BMW."

He drove a BMW that summer they met, Susan remembered, a clunky old black two-door with ripped upholstery and holes in the floor mats. It had California plates, which seemed so cool and foreign and exotic to her at the time she wondered if that might have been part of the attraction. She looked at him closer now, in his board shorts and T-shirt. He had thickened just slightly around the middle, but he was still handsome in his somewhat offbeat and slightly nerdy way. Then she put those thoughts out of her mind.

"So how are you holding up, really?" he asked. "Because seeing him suffer . . . it eats me up inside. If I don't feel like crying, I feel like screaming."

"I'm okay" came out before she could even really decide if she was, a sort of automatic response she'd developed over the years, it seemed, no matter how horrible she felt. I'm fine. Everything's great. No worries. She used phrases like that constantly. Also, she often found if she turned the question around and said, "But how are you?" to whomever asked, it would also deflect the attention away, and before you knew it, that person would be off yammering away about their own problems.

"Yeah. You seem pretty together. Sometimes I think that's what I liked about a woman like you."

"A woman like me? What does that mean?" Susan asked.

"Oh, come on, you know. Kind of emotionally shut down, I guess. You've always been like that. Kind of, well, cold. Kind of like my mother, if you really want to analyze it all," said Andrew.

"I am nothing like your mother," said Susan.

Then she shut down. They had arrived at the market and she practically leapt from the car before Andrew had even parked it. Inside, she cruised the unfamiliar aisles somewhat messily but, finding what she needed, determined to focus on the task at hand.

Later, back in the kitchen in the beach house, she poked at the bacon—a good, thick-cut applewood-smoked she had found—sizzling in a cast-iron skillet and set out an assembly line to put the sandwiches together because the number of people having lunch at the house kept going up. First Mr. Ritter, stooped, blind in one eye but surprisingly spry, Susan thought, extricated himself from the hole he was patching in the roof, then the shockingly tan and excruciatingly smooth-faced retired media mogul wandered over from next door, and finally, they were all joined on the deck by Linda's father, Robbie, and his boyfriend, Steve. Susan watched the group assemble on the deck, amused to see Mr. Ritter and Hans jockeying for position and nearly coming to blows over which one would help Edith Vale into her chair. She watched Linda fuss over the twins, Andrew move next to Henry, who was gazing at something off in the distance in the sea Susan looked for but couldn't pinpoint, and Robbie Landesman with his head close to the media mogul, who had come to make another of his enormous all-cash offers for Edie to sell him the house so he could knock it down and expand his own.

It suddenly struck her that while all this life was going on, she had spent the last few years holed up in her little box of an apartment in Brookline, barely seeing her son—barely making much contact with anybody—essentially dividing her life between insane, grueling hours on the line at the restaurant and then long, deep sleep. Suddenly she felt almost breathlessly alone, and before she knew what she was doing, she had fished her phone from her pocket and dialed Mike Finley.

"Hey, sweetheart," he said in a sleepy voice, and a picture danced into her head of a warm, slumbery Mike wrapped up in his sheets. "What's up?"

"Oh, I was just . . . um . . . I was wondering if you're remembering to pick up my mail."

"Yeah, yeah. That's the only reason you called? To be a nag? Because all you get is junk and bills. Just like everybody else."

"Well, and to say hey."

"Hey."

"How's work?"

"Babe, the planes keep coming, planes keep going."

"Is that some sort of a hint?"

"How so?"

"About me getting on a plane and coming to see you."

"Hmmm. Could be it is."

"By the way," Susan said, "don't lose track of any planes because you're distracted by my voice."

"That is so not funny," said Mike, gravely serious.

"Well, you're always joking to me about . . ."

"Gotcha! Ha!" He was laughing now, and even Susan smiled a little.

"All right. That's real hilarious."

"You find a job yet?" he asked, because she had mentioned she was looking.

"There's a couple of leads. I should know in the next couple of days. In fact, I may have you send me my knives."

"Oh. Okay."

"How's the kid?"

"He's . . ." Susan broke off because suddenly she noticed the hefty slices of the country white loaf she had bought and then laid out on a sheet pan under the broiler to toast were in danger of burning. "I gotta go." She ended the call before Mike could say anything more and pulled the pan from the flame just in time.

She broke down heads of iceberg lettuce and sliced tomatoes into thick slabs. She spread each piece of toast with a generous glob of mayonnaise. Jars of Best Foods lined the walls of Edie's beach pantry, along with can after can of New England–style clam chowder, boxes of oyster crackers, more Triscuits, a giant stack of what seemed to Susan like some strange obsession of Edie's for Cut-Rite Wax Paper, and yes it *absolutely has* to be Cut-Rite, and bags and bags of Lays Potato Chips. She laid down the lettuce and tomato on one slice of the toast, sprinkled them with salt and fresh cracked pepper, then came the crisp bacon. She topped them off with the second slice of toast, then ran her knife down each sandwich to create neat triangles. She set each one on a plate next to a generous pile of chips, put the plates on a large tray, and carried the whole thing out to the deck, where Edie, in between sips of the mimosas somebody had mixed, clapped her hands together and said, "Oh, Susan, what a perfectly marvelous lunch."

Griffin Barnekie stood on the sand at the bottom of the steps to the house, looking up at them. Susan thought he might be drooling. She grabbed one of the plates and took it down to him. He tore happily into his BLT, reminding her of some big sloppy puppy who hadn't eaten in days.

"It's delicious," he said in between massive bites.

"I cook for a living," said Susan. "I'm a chef."

"Well, you have found your calling."

"I wasn't fishing for compliments. But thanks. And you? What do you do?"

"Well, I surf."

"Yeah, I got that."

"Plus, I'm in a band. I play the drums. We totally rock. You should come hear us sometime."

Susan smiled. She watched as he continued to eat with relish. As always, it made her happy to have a satisfied customer. Of course, there were other times the rote and monotony of restaurant cooking made her nuts, endlessly banging out the same dish over and over and over. Or she'd want to scream at diners about how they should be home cooking their own damn dinners. And stop fucking taking pictures!

Now, Griffin finished the sandwich and licked excess mayonnaise from his fingers.

"So, we still have a deal, right?" Susan said.

"Yes, we do," he said and gave her another crooked smile.

***

After lunch, Andrew took Linda and the twins for a long walk up the beach. Susan watched as they got smaller and smaller, watched Linda on one side and Andrew on the other as each took a hand of a twin, who were holding hands too, and there was that little family unit she once longed for with Andrew and Henry. She had to fight the odd urge to run after them, shouting, "Wait, take me too!" When she could see them no more, she sat down on the deck and rolled a joint for Henry.

Edith Vale sat in a rocker nearby with knitting in her lap. She seemed engrossed in what looked to Susan to be a scarf or earmuffs, but she could tell Edie kept looking over to watch until finally she said, "Well, somebody seems to know what she's doing."

"You know, Edith," Susan said, "when you eat out in a restaurant, even the fancy restaurants you like to go to, I'd wager a good six times out of ten, the guy who cooked your meal is stoned."

Edie huffed and went back to her knitting. Henry grinned. If it felt strange, like she might be struck dead or something by handing her son the tightly rolled joint, Susan tried not to show it. She even held the lighter and coached him on how to inhale and keep the smoke down.

"Well, this is certainly different than when me and Zach Julian tried to do it," Henry said.

"Don't get too used to it, Mister Man," came from Edie, in between the snappy clickety-clack of her knitting needles.

"She's right," Susan said. "This will end when you get better."

"What if I don't?"

"Don't what?" Susan asked.

"Get better."

There was silence. She had no answer to that. She looked to Edie, who sat there, her mouth open, her knitting needles frozen midstitch.

Then Henry said, "Whatever," and continued to take puffs. Almost comically, he held it out to Susan, who could sense disapproving eyes and declined.

Whether it was psychological—some kind of placebo effect—or not, something seemed to have worked. Just a short time after he smoked half the joint, Henry polished off nearly an entire bag of potato chips, and he held it all down too.

***

When they got back to Pasadena, they found Evangeline and Blanca in club chairs in the library listening as Luz read aloud from a book. Susan watched as Henry stopped dead in his tracks when he saw Luz. She had figured there was some sort of crush activity going on by the way it always seemed as if he couldn't get a word out or the way he was trying to look all casual and nonchalant but would trip over something or bang into a wall when she was around. Now, before she could really think it through and stop herself, she tried to be helpful.

"Well, look who's here, Henry," she practically shouted, "Luz!"

Henry looked mortified.

Susan realized she had committed some horrible mistake. Here she was making headway, and now he had one more thing to hold against her forever. But he made a miraculous recovery, it seemed, and all on his own. He simply smiled and tossed a very casual greeting Luz's way as he headed for the stairs. Susan assumed he must still be stoned. Luz pretended to keep reading, but Susan could tell she was watching as Henry headed upstairs and into his room. For some reason, this made her smile.

XII.

Of course the place was gone. All the good things went away, thought Edith Vale, as her old turbodiesel chugged north and passed the spot on Interstate 5 where, for years, there was that funky little diner where they'd stop when she, Frank, and Andrew drove from Pasadena to Tahoe for their annual winter vacation. Now some massive gas station and truck stop had taken its place, vulgar and ugly like everything else new. She always looked forward to the diner, which had a giant neon sign in the Googie style that shot up into the sky like a starburst and could be seen like a beacon from miles away, the halfway point of the journey. There, they'd fortify themselves with warm white toast slathered in good sweet butter and slipped into wax-paper bags, alongside cups of steamy hot chocolate, which they'd take back to the big Pontiac wagon Edie drove in those days and nibble on and sip after hitting the road again, as Frank never wanted to lose any time on the slopes by actually sitting down inside the diner for the snack.

The trip to Tahoe was always the longer of the ski trips they'd make through the winter. Smaller ones were made to local mountains—Big Bear or, even better, Waterman in the San Gabriels and barely an hour north of Pasadena, albeit on a road of frighteningly treacherous curves. Sometimes Edie would go on those day trips with Andrew and Frank, but sometimes she'd let the boys go alone and stay home so she could catch up on her magazines. She loved that quiet time, made even better with a warm bubble bath, a daiquiri, and a couple of Miltowns. Indeed, those days were like minivacations, the house so peaceful, and she didn't need to sit down and make plans and lists or even pack a thing.

"Mrs. Vale, when are you going to let me drive?" said Henry from the passenger seat, jolting her from her reverie, asking the same question for the third time since they, along with Zach Julian, who was strapped into the backseat, set out for Sonoma.

"You're not allowed to drive on the freeways," said Edie.

"I have a full license now. Susan saw to that, remember? Passed all my tests and everything, ma'am. So, yes, I am."

"Later, then. After we stop."

Henry turned to face Zach. "You heard her, right? I get to drive after we stop?"

Zach, bobbing his head to some tune coming from his earbuds, gave Henry a thumbs-up.

Edith Vale was driving the boys to visit Henry's grandfather because Andrew was called to Chicago after the passing of a longtime client, and Susan, still new to the job she had landed, was working through the weekend. She thought of saying no, of making Henry postpone the trip, but Zach Julian had already arrived from the East Coast, and anyway, it was still nearly impossible to say no to Henry even though every day he was gaining strength. His hair was growing back in too, thicker and fuller than before, Edith thought.

The rounds of chemo had ended, and that, along with all the marijuana he was smoking, seemed to have made a difference. He had been eating like crazy, everything Susan or Edie or Blanca put in front of him, it seemed. He gained weight to the surprise of his doctors. He was starting to look like his normal self again, so that soon it was almost as if the whole nasty episode was like some dream, Edie thought, or like a story a friend told her about a stranger when all she had to do was nod and cluck with sympathy but then she could get on with her day. And the changes Edie noted weren't just physical. Henry seemed to grow mellower, more easygoing, less prone to brooding or sending those accusatory glares her way like he used to. Of course, that could also be due to the fact that he had looked deep into something dark and scary and he survived, and maybe that could explain an attitude change too. Edith couldn't be sure. The only problem was they needed to now draw a line about the drug taking, and none of them—she, Andrew, or Susan—seemed willing to do it, to say to Henry that he had to stop now that illness and frailty were behind him. Maybe his grandfather could broach the subject, Edie thought, but then she recalled how she heard years ago from Oatsie, who heard it from her husband, Pat, that Frank Entrekin in the late 1970s had gone through a period when he was growing massive amounts of pot on his land and smoking a good bit of it too.

Sometimes, Edith Vale marveled about how far Frank had detoured from the path they embarked on when they first met. Both were guests at the wedding of Edith's roommate at Vassar, a Farmington girl who dropped out of school in their senior year to marry one of Frank's roommates at Yale. The wedding was a little bit of magic. She could still picture the huge terrace overflowing with pots of vivid red geraniums behind a vast house in Westchester County with a lawn of emerald green that swept majestically down toward the Hudson, the river all shimmery under the light of a full moon. She'd never forget the moment she laid eyes on Frank. The meal had been served—pineapple cups followed by chicken à la king—and Lester Lanin and his band were playing "The Hukilau Song," an up-tempo, lilting tune that brought Edie back to Hawaiian vacations with her mother, father, and Evangeline, when Frank caught her eye from two tables away. He looked so dashing, chestnut hair slicked down with brilliantine, in a dinner jacket, crisp white broadcloth shirt, and bow tie, and when he held out his hand and escorted her to the dance floor, she felt funny little stirrings and flip-flops deep down inside. They kept dancing as the band took them on a veritable world tour, with stops in France ("I Love Paris") and Latin America for a mambo or two.

"What is it about you?" said Frank as he expertly negotiated the sea of taffeta and silk swirling around them. "There's something different. I can't quite put my finger on it."

"I don't know," said Edie. "These are mostly East Coast girls. I'm from California."

"That's it! Me too! I knew I recognized something!"

His eyes twinkled and his whole face seemed to open up in a dimpled grin.

It might have been the champagne; it might have been nerves or exhaustion even, as the day had been packed with activities; it might have been his hand and the pressure he applied just at the small of her back as they danced; or maybe it was Frank's heady scent, a curious, spicy blend of cigarette smoke, bourbon, and some musky aftershave, but by the time the orchestra dove into "Old Devil Moon," Edie was as hooked on him as he seemed to be on her. He wasn't her first steady boyfriend, to be sure, but he was the first one she thought she might really want to marry.

He had been raised in San Francisco, in Pacific Heights. He had been sent to the kinds of schools that would mold him into something morally upstanding, she thought, into a man who would dedicate himself to somehow making the world a better place. He talked of the Air Force after college, and Edie would imagine him strapped into a cockpit, soaring through the clouds in search of his enemy. Which was why it was something of a disappointment when, instead, he entered law school like his father, and then into trusts and estates at the Los Angeles outpost of the San Francisco firm where his father was a partner. Oh sure, he was sent to trailblaze the path into an ever expanding Southern California—and yes, it pleased the newlywed Edith, who missed Pasadena during her college years, but she thought she had seen something heroic in Frank, and soon all that was gone.

Not that she dwelled on it too much in those early years after they wed at the Episcopal church downtown. Edie still had fond memories of the day, of the flowing, off-the-shoulder, silk Anne Lowe gown she and her mother picked out at Bullock's, of the reception back in the garden of the house where she had grown up, of the carefully selected menu of limestone salads and hearts of palm followed by chicken cordon bleu, and finally a three-tier masterpiece from Hansen's in Los Angeles, a bridal white cake with layers of rich almonette creme.

In those early years, Edie was more concerned with problems they seemed to be having in starting a family. At first she didn't give babies much thought—she and Frank were having too much fun to really notice, it seemed—but then, when her sister and her friends all started getting pregnant, Edie began to wonder if something wasn't right. The doctor assured them both that all parts were in working order, but two years in, Edie had yet to conceive, and then when she finally did in the third year of their marriage, she miscarried, and that happened not just once but two more times, all of them, if anybody really wanted to know, causing a gut-wrenching sadness that was difficult to overcome, not that Edie would tell anybody because she didn't feel it necessary to share feelings like that. No, she soldiered on, but for the first time in her life, she felt like a failure—like she couldn't do the one thing she was designed and schooled and molded to do—and since she couldn't control what was happening in her womb, she began to demand perfection just about everywhere else, and that was probably actually the beginning of the end of her marriage to Frank, who became the target of constant criticisms until, finally, when Edie was past thirty and Andrew came, she turned most of her attention to her son, and so she may not have noticed that Frank was miserable. Until the day he announced, after a tennis game at the club, that he wanted to quit his job, move north, and raise goats.

Edie, fishing the olive out of a martini as she'd skipped lunch and was just famished, said, simply, "Are you absolutely mad?"

"No," said Frank. "But I am suffocating. Slowly but surely, day by day, I die a little bit in that office."

"Oh, for God's sake," said Edie, rolling her eyes, and signaling for the waiter to refill her glass.

She figured it was a phase, that next would come the adorable imported red convertible and the younger girlfriend, both of which were mainstays all through Pasadena. Indeed, the sight of all those middle-aged men wrenching and contorting their often flabby bodies so they could slide in and out of their little sportabouts always made her secretly smile. She'd wave but silently hope they'd get the pinched nerve or the slipped disc they deserved. Indeed, Edie had long suspected that Frank was cheating already, and deep down, she knew it was true. He was, after all, tall and handsome, even with the trait that kept getting passed down the male line of Entrekins, the protruding ears and prominent nose. He was a vital presence, charismatic, always chatting and gregarious even among strangers, always able to fill up the biggest rooms just by being there. Really, all the husbands were having affairs, it seemed, picking girls up in bars during those long lunches or on the business trips they all seemed to be on in those days, flying here and there on sleek Boeing 707s at the height of the jet age.

But like her mother before her and like most of her girl-friends, Edie simply ignored all the signals—the random hotel matchbook when she hadn't gone anywhere or the receipt for a gift she never received—or pretended they didn't exist. Then there was the strange hypochondria Frank suddenly developed. This could have tipped her off that something was amiss too; suddenly, he had this disease or that ailment, he was sure of it, or there would be a "Come feel this lump, Edie." There was a very bizarre obsession with his bowel movements around this time too, whether he had one and what type it was, not that Edie particularly cared to know. She herself would turn on a faucet when she tinkled because that was the polite and proper thing to do. Why did she really need this information about his bodily functions and whether or not it meant he was a goner? It was annoying. When these things really started to gnaw at her, an extra Miltown always did the trick, taking the edge off, especially if washed down with another highball, and then would come a nice, pleasant numbness.

Anyway, midlife crisis or no, she had no interest in tromp-ing through goat shit or molding curds and watching them age or tie-dyeing things or wearing big batik caftans or shopping at some unclean organic co-op where the ladies had stopped shaving their legs or, worse, under their arms. Because that's how they lived up there in Northern California—Edie was absolutely certain of that—with all their protests and causes and something about eating grapes she could never quite grasp. No, she intended to stay right in Pasadena, where she had her clubs, the girls, and her charity work. She never thought Frank would do it anyway, didn't think he had the guts to chuck it all, but he surprised her and quit his law practice. He bought a rambling piece of property outside Healdsburg and filed for divorce. Edie didn't budge. Andrew would fly up every other weekend and spend half his holidays with his father, who grew long sideburns and then a beard and would frequently forget to bathe.

Edie spent a few years alone, not minding it, if you really wanted to know, coming and going as she wanted, not trying to please anybody else. She dated here and there, but that was mostly just awful at her age, until one of the girls, her dear friend Bunny Vale, discovered a lump in her breast. Of course, it terrified Bunny to no end, so she said nothing and, like Edie might have done, ignored the whole potential unpleasantness, but time passed and the mass got bigger, and finally Bunny went to the doctor, but it was too late. She died soon after, and Anderson, her loyal, faithful, but somewhat stodgy and old-fashioned husband, was left alone and clueless, rattling around their big brick house in San Marino. Until Edie realized they were an ideal match and snapped him up before the other widows and divorcées had a chance. And they were happy, mostly because Anderson knew to keep his mouth shut and not contradict her and wear what she told him to wear and write a thank-you note when somebody did something nice and close the bathroom door at all times and try not to get on her nerves or . . .

"I have to pee like a fucking horse." Zach Julian's announcement from the backseat of the Mercedes snapped Edie from the past for the second time that trip.

"Young man," she said, "use that kind of language again, and you'll be walking back to Pasadena."

"Yes, ma'am," said Zach, clearing his throat and shifting in his seat.

Henry stifled a laugh but said, "Man, I could go for a piss too."

"You have to what?" Edie shot back.

"I mean, um, I sure could use a comfort break, Mrs. Vale."

Edie smiled tightly and signaled for a turn toward the exit.

***

"Well," said Edith Vale into the phone, "the truth of the matter is he's totally let himself go."

"*Que?*" said Blanca. She was talking from the kitchen of Edie's house in Pasadena. Edie could hear her spaniels yapping in the background, could picture them running in frantic little circles around Blanca's feet, and she felt a little ache of longing, even though she'd barely been gone a day.

"I mean whatever hair Mr. Entrekin has left is all wild and growing willy-nilly and, well, grey, and he's got such a belly like you wouldn't believe."

"*Que? No comprendo.*"

"Listen, I just wanted to check in and see how things were going. Are my puppies okay?" Edie shouted, thinking Blanca simply couldn't hear her, now looking for a place to flick the ash from her Parliament. Heaven forbid, she thought, Frank should properly equip his guest room. Oh sure, this was a working farm, set high on a rolling green hill, with blustery Tomales Bay churning in the distance, but still one shouldn't forget the little niceties that made life bearable, Edie thought, as Blanca rattled on.

"*Necesito ayuda.* We need to have more help," said Blanca. "Again, today, she walked out in the middle of the shower. This time she was outside and down the block before I could catch her. She had no clothes on!"

"We'll talk when I get home. Toodles."

She hung up on a protesting Blanca, because she was about to set fire to a recent manicure. She rushed into the bathroom, and—oh, to hell with it—flushed the spent butt down the toilet. Let Frank worry if the system backed up. She paused at the sink to rinse her hands. Then, a tiny gasp escaped when she caught a glimpse of herself in the mirror, because Frank also hadn't gone to the trouble to properly light the guest bathroom or even hang a proper shade over the window, so that in the harsh glare of the sun streaming in and without her face on yet or her hair shellacked back into place, she saw that scary old woman she'd occasionally spot in passing reflections when she wasn't properly prepared or lighted or holding up a hand to shade the sun or fortified against what she might see.

"Oh, for crying out loud," Edie said to herself.

She grabbed a towel and hung it from the top of the window frame to block out the sun. There, that was better. Now she turned back to the mirror and grabbed her makeup bag. She didn't use much in the way of makeup—that would be coarse and vulgar—but a little subtle help never hurt. First she brushed on a featherlight coat of foundation, just enough to smooth over the imperfections. Then she added a touch of a nice cream blush to her cheekbones and a little shadow to bring out her eyes and then just the teeniest dabs of mascara. She rolled on a coat of pink lipstick, poked and prodded at her hair, spraying a few stray strands back into submission, so that now when she assessed her reflection, there was Edith Vale again, all set for the jaunt to the bay with Frank and the boys. Back in the guest room, she decided on blue jeans, a black wool turtleneck from Talbot's because she figured it would be freezing by the water, and a charcoal tweed Chanel blazer she bought nearly thirty years earlier. Not bad for an old dame, Edie thought, as she headed for the stairs.

***

Only a half hour later, Edie looked like a fright again. She had agreed to ride to the bay in Frank's truck but didn't realize there was no back window to the cab. It had gotten smashed or some such thing, and of course, he didn't think to repair it. So what started out as a mild breeze inside the truck—at first welcome because of the pungent smell of goats that seemed to be seeping out of every crevice—turned into something like gale force winds as the truck went faster, and of course, Frank drove like a maniac, if you asked Edith. When they stepped out of the truck at the little fish shack in Marshall, Frank, Henry, and Zach Julian were grinning stupidly and pointing at her head. Edie reached up to pat at her hair, found nothing where it should be and, fighting a dizzying sense of disorientation, knew something had gone wrong. She dashed inside the restaurant and made a beeline for the bathroom.

"Oh my God!" she said when she looked in the mirror, because somehow, the back portion of her hairdo had been blown out to the sides, and then somehow, it all turned north so that the bottom portion now stood straight up, as if she had been hung upside down.

This time, no matter how much she fiddled with it, the hair wouldn't budge. When a large clump actually broke off, she realized this was an emergency and called for drastic measures. She ran warm water in the sink, stuck her head under the tap and rinsed out all the spray. She wrung out as much water as she could, stood under the hand dryer for a few minutes, then pulled all the hair back and tied it into a neat ponytail with a rubber band she fished from her purse. Next came the Hermès scarf she always had tucked into her bag because one never knew. She threw it over her head and tied it loosely at her neck, so it looked casual and carefree. Finally, since she was feeling vulnerable with her helmet suddenly gone, she put on her big pair of dark sunglasses, even though Oatsie, Evelyn, and Tish always claimed they made her look like a bug.

"We should have taken my car," Edie said as she rejoined the boys at the table by a window overlooking the water and pretended they weren't looking at her funny.

"You know, I could convert it for you," Frank said.

"Excuse me?" Edie said.

"That big old tank you drive. To vegetable oil like the sticker on the back says. I've got an old VW diesel I converted. Plus, you know, half the energy on the farm comes from methane we make with the goat shit."

Edith looked at Frank as if he were speaking some strange foreign language. She turned to Zach and Henry. "Do you boys have any idea what he's talking about?"

"Good Lord, Mrs. Vale," Henry said. "Hello? Going green? How many times do we have to explain this?"

"Watch that tone, mister," Edie said. "You may have been through an ordeal, but that does not mean you have license to be impolite."

"Yes, ma'am," said Henry.

Edie flagged down the waitress so they could order, and while she and Frank feasted on barbecued oysters and sourdough bread, washed down with strong Bloody Marys, the boys dug into fried shrimp and tartar sauce.

"You kids enjoying yourselves?" Frank asked as they finished up.

"Dude, where do the girls hang out in this town?" asked Zach Julian, prompting what sounded like a snort from Henry.

Edie looked at Frank.

He smiled, still all dimples, big ears, and teeth, she thought, although more grizzled and grey. "It's nice to know some things never change," Frank said. He winked at Edie, who pretended not to notice. "Anyway," Frank continued, "don't handsome boys like you already have girlfriends?"

Zach Julian pointed at Henry. "Well," he said, "he has Luz."

"Luz!" said Edie. "Blanca's granddaughter Luz?"

"Oh," groaned Henry, "my God. Zach, please shut the fuck up!"

"Henry!" said Edie.

Actually, she was curious to hear more, but Henry, she now noticed, was turning serious shades of red, and suddenly she worried about his blood pressure. So she changed the subject.

After lunch, they took a walk along a small pier that jutted into the bay. The wind was blowing hard, sharp icy gusts that stung at their cheeks and made their noses start to run. Edie watched as Henry broke off from the group and walked to the edge of the pier. He was looking at a small sailboat, a Sunfish, she thought, that had come unmoored and was now being tossed every which way on the roiling surface, coming perilously close to an outcropping of rocks, something banging rhythmically against its metal mast making a harsh clanging sound. For a second, she feared he would step off the pier and try to fetch the errant little boat. In her mind, she calculated the distance between them, not certain if she was close enough to grab Henry and pull him back. But he turned and started toward her.

"It's very cold out there, I bet," he said as he headed for his grandfather's truck.

Indeed, a shiver passed through her. She huddled into herself in an attempt to get warm as she started after him.

**

Frank's afternoon activity involved whistling for his two Australian shepherds, Whizzer and Zoom, and marching out to round up one of his herds of sheep for their annual checkup with the vet. Henry and Zach, reluctantly at first, decided to join him.

"Come on," Frank had said to Edie. "We could use your help too."

"Thank you," she said tartly, "but I am wearing very expensive shoes. I'd prefer they remain clean."

Instead, she drove into town in search of a beauty parlor that might be able to properly wash, set, blow out her hair, and spray it back into place, but she had been trusting that job to the same man, dear sweet Bruce, for so long she lost her nerve. Instead she headed to Sebastopol and wandered the antique shops. She picked up a small sterling silver pitcher at one, a well-worn copy of a classic gardening book in another, and a kicky old brooch in a third. In a fourth, Edie found herself gazing at a gleaming copper chafing dish of the sort that were popular around the time she first got married, and she was so absorbed in how odd her reflection looked in it that she was startled when she heard from behind, "Mrs. Vale?"

For a second she was irritated. She had been enjoying this solitary afternoon. Who could be bothering her now? Edith turned around to see Cis O'Shea waving at her from behind a counter filled with old costume jewelry.

"I almost didn't recognize you under that scarf," Cis said.

Edie hadn't seen Cis in years, ever since she shocked her mother and father by moving in with Oatsie's riding instructor, who not only was a woman, but was a woman nearly twenty years older than Cis. "Hello, dear," she finally managed. "Up here for the weekend?"

"Oh, no, I live up here now," Cis said.

She stepped from behind the counter and Edie saw she must have been at least eight months pregnant.

"With my partner, Brandi," Cis continued. "We own this store. We might open a café or a restaurant too because business here kind of sucks, if you want to know the truth. That's her over there," she added, pointing to a short, powerfully built woman with bluntly cut, close-cropped, salt-and-pepper hair, who was helping a customer carry a table to the parking lot by hoisting it high over her head.

"Oh," said Edie. "Well, then. Partner . . ."

"Actually," said Cis, "you remember that day when all those same-sex couples got married on the steps of city hall in San Francisco? We were there. We actually got married. Although we were never sure if it counted. So we flew to Vermont and got married there. We'll do it again here one of these days maybe."

"Oh!" Edie said, reflexively making a mental note to send a gift—two actually, since a baby was coming—"Well, Oatsie didn't say a word."

"That's because she doesn't know. About the wedding. Or this," she said, now running her hand over her swollen belly.

"How could she not?"

"You know my mom. She still goes to Mass every morning. She has enough trouble with the lesbian thing. But marriage? And this baby? She would think I'm going to burn in hell."

"I don't think you give your mother much credit," Edie said.

"Well, you tell her then."

"Far be it from me to gossip," Edie protested, a little indignation creeping into her tone now.

"Oh, come on. You—Mrs. Brookby, Mrs. Van Buren, my mother—you're like four old cackling hens. How's Andrew, by the way?" she said, the abrupt change of subject making Edie a little dizzy.

"He's fine. He's married. His son has a brain tumor."

"Oh my God," said Cis.

"Nonsense. It's all behind us now. He's going to be just fine."

"Well . . ."

It was an awkward moment. Edith broke it by grabbing the chafing dish, paying the bill, scolding Cis for not calling her mother more often, and rushing back out to the Mercedes for a Parliament.

***

Later, when Frank asked what she was doing with a chafing dish, rather than explain her run-in with Cis O'Shea—with that disturbing comment about clucking old hens still ringing in her head, and with the idea that Cis, once a candidate to marry Andrew, had married a woman and was having a baby, and wait, she thought, who was the father, because gosh, had things changed that much when she wasn't paying attention?— Edith simply said the first thing that popped into her head, that she had, on a whim, decided to cook them all her famous hobo steak, something she was famous for almost forty years earlier actually and hadn't made since Frank walked out on her. So while Frank went off to mix her a Manhattan, Edie pulled her phone from her bag and called Susan Jones, rousing her from a deep slumber.

"My goodness, dear, it's after four!" Edie said in a some-what scolding tone.

"Excuse me," Susan grumbled. Her voice crackled through the line like she had swallowed a handful of pebbles. She cleared her throat, then said, "Restaurant hours? I didn't get home until almost dawn."

"I thought your shift ended at midnight."

"Yes, well," Susan said, "I went out with the kitchen crew after closing and we all knocked back a few saki bombs."

"For what? Five hours? Until dawn? Come on, dear, nobody can drink that much saki."

"Well, then I . . ." Here Susan broke off. She coughed, and then cleared her throat again.

"You were with that child, weren't you?"

"For your information, Edith," said Susan, "Griffin is almost twenty . . . uh . . . something."

Susan had started seeing the man she met at the beach, the pot dealer, and Edie didn't approve, not one bit. Oh, Susan tried to hide it from her, from Henry and the rest of the family too, but they all figured out soon enough why she kept making those trips out to the coast, even at times when Henry didn't need a new supply or when Griffin showed up at the door in Pasadena. He'd wait at the door for Susan, a trippy grin on his face.

"I don't know what you could possibly see in some . . ."

"Did you wake me up for a reason?" Susan interrupted.

"Actually, I need a favor."

Edie directed Susan to the kitchen, to the spot over the sink and the old battered wooden recipe file, where she was sure the recipe was tucked away somewhere. It came from the old Chasen's in Los Angeles, from the days when she and Frank, newlyweds, would occasionally drive into town from Pasadena to have dinner with a client who lived in Beverly Hills. That was when Chasen's was still a modest shack; when it got bigger and glitzier, they stopped going, except that one time, a fund-raising dinner for the Reagans, and the Vales were cochairs, so Edie had to go. Susan finally found the card, not under H for hobo or S for steak or even B for beef, but under M because it was Maude Chasen who gave Edie the recipe. So after Frank returned from the store with what she needed, Edie retreated to the kitchen, where she wrapped nicely marbled New York strips in an extra layer of fat ("You'll have to ring for the butcher and ask for this *specifically*," she told Frank in a firm tone, even writing it down on the list and underlining it because he was such a ninny about these things) and secured the fat with toothpicks. Then she made a paste with a couple of cups of coarse salt and water. She mounded the salt mixture on top of the steaks and slid them under the broiler. After precisely ten minutes, she pulled them from the oven, removed the salt crust, flipped the steaks, topped them with the crust again, and slid them back in the oven. She took thin slices of firm sourdough bread and toasted them. She measured out the butter she'd need to complete the recipe, then went into the dining room for a last check of the tableau she had created before calling Frank and the boys in.

She had set the table carefully, with the best linens, candlesticks, and dishes she could scrounge up. She cut a spray of blue cornflowers she spotted in Frank's yard and arranged them artfully but casually in a small bowl she nestled inside a pretty wicker basket. She placed the chafing dish near her spot because part two of the recipe called for a little showmanship from the hostess, tableside service; she would pull the steaks from the oven, slice them thinly, and then proceed to the dining room, where she would swirl the slices in sizzling butter in the chafing dish as hungry eyes looked on. Then, she would fan out the slices of hot steak on the toast and, with a flourish, sprinkle fresh chopped parsley on top. Except for the boys, of course. Kids hate anything green, Edie knew. They'd probably ask for ketchup. Satisfied that all was in order on the table, she lit the candles, and then ignited the flame under the chafing dish. Back in the kitchen, she was slicing the steaks when Henry poked his head in.

"Uh . . . Mrs. Vale?" he said.

"Yes, dear?"

"Quick question."

"Yes, yes?"

"You won't get, like, mad or have a heart attack or a cow or anything?"

"Oh, for goodness' sake, Henry, what is it already?"

"Well, is the dining room supposed to be on fire?"

Edie spun around. She hadn't thought to check the reservoir of the chafing dish to make sure it didn't leak. Apparently it did. The entire table was engulfed in flames, which were now licking up toward the ceiling.

"Oh my God!" Edie screamed, then added, "It's not my fault! Call 911!"

Frank dived for the phone. Zach Julian grabbed a blanket from the sofa to douse the flames. Edie ran in circles and screamed some more until it struck her that she did indeed sound like some screechy old bird.

**

Later, after the fire department left, Frank took the boys into Healdsburg for cheeseburgers, and Edie sat in her room wondering if, like Evangeline, her mind was turning to mush.

"I mean, setting the dining room on fire," she said aloud, then almost started to laugh because it struck her as so absurd.

Luckily, damage was minor, mostly to the table and the ceiling, but still, Edie—usually so meticulous, so careful to get things exactly right, as they should be—felt as if she were letting things slip, and if that were true, it might be a slide into something more dire. A good vigorous walk is what I need,

Edie thought. She whistled for the dogs, and they trotted after her.

Outside the house, the air was cool and crisp. There was a stillness to it that Edie found calming. It was quieter here, more peaceful, she had to admit as she started to walk, Whizzer and Zoom at her heels. She hadn't gotten far when she heard a chorus of bleats. She turned around. There was a veritable sea of white fuzz, since Frank's herd of goats had decided to follow.

"Go away, stinky beasts!" Edie shouted, but that only set off a louder refrain, and for a moment she wondered if they might charge and trample her, payback for all those roast legs of lamb and mint jelly she liked to serve at Easter. Goats and lambs were closely related, she figured.

But the goats wouldn't budge and Edie wasn't sure she had the energy to continue this standoff. All right, then, a nightcap might soothe her nerves, so back to the house she went, pursing her lips and clucking in disapproval at the disarray in the dining room and heading straight for the bar. She was pouring bourbon over some ice when Frank came through the front door alone.

"Where are the boys?" she asked as she rolled the bourbon around, the ice tinkling against the glass, a sound that always seemed comforting to her, like a lullaby.

"Where else? With the girls?"

"What girls?"

Frank walked up next to Edie and poured a drink of his own. "One of the biggest clients for the milk my goats produce is this lady in Petaluma. She makes cheese. She's got a kid their age who was having a birthday party tonight, so I dropped them off. She said she'd run them back here later." Here Frank leaned a little closer and smiled. "You know what that means?"

"What?"

"We're all alone, you and me."

He was grinning, like a goofy little boy, if you avoided look-ing at the wild wisps of grey hair and the belly he'd developed. Still, it took a good full minute for Edith to comprehend that Frank said it in a way that was more than a little suggestive.

"Don't be ridiculous, Frank. I mean, really."

"What? We were married once, remember?"

"How could I forget? I remember you telling me how I smothered you. In fact, I clearly recall one of the last conversa-tions we had, where you said you couldn't breathe around me anymore."

"I was an ass at the end. I don't know if I ever said so, but I'm sorry for that. And you have to admit there were times we had fun."

"Yes, well . . ."

"You know what else I realized this afternoon, Edie?"

"I can't imagine."

"We were at the table at lunch waiting for you to come back from the ladies' room. And when I saw you coming, if I squinted, with the light just right the way it was, I swear to God, you could have been twenty-two again."

"Squinted? You had to blur your vision from forty feet away to make me look good! Is that supposed to be a compliment?"

"You know what I mean," Frank said.

The funny thing was she knew exactly what he meant. She squinted at a lot of things these days. Everything did look bet-ter with a bit of a blur all around it. Or with sunglasses on. That did wonders. Then Frank leaned a little closer, so close she could almost feel the heat of his skin.

"Get away from me," Edie said. She gave him a little shove, and whether or not she meant it, it came out more playful than not. She rooted around her pocketbook for a Parliament, hop-ing the distraction would bring him back to his senses.

He took the matches from her hand. "What are you going to do? Burn the rest of my house down now?"

"Ha ha," said Edie, aiming for light sarcasm, but she found herself starting to laugh for real as the image of her chafing dish in flames popped into her head.

"Remember when I used to do this, Edith Lee?" He placed one hand at the small of her back, pressing firmly, slowly moving his hand in a circle, so she almost instinctively moved even closer.

His familiar touch caused her to feel stirrings deep down inside, deep in her core. Edie was shocked; how could that sensation still be there? How was it possible? Did this reaction lay dormant, like some of the bulbs she had planted years earlier and had forgotten about, until suddenly one or two sprouted shoots at the first hint of spring? And Edith Lee? He used to call her that. "Edith Lee! Oh, Edith Lee. Where can you be, Edith Lee?" she'd hear coming from their bed, a giddy sing-song voice that meant Frank was feeling especially frisky. She'd be at her vanity in the bathroom, and she would rush through the removal of her makeup and the primping of her hair so she could race back into their bed. She'd jump under the covers, and Frank would yank her nightgown over her head and sometimes it felt as if they'd literally ignite when skin touched skin. She hadn't heard anybody say her name like that in years. It almost made her cry because that part of her life was long over, the part where she was so young and, well, agile. Because now, even though she was in good shape, she wouldn't consider moving so fast without worrying about pulling a muscle or, God forbid, breaking a bone. But also his using that special name made her knees go weak.

And then, in that instant, he kissed her. And then, in that instant, another image popped into her head, of young Frank the night they met, so dapper in his dinner jacket, with Lester

Lanin and his band providing the soundtrack, with images in her head of Frank in the cockpit of a fighter plane, soaring through the clouds, making the world safe, and suddenly she didn't feel like an old lady anymore. It was as if the years melted away, like they were both being magically transported back in time, and suddenly she didn't want him to stop.

XIII.

"Maybe now you'd like to tell me why you came home from your grandfather's with a black eye?" Susan asked again as they waited for Henry's latest MRI to begin.

Henry laid back and closed his eyes. For a second he didn't answer. "You asking me now because you know the drugs kicked in?"

"What? Why would I do that?"

"You figure I'm feeling no anxiety, no fear of claustrophobia. No pain whatsoever. You figure you'll get a straight answer out of me. But it wasn't truth serum that nurse just gave me, Susan. It was just a few milligrams of Ativan."

"I'm just curious is all," said Susan. "About the black eye and why Mrs. Vale has been in such a lousy mood."

"She swore us to secrecy. Me and Zach," Henry said.

"I won't tell. Scout's honor."

"Yeah, like you were ever a Girl Scout."

"I was a Brownie, for your information. A damn good one," Susan added.

"I thought Brownies were taught never to use bad language."

"Okay. A darn good one."

"Whatever."

"Fine. Don't tell me."

But the Ativan had kicked in, it seemed, because suddenly Henry got a little blabby. "She slept with my grandfather," he said.

"What?"

"Mrs. Vale. Well, they were in bed together anyway."

"Get out of here," said Susan.

"Lady, I tell you no lies," Henry said.

"My God. Edie made Mr. Vale sleep in his own room back in the day. I can't imagine her in bed with anybody."

"Who was in bed with whom?" asked Andrew, returning from the cafeteria with cups of coffee, as he walked in.

"Henry says your mother slept with your father."

"Get out," said Andrew.

"Of course," Henry added, "that was after she set fire to the house."

"Oh God," said Andrew. "Don't tell me she cooked hobo steaks."

"She called me for the recipe," Susan added.

"Well, she tried to cook them. Anyway, later that night, me and Zach got dropped off at this party. That's where I got the black eye. When we got home . . ."

"Whoa," said Susan. "Back to the black eye, please."

"There was this girl at the party. She asked me why I got a buzz cut. I told her I had brain surgery. For this tumor. And she's all like, 'Oh my God,' 'Oh, you poor thing,' and 'How awful,' and blah-blah-blah. So Zach dared me to ask if I could feel her up. I did. And she got all bent out of shape and, like, slugged me."

"Well, you got what was coming to you, didn't you, bub?" said Linda Landesman, who had charged into the room with

Serenity and Alexander. The twins wriggled free of Linda, climbed up to the platform where Henry was laid out, and were trying to poke their heads inside the machinery of the scanner.

"She's right," said Susan. "But that still doesn't explain Mrs. Vale's bad mood."

"Or the new hairdo," said Linda. "What's up with that?"

"Okay," said Henry, "so this lady in Petaluma who makes cheese? She's supposed to drive us back to Grandpa Frank's. So we all pile into this smelly old truck she drives. I mean, I'm talking you're almost gagging kind of smelly. Anyway, we get back to the house, and she's like, 'I'm going to pop in and say hi to Frank.' And we're like, 'Suit yourself, cheese lady.'"

Here Andrew interrupted. "Could we maybe try 'We *said*, "Suit yourself, cheese lady?"' instead of 'We're like'?"

"Jesus, all right already. Anyway, so she goes upstairs, and two seconds later, there's this god-awful scream, so we rush up there too, and cheese lady is standing in the door, and Mrs. Vale is in bed with Grandpa. We couldn't see much, mind you, but I'm pretty sure they were both, you know, like nude? Which, honestly, is an image I don't know if I'll ever be able to get out of my head. So the upshot is it turns out cheese lady is sleeping with him too, and Mrs. Vale's like, 'You are an animal, Frank,' and Grandpa goes, 'Come on, Edie. Be reasonable. We're all adults here,' and that's when she told me and Zach to pack our bags because we were leaving that instant."

Henry finished the story just as the door swung open and there was Edith herself, and when she saw them all staring at her, she said to Henry, "You told them, didn't you? After you swore you'd keep it a secret."

Henry gave her a sheepish little shrug. "Sorry," he said. "It was just too juicy to sit on."

"Oh, you're all just awful," said Edith. "Now I'm off to the airport to pick up Gigi. Who's coming with me?"

Evangeline's daughter was not a popular family member. Edie got no volunteers. Finally, she turned on her heels to leave, nearly plowing down the technician, who had come in to shoo them all to the waiting room so the examination of the inside of Henry's head could continue.

***

Later, Susan tried not to eavesdrop. But with the door mistakenly left open a crack, she could hear Henry and his therapist, even though she was in the waiting room trying to tune them out. She flipped the pages of one magazine loudly. She tried to focus on a recipe for peanut brittle she found in another.

Still, she heard the doctor ask, "Would you like to talk about how it feels?"

"How what feels?" Henry answered in a voice Susan recognized as peeved and put-upon.

Good luck with that, she thought, unable to suppress a small grin.

"You tell me," said a persistent Dr. Greene.

"How about for a change, you tell me, because if you really want to know, I'm kind of sick of hearing myself yak about everything."

Again, Susan smiled. Seeing this doctor had been Linda's idea, and Susan wasn't so sure she disagreed. When they first learned he was sick, she watched as Henry seemed to go through all the classic stages she'd always heard about. Denial seemed easy. It ran in the family in a direct line down from Henry's grandmother, Susan figured. If one didn't think about something bad or unpleasant or sad and didn't talk about it, nothing bad would happen. Then, she watched as Henry got mad. He quickly grew tired of all the doctors and all the poking and the prodding, and then the process that was supposed to make him better only made him feel worse, and he got angrier. Until one day he exploded, yelling at them all to leave him the hell alone already. He bolted upstairs to his room. He slammed the door. He threw things around. They could hear the shattering of a glass pane, and Susan thought she detected a small gasp from Edie, who seemed so connected to her house. This was when Linda, having weathered a recent life crisis of her own, stepped in and insisted Henry get help with his feelings. But by the time Linda got a referral and Henry reluctantly agreed to meet the guy, his anger seemed to have morphed into a kind of acceptance, which on the one hand was a relief and on the other made Susan feel even more afraid. Meanwhile, Linda tried prodding her to see a therapist to deal with her own feelings. Susan knew it wasn't a bad idea. But, like Henry, she hated talking about herself. Yes, she felt rage over what was happening. Other times, she felt so sad she wasn't sure if she could get out of bed. Somehow she managed to concentrate on helping Henry get better, and that's how she dealt with it.

Now, she tried to focus on the magazine, this time an article on the benefits of moisturizing, which Susan knew she never did enough of. At some point, she must have fallen asleep. The next thing she knew somebody was poking at her. Susan opened her eyes to find Dr. Greene leaning over her. She attempted a smile, but something about this man—maybe the bowl of sugarless candy or the leather sandals he always had on or his pale papery skin so thin she could see blue veins in his skull or the fact that this office always smelled like banana bread—and Susan hated banana bread—something about him just got on her nerves.

"Hi. What?" said Susan, feeling suddenly compelled to add, "I just started in a new kitchen. I work nights."

"We thought maybe you'd like to join us," said the doctor.

"Oh," Susan said. "Um . . ."

A part of her was, of course, afraid of what Henry might say about her or about her parenting skills or lack of them or their relationship in general. She wasn't sure if the doctor noticed her eyes dart around in search of a quick escape, but there was none, so she followed him into the office, where Henry's smirk seemed to be saying that if he had to suffer, she'd have to as well.

"First of all," Dr. Greene began, once Susan settled onto the couch next to Henry, "we were talking about the MRI coming back clean."

"We're all thrilled about that, naturally," Susan said, although she couldn't quite read the look on Henry's face now.

"And then I asked Henry how you two were getting along, and he said, 'Why don't you ask her yourself?' and so I thought it might be beneficial for you to join us."

"Oh," said Susan, silently breathing a little easier because the question wasn't so hard, "well, we're getting along great. Aren't we, sweetie?"

"Right," said Henry. "I especially like her pot dealer boyfriend. I'm not so sure about the other guy she seems to be seeing too."

Dr. Greene looked at Susan. "Whoa. Wait a second," she protested. "First of all, Griffin is not a pot dealer. He's a drummer in a band. And a sometime professional surfer. And . . . um . . ."

She noticed that this elicited a longer appraisal from the doctor. She tried to clarify the situation. "Second of all, while I have been involved with Mike in the past, as of right now, we are simply good friends."

"Right," Henry said, although he seemed to be smiling slyly, as if he knew more.

The truth was, with all that was going on, she wasn't looking to date anybody. She didn't actually mean to start sleeping with Griffin Barnekie and certainly didn't need any added complications, that was for sure. But every week or so during the worst times for Henry, she would make a marijuana run. Most of the time, she'd meet Griffin in front of Edie's beach house, but one afternoon, he called her from his own place and asked her to come up there. So Susan drove further north, took a nearly hidden cut-off, and wound her way up a steep, narrow road into some canyon that had recently burned and still showed the evidence, with its Mars-like barren landscape and charred, spindly trees poking up out of dirt scorched black. She followed his directions and arrived at what was left of one house after the blaze passed through on its unstoppable march to the sea: a chimney and stone hearth, and the partially melted remains of an old stove. The house was gone, but the land was springing to life again, even if it still sometimes smelled of fire, so that patches of green had sprouted here and there, along with unexpected splashes of native color, and all around her was the sweet, spiky scent of sage. Parked to one side of the burned-out house was a rusty Airstream, and that's where Susan found Griffin that day, curled up in a makeshift bed with Dora, a big old black Labrador, by his side. He told her he had grown up on this property, but after the fire, his parents, who had been planning to rebuild, instead split up and had been bickering over custody of the land ever since.

"Which is awesome for me," Griffin had told her, "because neither of them gives a damn that I'm camping out here."

That day, when he jumped out of bed and moved around the little trailer in his boxers, Susan tried looking every which way but right at him, taking in the drum set in the corner and the stack of flyers for his band's latest gig, but she couldn't help it and kept peeking anyway. He had the sort of body she always found attractive. He was long and lean, all ropey muscle, it seemed. Then there were all those tattoos on his arms and in other places she noticed. Later, she'd figure out the reason she jumped into bed with him after he had rolled her a few joints and she was getting all set to leave; they'd been taking turns—she, Andrew, and Edie—shuttling Henry back and forth to chemo appointments. All around her, suddenly, everywhere she looked, was sickness and decay and the sort of fear she could actually smell, despite frequently valiant and often touching attempts at all-around good cheer on the part of nurses and other aides, and here she was at Griffin's in what appeared to be a veritable garden of destruction, but he was all health and vitality, something to grab on to and hold tight because, maybe, some of it would rub off and she'd pass it along to her son.

She thought it would just be that one time. Never again, because, well, for one thing, he wasn't even thirty and she had forty coming fast down the pike. But Griffin kept showing up, first at Mrs. Vale's and then at the restaurant, a venerable old Pasadena steak joint where Susan had landed a job as executive chef with a mandate to revamp a stale menu and reinvigorate a staff that had grown stale too. Griffin would wait for her in the alley out back, where the kitchen crew would gather for smoke breaks. He swore up and down he wasn't really a dealer, but if one of the guys wanted to buy a joint here and there, he would oblige. Susan would get mad, but then Griffin would offer to rub her back or massage her feet after standing all night, and who could say no to that? They settled into something like a relationship, but Susan couldn't be sure if it was anything more than physical. Then came the morning she was driving up to Mrs. Vale's, and she thought her former mother-in-law might be in trouble with the FBI. There was a beige nondescript sedan parked by Edie's Mercedes. There was a tall chunky man coming out the front door in a blue suit and dark aviators, hair precisely clipped and neatly combed into place.

It wasn't until she was nearly at the door herself and the man grinned and said, "How're you doing, babe?" that she realized it was Mike Finley, and that he'd come looking for her.

"Oh my God," Susan answered, "what are you doing here?"

"Brought your mail." He held up a small stack of mostly bills. "Thought you might want these too." He had her knives, zipped tightly in their case, which she did indeed miss. "It was hell getting them through security, I'll say that."

"You came all the way out here to bring these to me?"

"Well, that and there's a training program that the Air Traffic Control Association is putting on, and I have to pass it if I want to get bumped up to this supervisor position I'm after. So I'm spending the next month at the Radisson. At the airport. In Los Angeles."

Susan smiled up at Mike. When he wasn't watching football or hockey or baseball on TV, he was a huge fan of the cable channel that played nothing but classic movies. So he pronounced Los Angeles with a hard g and sounded like he stepped out of some black-and-white picture starring Barbara Stanwyck. He was a welcome visitor for another reason. He came from the time before she set out to see Henry, before all the bad stuff, so it felt like a reminder that her life wasn't always filled with anxiety and dread.

"Well," said Susan. "It's good to see you. You look . . . um . . ."

"Yeah, yeah," said Mike, "I know it. I got fat."

"Get out of here. You are not, um . . . exactly fat . . . but, what have you been eating?"

"Well, for lunch today? A patty melt and an order of wings. Oh, and curly fries."

"So, like, you're trying to commit suicide?"

"Maybe I just miss your scrambled eggs at three in the morning."

"I hate to tell you, but those aren't exactly low calorie."

"Yeah, but they come with a side of you."

Susan felt herself flush. "I have a confession to make," she suddenly blurted out, had felt a sudden urge to come clean.

"Wait," Mike said, "let me guess. You're dating some surfer dude?"

"What? How did you . . . Oh, goddamn her," Susan said, thinking Edith Vale couldn't keep her mouth shut.

"It wasn't the old dame. The kid told me. While I was waiting for you."

"Oh. Nice."

"Hey, even back home, we were never exclusive, remember? You never wanted to be."

"Yeah, but I was never really dating anybody else."

"Yeah, well, neither was I. So is this serious?"

"I'm not sure what it is," Susan had to admit.

He left that day telling her he was there if she needed him, that she should swing by the Radisson anytime, and Susan found that oddly reassuring.

She was forced to tune back in to the therapy session when she realized Dr. Greene and Henry were both staring at her, waiting for the answer to a question she didn't hear. "I'm sorry. What?" she said.

"I was just looking for your reaction to Henry's suggestion about homeschooling."

Susan looked at Henry. They had decided that Henry would be kept in Pasadena for the upcoming school year to be closer to the doctors and to them all, just in case. Nobody had ever discussed homeschooling. "Are you serious?" she finally said.

"Yeah," said Henry. "You and Dad and Mrs. Vale and Linda could take turns being my teachers. Just think of the fun we'd all have."

Susan turned to Dr. Greene. "I hope you understand he's pulling your leg. I can almost guarantee he has no interest in being homeschooled."

"Hmmmmm," murmured Dr. Greene, who then began to stroke the thin strip of a beard he had grown just under his lower lip.

Susan started to fixate on the little patch of hair, then looked away until she noticed those open-toed sandals and that he had one really dirty nail.

"Well," continued the doctor, "then why would he suggest it?"

"Because, and believe me I can understand this part, he doesn't want to start a new school with new kids he doesn't know and because, truthfully, he thinks he could get away with lying in bed and watching TV or playing Xbox all day if he were homeschooled. Isn't that right, sweetie?"

Henry smiled tightly. "I thought we were talking about you and your juggling two guys," he said.

"Again," said Susan, "one I wouldn't exactly call a boyfriend and the other just a friend. But maybe we should talk about your love life, Henry?"

Here, Dr. Greene looked at Henry, who had clammed up.

"He's got this thing for this girl—Luz—everybody in the family can tell, but he never seems to have the nerve to do anything about it," Susan said.

Henry looked mortified. He opened his mouth, but nothing came out.

"Seriously, I think there are self-esteem issues you could be working on, and now might be the time for it."

But Henry clearly wanted no further part of this discussion. He stood and left the office and refused to come back.

***

Later, in the library back at Edie's house, it was cocktail hour, something Edie clung to with a near-religious fervor, it sometimes seemed to Susan. Not that she didn't happily accept the dry Manhattan that Edie just mixed.

She was settling into a chair when Evangeline turned to her and said, "Those dogs are plotting against me." She pointed at Edie's King Charles spaniels, who sat in the corner playing tug-of-war with some old chew toy and making contented grunting noises.

"Oh. Well . . . ," Susan started and then broke off, not quite knowing how to respond.

"What are you talking about, dear?" asked Edie as she settled into her own chair near the roaring fire Blanca had stoked in the hearth, her Manhattan in one hand and a fresh Parliament in the other. "They're dogs. They do not plot."

"They look at me funny. They're shifty. I'm warning you. T-R-O-U-B-L-E."

Edith glanced over at Susan and gave a small eye-roll, then simply nodded at her sister and sipped her drink.

Susan felt a rare tug of affection for Edie in that moment, as if they shared a little secret. Sometimes it made her heart ache that she never got to know her own mother. Sometimes she wondered what her mother would be like at Edie's age, wondered about both her parents really. Would they be one of those happy old married couples who finish each other's sentences and dress alike and walk with their shoulders brushing, or would they have grown peevish and prickly, annoyed with the sight of each other? Would they even still be married at all?

"And who is that absolutely enormous woman in the room next to me?" Evangeline continued. "What kind of hotel is this?"

"Oh for goodness' sake, Evangeline. It's your daughter, Gigi. You know that."

"That is not my daughter," Evangeline insisted.

"Tell her, Susan. It is indeed Gigi."

Susan tried to convince Evangeline but didn't have much success either. She had met Gigi a few times. It had been several years since she'd seen her, but the truth was she almost didn't recognize the woman who hauled herself out of the car with considerable effort when Edie returned from the airport earlier that afternoon. Gigi was enormous, a tiny head with no discernible neck perched on a body that resembled a lumpy, overripe pear. Not helping matters was the flowing, somewhat garish caftan she wore with tons of big turquoise jewelry. Oh, Susan had heard the stories from Edie before, about how Gigi was always a difficult child, and apparently not much had changed, because Gigi started complaining the minute she set foot in the house, pulling Susan aside when everybody else knew to scatter and going on about the narrowness of the seat on the plane, the rudeness of the flight attendants, and the problems with her health (asthma, a bad case of sciatica, bum knees). Things only seemed to go downhill when Evangeline got a look at her daughter, decided she must be some new nurse who had come to take her blood pressure, and locked herself in her room.

Later, they all gathered for dinner, which was meant to celebrate the good news Henry had received from the doctor, and so Edie had put him at the head of the table with Susan on one side and his father on the other, opposite Linda and the twins. Susan offered to cook, but Edie insisted that Blanca would do a better job with Henry's favorites—tomato soup, creamed chicken and peas on toast, and butterscotch pudding, and so Susan just sat back and tried to enjoy the evening. She exchanged pleasantries with Linda and the twins, and even with Andrew, who had returned from his trip to Chicago with what seemed to Susan like a cagey grin, like he might be in on some private joke. Well, that was none of her business any-more. The only thing that seemed to be amiss was that Susan noticed that, for once at Edie's table, she didn't feel the poke of wet noses at her ankles.

"No puppies tonight?" she said to Edie.

"Are the dogs in there with you?" Edie called out to Blanca in the kitchen, and when Blanca shouted back that they weren't, a rare look of alarm passed across Edith Vale's face. She turned to Evangeline. "Where are my dogs?"

"I told you, they were up to no good."

"Mother," said Gigi, in between bites of the creamed chicken, which at first she'd expressed concern about, what with her irritable bowel, her gluten issues, her lactose intoler-ance and all, but now was devouring it as if somebody might swoop down and make off with her plate, "that's crazy."

"Where are they, dear?" Edie repeated, a little more emphatic this time.

"I let them out," said Evangeline.

"Into the backyard? Where it's all nice and fenced in, right, Aunt Evangeline?" asked Andrew.

"Oh no. I opened the front door and I told them to go."

"Oh, Good Lord," said Edith. She jumped from her chair and ran for the door.

Susan grabbed Henry and they followed Edie, as did Linda, Andrew, and the twins, Blanca trailing behind with an apron pocket full of treats. Gigi stayed behind with her mother. Outside, they fanned out in every direction, calling the dogs' names. Susan followed Henry around the corner. They headed up the pitch-black cul-de-sac behind Edie's house. Susan scooted up a dark driveway because she heard what could be the dogs, but they weren't there. She returned to the street. Henry was gone. For a second, in the gloom, in this unfamiliar place, a panic overtook her, as if she'd never find him again.

Suddenly she wasn't calling out for the dogs but was calling Henry's name, louder and with growing urgency until she couldn't help it and she lost all control of her emotions and started screaming. Her voice sounded alien and screechy, like it was coming from some different person altogether, like a crazy person, she knew, but somehow she couldn't seem to stop it. Then Henry popped up next to her as abruptly as he seemed to vanish, and she launched into a tirade about never leaving without telling her where he was going and exactly when he'd be back.

Henry just stared at her. "Jesus," he said after a moment, "why are you screaming at me?"

"Because you got sick!"

There it was. The words popped out of her mouth and seemed to stay suspended in front of them like the ones in those cartoon bubbles.

"Wow," Henry said. "Mad at me because I got sick? That's pretty screwed up. You might want to bring that up with the shrink."

Now another torrent of words came tumbling from her mouth, along with a flood of tears. "I'm sorry, Henry. I don't know what I'm saying. I'm just afraid. There's no rule book for this, it turns out. And that was a horrible thing to say. I'm horrible. I'm a terrible, horrible mother. I guess I don't have to tell you that. I just wonder if you'll ever be able to forgive me. Because I may never be able to get you to understand it. But I swear I always did what I thought was best for you. And if I could switch places with you right now, I would."

Henry looked at her for a long moment. "How about you quit being such a big drama queen and just chill?" he asked.

She took a deep breath. She wiped at her eyes with a sleeve. "Okay. All better. I'm calm," said Susan. "Don't I seem calm and together?"

"Yeah. Right. Let's find the dogs then."

Susan followed as Henry continued the search. It took a few minutes before she realized he never said a thing about forgiveness.

***

It was Blanca who found Freddie and Min trying to knock over a trash bin a few doors down from the Vales'. She had scooped both dogs into her arms and trotted them back to the house, depositing them at Edie's feet before nearly passing out as she tried to catch her breath. She was still there, taking in big gulps of air, when Susan and the others returned and they all started to head back inside.

"Missy, we need help," Blanca finally managed to say to Edie.

"Help? With what?" said Edie.

"*Su hermana.* Your sister. We can't do it ourselves, you and me, anymore."

Edie waved that idea off. "Oh, pish tosh, of course we can. We're doing perfectly fine."

Blanca shot Susan an imploring look. "You've seen. Tell her."

Indeed, Susan had noticed a gradual deterioration in Evangeline. "You know, Edie, it does look like you could use more help," she said.

Edie remained unconvinced. "I think we manage this ourselves, thank you."

But Blanca had stopped. She was pulling at what appeared to be a cramp that had developed in her side. "Missy," she finally said to Edie, "I'm seventy-seven years old."

They were almost at the house. Susan, following behind, almost crashed right into Edie, who had stopped dead in her tracks and looked stunned, as if Blanca had turned and slapped her in the face.

"You . . . what?" Edie managed to ask.

Actually, this was something of a shock to Susan too. Blanca didn't seem to look any different from the first night she saw her, but that was nearly twenty years ago: same squat, sturdy frame, same jet-black hair, same smooth skin.

"I'm seventy-seven, Missy. I get a little tired."

Susan watched as Edie simply gathered up the dogs and walked into the house. She marched right up to her room and wasn't heard from again the entire night.

***

Somewhere around dawn, Susan was woken by a crash. It sounded like it came from the kitchen, and because Henry had recently been finding himself hungry at the strangest of hours, she climbed out of bed and went down to investigate. She found Edie in a bathrobe on her knees, holding up two sides of a plate, a piece of Royal Crown Derby bone china with a floral design Susan knew was from her own mother's collection.

"I think a little super glue, and we can put this back together, don't you?" she asked when she saw Susan.

"Yeah. It looks like a clean break. Is everything okay, Edie?"

Edie rose and set the pieces down on the counter. "I thought I'd bring Blanca breakfast for a change. So I have toast. With lots of yummy sweet butter and honey. And tea. Piping hot." She placed the toast on a new plate and set it down on a breakfast tray. "Be a dear, Susan, and grab the teapot."

She picked up the pot—also Derby in that floral pattern, so she moved very, very slowly—and followed Edie to the door to Blanca's little white square of a room off the kitchen. Edie knocked.

Blanca, her hair in a net, bundled up in an old fuzzy robe and slippers, cracked open the door. "What have you got there?"

"I brought you breakfast!" Edie chirped.

Blanca eyed the tray with suspicion. "That's what *you* eat for breakfast," she said. "I like menudo. The stomach of a cow."

"Oh, don't be revolting," Edie said. She pushed her way into the room, ordered Blanca back into the bed, and set the tray down before her.

Susan poured the tea and turned to leave, but Edie grabbed her arm. "No, you stay. I have something to say. I could use moral support."

This should be interesting, Susan figured, and so she perched on the end of the bed too.

"Do you want to retire?" Edie asked as Blanca poked at the toast. "Is that what you want? Because we've talked about this, remember? It's all planned. I will take care of things. You won't have to worry."

"Who said anything about retiring?"

"Well, I was just . . . I mean, last night you seemed rather . . ."

Blanca turned to Susan. "Didn't she say that was my tea?"

Apparently, without thinking, Edie had plopped a cube of sugar into the cup, stirred it around, and was about to take a sip. She handed it back over.

"Anyway," Blanca said, stretching out and wiggling her toes as she sipped the tea, "I don't want to stop working. What would I do with myself? Like I told you, Missy. We just need some help."

"What about one of your daughters? Didn't you tell me Maria needed a new job?"

Blanca seemed unsure. "We could try," she said.

Now there was silence. Susan, anxious to get back to bed, stood to leave, but Edie grabbed her arm and pulled her back down. "I couldn't sleep at all last night," Edie said. "I kept think-ing about something."

"What already?" said Blanca.

"You've been working here over forty years."

"Yes. That's right."

"Why do you stay? Why in heaven's name do you put up with me?"

Now they had Susan's attention. She was curious about how Blanca would answer that one, but Blanca calmly took a bite of her toast and a long sip from the cup of tea.

"I don't know," Blanca finally said. "There are worse jobs, I guess."

Edie seemed unsatisfied by this and pressed on. "But I can be so . . . oh, let's face it. I must be impossible, sometimes, to work for."

"Sometimes?" Blanca asked. Here, Susan could swear Blanca winked at her.

"Well," Edie said in her own defense, it seemed, "I'm a per-fectionist. I know that. Also, I know I can be persnickety and I can be opinionated about the way I like things done."

"Plus," added Blanca, "you get obsessed about things. *Compulsivo*. It can be very irritating. And always with the nag-nag-nagging. Like, if you say, 'Blanca, *por favor*, please clean the top of the picture frames,' then you don't have to ask me twenty-three times if I did it. And then check it to make sure I did."

Edie huffed and puffed. Susan half expected her to storm right out of the room. She didn't. "Well, I just have to say one thing," Edie continued. "I don't know what I would do without you. Honestly, I don't. If you left, I would be absolutely lost. And if I'm really so awful, if I have been in the past, and when I will be in the future, I'm sorry."

Blanca took her time forming an answer. Susan almost felt a shift of power taking place, like a strong gust blowing from one side of the room to the other. "Lighten up, Missy. You're not so bad," Blanca said.

"Great," said Edie. "I'm not so bad." Then she turned to Susan. "I suppose that's what you think too? That I 'could be worse.' Or that I'm 'not so bad.'"

For the second time that day, Susan opened her mouth but couldn't find the right words. The truth was she wasn't sure how she felt anymore about Edie.

"Well, that's nice. That's just wonderful," said Edie, filling the awkward silence that had fallen. And before Susan could stop her, Edie turned and left the room.

XIV.

Henry figured it was ironic—at least he thought that was the right word; he wasn't exactly sure how to define *irony* and made a mental note to Google it—that it was Mrs. Vale who was responsible for his hooking up with Luz. Or, well, getting close to hooking up. Or, well, sitting across from each other— knees almost touching—in a booth in what was once a classic 1940s diner in the Westlake district of Los Angeles, a place that looked frozen in time, with all its Formica and Naugahyde intact, the only change being it now served foods from Oaxaca, and Henry was pretty much the only white kid in the place, and a lot of the other customers seemed to be sending dirty looks his way.

Earlier that day, he had been in his room, running a hand over his scalp, absently marveling that what had started out as fuzz, like you'd find on a ripe summer peach, had grown out so fast. Indeed, hair pretty much now covered the scar left from where the doctors had drilled a hole in his head. He had run a finger over the scar. It hardly itched at all anymore either so he wasn't always scratching his head madly, which made him feel like some monkey at the zoo. Still, the hair wasn't long enough to brush, and it tended to stand up and tuft out in odd places. He had come to the conclusion that he looked like an even bigger dork than ever as he headed downstairs to get something from the kitchen, all the while wondering if he'd run into Luz, who was at the house all the time now because Mrs. Vale had hired her to help with Evangeline.

First they had tried Luz's aunt, Blanca's oldest daughter, Maria, who would begin her shift in a responsible way, but then she would disappear, only to be found in Blanca's room, nodding along with or chattering back to one of her telenovelas. Or she would get in long, involved phone calls or elaborate texting with her latest boyfriend while Evangeline drifted this way or that during their afternoon walk. Even Henry could see Maria wasn't going to last. Mrs. Vale was all set to call an agency, but then Luz appeared at the front door, surprising even Blanca, and asked for the job. She would need the money for college the following year, Henry overheard her telling his grandmother, and so Edie decided to give her a chance. Luz would show up midafternoon and stay through giving Evangeline her dinner and a bath. She'd read to Evangeline in the library most afternoons too. Henry would lurk at corners and follow her around but stayed just out of sight as much as possible.

Downstairs, Henry now found his mother all set to leave for her new job, looking at something in the library, and when he joined her, he saw Luz. She had fallen fast asleep, a book open in her lap. She wore a white tank top and faded jeans that had holes at the knees, so Henry could see soft brown skin. A cross dangling from a gold chain around her neck rested in the nook between her breasts. Henry decided right then and there she was the most beautiful thing he'd ever seen; he couldn't take his eyes off of her.

He snapped out of this trance only when Evangeline said, in a loud whisper, "She has to take two buses and two trains to get here. Plus, she told me she's going to summer school."

"Well, clearly she's exhausted," Susan said.

"Who's exhausted?" asked Mrs. Vale. She had come in from the garden. She wore a favorite gardening outfit, kicky red capri pants and a perfectly enormous straw hat. In one hand she had razor-sharp pruning shears and in the other a fresh-cut bunch of vivid yellow roses that smelled sweet and citrusy. "Oh dear," she added when she saw the sleeping Luz.

"Maybe this job is too much after all," Susan said.

"You could pick her up and drive her home, you know," Henry said, "instead of working her to death and then she has to make that commute."

Mrs. Vale clucked and fussed with the flowers. Then she said, "I have a better idea. Susan, dear, wake her up."

"I'm sorry. I'm late for work as it is."

Susan headed for the door. Henry watched as Edie gingerly poked at Luz until she roused. She looked up, at first a little confused, then smiled when she saw Henry, who dared to smile back.

"Do you drive, dear?" Edie asked Luz.

"My father taught me," she said. "I got a license. Yes."

"Come with me then."

Henry followed as Edith walked Luz out the back door and down the driveway. They wound up at the difficult-to-access, rarely used garage. Edie pulled open the heavy double doors, and there, under a thick layer of dust and soot, sat her big old wagon, a forest green Pontiac Catalina, with its faux wood paneled sides, its three rows of seating, and with the ski rack Frank had struggled to install one Saturday all those years ago still rusted solid to the roof and the fading *"Re-elect Nixon in*

'72!" sticker still on the bumper, the same car Edie turned over to Blanca until the cataracts forced her to stop driving.

"What do you think? Do you think it will start?" Edie asked.

Luz looked at Henry. The best he could manage was a shrug.

"Oh, well, let's try," said Mrs. Vale, smiling broadly, so to Henry, at least, it looked as if they were about to set off on some fabulous adventure.

He dove into the back. Luz took shotgun next to Edie, who reached under the seat, and there were the keys, just where she stashed them. The gas-guzzling V-8 sprang to life with a shockingly throaty roar. And though it took some coaxing to move the gearshift into reverse, the wagon rolled out of the garage with ease.

"I suppose we should take her around the block to see if all systems are in order, don't you think, Henry?" asked Mrs. Vale as she pressed the windshield spray button furiously, and the wipers started a slow sweep back and forth.

"Whatever," said Henry, though secretly he was hoping she might suggest a longer road trip, hopefully one where they could get lost for days. They'd pitch a tent—in the mountains, say—and huddle close. Of course, they'd have to ditch his grandmother in this scenario.

But all they did was circle the block. They stopped at the gas station at the corner so Edie could have the fluids and tires checked. Then Mrs. Vale handed Luz the keys, insisting she take the car, that it would cut her travel time by at least half, adding that she would include gas and upkeep money now in her salary. "I can drive," Luz said, "but I don't know the route back home. I'd get lost for sure."

"Silly me," said Edie. "Of course, because you've never done it." She thought for another moment. "Here's what we'll do.

Henry, you ride with Luz. I will lead you in my car so you can learn the way to go, and Henry will come back home with me."

So that was the plan. Mrs. Vale went off to get her pocketbook and keys. Henry tried to smile in a not lame way as Luz pointed the Pontiac toward the street, following Edie's Mercedes, but the way ahead was suddenly blocked as Evelyn Brookby's Lincoln Continental pulled into the driveway. Edie had forgotten her dinner date with Oatsie, Evelyn, and Tish. So she informed the ladies they'd have to make a predinner detour and told Luz to follow Evelyn.

In the Pontiac, Henry sat as far to the right on the huge bench seat as he could until Luz finally seemed to take control of the situation and began a conversation. "Your grandmother seems like a nice lady," she said as she steered the big old wagon onto the southbound Pasadena Freeway.

"Well," said Henry, "she's okay. If you like out-of-their-mind control freak types."

Luz smiled. Henry tried to find something—anything—on the AM radio and got nothing but static and little bits of some talk show where the guy was talking about the dire situation somewhere in the world that was about to explode. He turned it back off.

Luz tried again. "It's nice, though. That she's seeing that her sister is being taken care of."

"I guess," said Henry. "Although personally, I'd have kicked the old bag out on her ass."

This had the desired effect of making Luz laugh, which made him feel powerful, strong in some new, appealing way. Henry laughed a little too and filed the line away so he could tell Zach Julian about it later. During the remainder of the ride, Henry helpfully indicated when the car ahead would signal for turns—that is, when Mrs. Brookby, the top of her hairdo barely visible behind the wheel, remembered to. Most of the time, she

weaved in and out of lanes or sped up suddenly, rocketing from
stop signs like a bullet and just as suddenly slamming on the
brakes, as if it had already slipped her mind she was being followed by people who needed guidance, although every minute
or so, Henry noticed Mrs. Vale's head start a rotation, as she
craned her head around to make sure they were there. When
they pulled up and parked the Pontiac on the street where Luz
lived in the Westlake district of Los Angeles and it was time to
say goodbye, Henry fumbled in silence for words, finally managing a lame "Oh. This is nice."

"Yeah, if you enjoy dodging bullets and tripping over crack
pipes," said Luz.

"Um," said Henry, starting to sweat.

"Please, don't patronize me," Luz continued, only now there
was a note of something like annoyance in her voice. "This
neighborhood sucks, and my mom's apartment is a shithole.
You ought to know that. You've been here before."

"I have?"

"You don't even remember?"

"I . . . uh . . ."

"It was a whole weekend, Henry. Like ten years ago. Your
grandmother went on some trip, and I don't know where your
dad was. The inside of the house was being painted or something, so my *abuela* brought you here. I guess it was no big deal
to you, though."

Henry racked his brain for words. Eliciting sympathy
seemed his only out. "You know I had a tumor. I was very sick.
Near death, even."

"Right."

Now came impatient honking from Mrs. Brookby in the
Lincoln, which was blocking the street as the ladies waited.

"You better go," Luz said.

"Yeah." Henry tried to come up with a way to say he was sorry. Again, he fumbled. He fled from the car without another word and felt like an even bigger jerk.

***

A few minutes later, settled into the cushy backseat of the Lincoln between his grandmother and Tish Van Buren, with Oatsie and Evelyn up front, Henry was mortified by the conversation that was unfolding, something about Mrs. Vale needing to make a stop at the drugstore for what she called adult panty liners for Evangeline, which prompted Tish to say, "Oh, Edie, please, just call them what they are: diapers," and then Mrs. O'Shea started to go on, at length, about her own mother's incontinence—"Every time she laughs," Oatsie said, "she pees!"—and Henry wondered if it would be impolite to cover his ears or hum really loud. Then Mrs. Brookby nearly ran a red light, only stopping after the other ladies started screaming. They were near MacArthur Park, and as they waited for the red light to turn green, Edie pointed to what looked like a small coffee shop wedged between a shifty-looking travel agency and a down-on-its-heels pawnshop.

"My mother," Edie said brightly, "used to take us there after shopping trips downtown. I remember it distinctly. They had the most marvelous desserts."

"Oh yes," said Oatsie. "I adored the coconut ice cream ball."

"With that wonderful chocolate fudge sauce," added Tish.

All the ladies gazed wistfully at the place, lost in tooth-achingly sweet memories, it seemed to Henry. Then he took a closer look at it. "Oh, shit!" he practically shouted.

"Henry!" said Mrs. Vale, while the other ladies squawked.

But a memory of his own had flashed into his head of a stout, round-faced Latina in a starched waitress uniform placing a plate before him of something unfamiliar, two small discs wrapped in something green, banana leaves, it turned out, which when unwrapped, unleashed the strong, earthy aroma of steamed corn. He remembered sitting in a booth next to Luz, their legs swinging back and forth under the table, Blanca opposite them, as they devoured the tamales, and now he realized he needed to see Luz and apologize for not having remembered. And so just as the light turned green, while an oblivious Mrs. Brookby was chattering away and the car hadn't moved, he climbed over Mrs. Vale, opened the door, and leapt out of the car. And even though he could hear his grandmother yelling for him to come back that instant or else, Henry ran, darting through traffic to reach the sidewalk on the other side. When he was in the middle of all the treatments—the chemo and the radiation—he had often felt utterly depleted, startled at the inability to make himself move at anything faster than a crawl. Now, with strength back, it felt exhilarating to move fast.

He kept on running, all the way back to the apartment building where Luz lived, slowing only once to glance at his caller ID, which of course lit up with Mrs. Vale's name, so he hit "ignore" and ran harder, past small noisy bodegas teeming with customers, past what appeared to be an encampment of the homeless in a little tent city that had sprouted among the dusty weeds in a vacant lot. He ran past more than a few rough-looking kids barely his own age, who glared at him with suspicion. It crossed his mind that people got shot in neighborhoods like this, with actual bullets. But he kept going. He squeezed through the front door of Luz's building as a woman who reminded him of Blanca was coming out. He took the stairs two at a time, up three stories, so that when Luz's mother opened the door and gave him the once-over, he had to struggle to catch his breath. All at once, words came tumbling out, and Luz, happy he had come back, invited him in. But as they sat on a couch in the living room, they realized everybody was staring—Luz's mother and her aunts and various cousins Henry couldn't keep straight.

Finally she asked if he was hungry, and so before long, they were back at the old time-warp coffee shop that now served Oaxacan specialties, trying to talk, though Henry's phone continued to interrupt, first a rather screechy Mrs. Vale, then his mother screaming over the clattering of pots, then his father calling from his hushed office, all asking the same questions about whether or not he'd gone crazy and what was he thinking jumping out of a speeding car (even though—hello?—the car wasn't even moving), and how would he get home? He swore up and down he'd be fine, that he could take the subway if he had to because isn't that what Blanca and Luz had been doing all this time anyway, the subway and the bus?

Then he turned the phone to silent and said to Luz, "So. Anyway. It's sort of, well, ironic, isn't it?"

"What is?"

"That we're sitting here now. Waiting on an order of tamales again. Just like all those years ago, when we were kids."

"I guess that depends on how you define irony," said Luz.

Suddenly it felt like he had a ball of cotton in his throat, and there was a tingling sensation behind his ears. He could feel himself beginning to flush. "Um. Well, how do you define it?"

"There are a couple of definitions, of course."

"Naturally," said Henry, hoping he didn't sound totally without even the hint of a clue.

"Well, there's Socratic irony, which means . . ."

He had forgotten one important fact about Luz Guttierez: she was a major brainiac, had been since childhood. Indeed, some might have called her bookish or, worse, a dweeb. Now he recalled she was even in glee club, for God's sake, and had a fondness for entomology. There were times he recalled when Luz would be at his grandmother's house and she'd amuse herself by chasing down spiders or a certain butterfly she'd spotted flitting around the yard. She'd ferry these finds home in the empty Best Foods mayonnaise jars Blanca kept under the sink. One time she discovered and brought to Mrs. Vale, wrapped meticulously in a sliver of sky blue tissue from the powder room off the front hall, a termite. At first, Mrs. Vale insisted it was an ant, but Luz pointed out that it had wings, that there was probably a colony somewhere, literally thousands of them boring through the wood framing of the house as they spoke. This caused Mrs. Vale to shriek that her house would be the death of her, and soon they were all packed into the big old Ritz-Carlton near the Rose Bowl while the house was tented and fumigated.

Now, as Luz continued to define Socratic irony, Henry was starting to feel dumber and dorkier than usual. Thankfully, here came the tamales, plates of two small neat bundles like he remembered, wrapped in banana leaves, delivered, he suspected but couldn't be entirely sure, by that same waitress whose sweet face was now etched with deep lines and creases.

He was hoping the delivery of food would allow a change in subject altogether, but Luz finished her definition, and then was saying, "and then there's the kind of irony maybe you're thinking of. You know, sort of an inconsistency between the actual result of a sequence of events when you compare it with what the normal result would be."

"Yes! Precisely," Henry said, even though he was completely lost. But he tried to cover it with a compliment. "You're pretty freaking smart. How do you know this?"

"Dude, I took AP English last term, but you go to a fancy boarding school, so you should know this too, I'd think."

"Yeah. Well . . . anyway, what else do you know?"

Luz unwrapped a tamale and dug her fork into the soft, heady-smelling masa to reveal meltingly tender shredded pork bathed in rich dark mole the color of rust. "Why don't you test me. Ask me something—anything—and I'll see if I can answer it."

Henry brought a search engine up on his phone and started firing random questions at her. "What's the capital of Peru?" and "Who was president in 1813?" and "What is the Latin name of the live oak trees that line Mrs. Vale's driveway?"

"Lima. James Madison," and after a brief pause and a false start, "*Quercus virginiana.*" Luz had answered every one of them. She smiled. Their knees brushed against each other.

Henry felt a jolt in his groin that made him flush again. "Jesus," he said. "Is there anything you don't know?"

She gave him a little shrug.

"Okay," Henry said. "Now I know I get it."

"Get what?"

"Why you got early acceptance at Stanford with practically a full scholarship."

"Yeah. Well. And I'm a nervous wreck about it all, if you want to know the truth."

"Really? Why?"

"Why? Seriously, Henry? What do I know about a place like Stanford? It's a whole other world, if you think about it. I mean, Palo Alto? And they'll put me with some roommate I've never met from God only knows where. Sometimes I think I should have just stuck with applying to USC and UCLA or Claremont or Loyola and stayed closer to home, lived at home, even. I think that's what my mom would want anyway. But I wouldn't expect you to understand anyway."

Abruptly, she got up and dashed to the bathroom. Henry realized she was crying. Now he sensed the looks of other customers had turned to glares, like daggers pointed in his direction. He felt himself flush with shame, even though he wasn't exactly sure what he had done. He went to the bathroom door. He knocked on it and got no response. He got no response after more knocking, but then the door opened, and Luz, dabbing at her eyes with a piece of Kleenex, hustled to the table. He settled back in across from her, desperate to see her smile again.

"I don't know what I did, Luz. But I never meant to make you cry. So whatever it was, I'm sorry," he said.

"You know what, Henry? The thing is, I'm just a little scared. Okay, terrified, if you want to know the truth."

"Of what?"

"I don't know. Of being different. Of being laughed at maybe. Like nobody up there will get where I come from or how hard it might be to leave. Or how much pressure I'll be under, like I have to represent. For a whole neighborhood or a culture."

"You'll do great," Henry said, even though the truth was he knew he had no clue about what it might be like to have to straddle two worlds.

"You think?"

"I do."

He took the last bite of his tamale, savored it really. "These are so delicious. How do you make these?"

"Oh," Luz said, "I used to watch my grandmother do it. Not Blanca. The other one in Guatemala, my father's mother, who was real old-school. It would take all afternoon. She'd set up like an assembly line, and I'd get to help with wrapping them up in the banana leaves once they were stuffed. She'd stew pork a real long time. Hours, until your mouth started to water from the smell. She'd make a dough from fresh masa and some other stuff. I think there's *achiote*, which is a . . ." She broke off, was quiet a minute, then asked, "I do sound like some big annoying know-it-all, don't I?"

In fact, the memory of watching her grandmother make tamales had caused her face to light up again, as if all bad thoughts and negativity had been banished by recalling being fed something not just tasty but that also seemed to nourish the soul. "Nah. It's all good," he said.

"Because really, what you asked before? Is there anything I don't know?"

"Yeah?"

"There's lots. A ton of things I haven't figured out. I think there's stuff I'll never be able to learn."

"Like what?"

She thought for a moment. "Well, like water. I'm afraid of the water. Not pools so much, although I'm not so fond of them either because you never know who might have peed in one. But the ocean. The ocean scares me."

"Why?"

"Maybe because it's something I can't control. Like a rip current or a tsunami. Like you can get carried out to sea and nobody will be there to bring you back."

"There are ways to get out of a riptide."

"Well, anyway, I don't know how to swim."

He smiled and signaled for the check.

XV.

Susan Jones stood before the cracked mirror in the employee washroom of the restaurant about to perform a sort of pre-work ritual, a psyche-up for the battle of dinner service, even though she hadn't been hired to work the line. She had been brought in as executive chef of this place, Chadwick's, an old-time Pasadena institution tucked discreetly in an alley just north of Colorado Boulevard, where it had been since its founding in 1926, when it functioned mostly as a speakeasy. As executive chef, she'd be mostly managing the kitchen staff, expediting, and doing all the ordering and buying. But since her dinnertime line guy was right now having his appendix removed, she would man his station at the grill, and she felt a little rusty after all this time away from the stoves. So she holed herself up in the washroom and took a moment to bring her head into focus. She pulled her hair back tight and secured it in a neat ponytail at the nape of her neck. She splashed water on her face. She cinched a clean, starched apron tightly around her waist and took a few deep breaths. And it worked. Even though her image was distorted, sliced in half by the crack in the mirror and disjointed, like a Picasso, she looked pretty badass, she thought. And the truth was part of her missed the line because when things ran smooth—with all cylinders firing—the adrenaline pumping through her veins would leave her with a sort of high.

Her mandate from the owner, an elderly granddaughter of the founder of the place, had been to update the menu, mostly, Susan figured, so she could ultimately sell it since it had been going steadily downhill for years. But then the tough old bird fought every change Susan tried to make. She thought about quitting, but then she looked at her bank statement. Whatever cash she had managed to sock away before leaving Boston was somehow dangerously depleted, even though she was living rent-free at Edie's house. Of course, she was still paying rent on the apartment back east, and her aging Volvo suddenly seemed to be coming apart at the seams, needing first a battery, then brakes, and now, from the looks of them, most likely new tires too. She was giving Henry cash now and again for God only knows what because every now and again he'd ask her and she found it difficult to say no. So she stayed on the job, and all the standbys stayed on the menu, the Salisbury steak, the chicken Tetrazzini, the schnitzel Viennoise, Edie's favorite shepherd's pie, and a chicken Madras, with canned pineapple served over white rice. Susan fought for and finally got one concession: a special of her choice each night.

So she added a simple steak frites or a small roasted chicken for two or a braise of some kind, every now and again slipping in something daring, like quail or sweetbreads, upgrading the quality of the ingredients where she could and making sure the execution of each dish was perfect. In fact, Susan hired a whole new kitchen crew—the crusty old waiters were not to be messed with—and made execution the focus all around so that even the tired dishes were coming out of the kitchen with a freshness and a flavor that had been missing for years. She also fought for the hiring of a crack mixologist she'd once worked with back east to oversee the bar and create a cocktail menu, with the understanding that all juices—lime, orange, grapefruit, or whatever was in season—would be freshly squeezed. That was a day that Susan relished, tasting the various drinks and deciding what went on the menu, an alcohol-fueled afternoon that ran into the evening, that ended up with the entire staff out cold on the floor when they were supposed to be rehearsing for the reopening. They found a stash of copper mugs hidden deep under the bar, so making the cut was a Moscow mule, a zesty combination of vodka, ginger beer, lime, and simple syrup. There was one of Susan's favorites, a salty dog—a greyhound, but with the glass rimmed with coarse salt—and a mojito, with tons of freshly muddled mint. Since Edith Vale insisted Chadwick's was always home to one of the finest Manhattans in town, one was named in her honor.

So business started to pick up, and two hours after Susan's deep breathing in the bathroom, she was sweaty and lightheaded as she banged out orders, flipping steaks on one side of the grill, poking at a piece of halibut with a finger on the other, then spinning to pull orders of the roast chicken from ovens and getting blasted with furnace-like heat. She managed to stay on an even keel until she noticed orders of the smoked salmon appetizer going out.

"Did you prep those?" Susan said to Stacy, the cooking school newbie who was in charge of salads and cold apps, pointing at the toast triangles with the end of a wooden spoon.

"Um. Yeah," Stacy said.

"They look like shit. They're brown on one side and not the other. I told you I wanted even triangles, uniformly toasted. On both sides. How many times do I have to say it?"

Stacy swiped the plate back from Susan and muttered something nasty just loud enough for Susan and everybody else to hear. Susan didn't often have meltdowns. She was rarely a screamer, like a lot of people, men mostly, who ran restaurant kitchens. But occasionally she would lose it, usually when something frustrated her, like a gazillion orders of seared ahi tuna or when she found something being done in a sloppy way, as if nobody in the kitchen cared. Like now, so she started screaming, a litany of obscenities flying from her mouth as fast as she flipped the steak, swirled butter into a pan to sauce the fish, and pulled a batch of fries from hot oil. She was aware that the entire kitchen crew was staring at her like she was a madwoman, but really it felt good to scream like this, as if she was venting months' worth of steam about things that had absolutely nothing to do with the restaurant.

What she wasn't aware of was four fresh sets of eyes. Until she heard a familiar voice, "Really, Susan, such a potty mouth."

She spun around. There stood Edith Vale, Oatsie O'Shea, Evelyn Brookby, and Tish Van Buren, all of them impeccably turned out in sweater sets and pearls, pocketbooks clutched in their hands, all of them bright-eyed and more than a little lubricated after copious samplings from the cocktail menu, apparently. The four had decided to have their ladies' night out at Chadwick's that week, and Susan, already red-faced from the heat and steam of the kitchen, went a darker shade of scarlet as she wilted before them.

She smiled sheepishly and dusted a plate of sole with finely minced parsley. "Did you ladies eat?" was all she could manage.

"It was delightful, dear," said Oatsie.

"I haven't set foot in this place since 1989," said Evelyn Brookby, "but I'll be back."

"Girls, maybe we should go. She's obviously busy," said Tish.

"Well, we wanted to pay our compliments to the chef," said Edie. "But we obviously caught you at a bad time."

"Oh, don't leave," said Susan. "Let me send out some desserts."

"Darling, we all shared a floating island, and it was divine," Edie said, "light as a cloud, just as we remember!"

"Although do consider putting the blueberry buckle back on the menu," Tish added.

Susan nodded.

The ladies left the kitchen, and the dishwasher, Luis, practically invisible under the huge stockpot he was scrubbing, popped up and said, "I don't know about anybody else, but that grey-haired one? She had one hot ass. For an old lady, I mean."

"I'd tap it," said Stacy.

Susan couldn't help it; she forgot what set her off and started to laugh.

And so one crisis was diffused only to be replaced by another when one of the wheezy old waiters tottered into the kitchen and said to Susan, "You've got a problem, honey doll. You better get out to the bar."

Which was where they found Mike Finley and Griffin Barnekie. Mike had recently been coming to the restaurant regularly, taking a stool at the bar for dinner. Griffin had swung by on his way to a gig later. Apparently, they had been trading angry glares from opposite ends of the bar. Now Mike had one of his meaty hands around Griffin's throat and had him lifted clear off the floor and pressed against the wall.

"Who's the marshmallow now, pencil neck?" Mike asked a squirming Griffin.

Griffin gurgled something unintelligible, like when he took Susan scuba diving off Catalina and talked to her through his mask and all she heard was gibberish and bubbly sounds.

"What the hell are you doing?" Susan screamed at Mike. "Put him down."

"He called me lard ass."

"Let him go. Now," Susan said.

Mike released his grip. Griffin dropped straight down and landed with a loud thud. "Ow. Jesus," he said. "This dude's, like, completely postal."

Susan realized all eyes in the room were on them, like this was dinner theater. Mike shifted from one foot to the other but looked like he might lunge for Griffin again. "Come with me," she said.

Susan led Mike through the kitchen—past more curious eyes—and out the back door to the alley, where they all went to smoke when they couldn't stand the kitchen anymore.

"Okay," she said, actually relieved to be out in fresh air. "What is going on with you?"

"What do you see in that kid anyway?"

"He's just fun. We hang out. He's teaching me to surf. He told me when you catch a wave, at just the right time, when you stand on top of it, it's like you can feel the power of the universe at your feet. And you know what? It's kind of true."

"Oh, please."

"Yeah, well, you never took me anywhere," Susan said. "You sat around like a big lump and waited for me to go to bed with you or bring you something delicious to eat."

"Here's the thing: When you told me about him, I acted like I didn't care. Like it wasn't a big deal. But maybe it is. Maybe I'm not so good with us just being buddies."

"Seriously? Really?"

"You know, you'd think it'd be fun staying at the Radisson for a month on Uncle Sam's dime. Ordering room service twenty-four seven. Watching pay-per-view. And not just porn.

Somebody cleans your room. Every day. But you know what? It gets old. So I've been evaluating my life. Doing a lot of thinking."

"Oh, that's never a good sign," Susan joked, hoping to lighten the mood, as she couldn't quite gauge where this conversation was headed. "By the way, when does this training thing end?"

"When those FAA boobs decide I'm ready to supervise a tower. Soon, I hope. Anyway, I'm not getting any younger. I'm missing things. Maybe I want them in my life after all."

"Like what?"

"I don't know. I get lonely sometimes. A wife? A rug rat or two? A house with a backyard. A hound?"

His mouth was turned down at the corners in a pouty frown. His arms hung loosely at his sides. Somewhere, in the scuffle with Griffin, his shirt had come untucked, and his hair, always neatly combed, was sticking up in odd ways. He looked like an overgrown, sad little boy. But Susan didn't have time for this now.

"Uh-huh," she said. "Okay. Right. I have to get back to work. You're going to have to leave. We'll talk later."

He started to protest, but Susan had already turned to head into the kitchen. It dawned on her that this was something new, having two men fighting for her attention after a long period where nobody seemed interested at all. The truth was she kind of liked it.

***

It was also true that she didn't have an actual date with Griffin that night. His band did have a gig at a club in Echo Park, and since Chadwick's was generally dead by eleven, Susan had said, trying to keep it all casual sounding, that she might try to stop by after work. But part of her did very much want to go. So all through the rest of the night, she tried hard not to keep glancing at the clock over the dishwashing station and count the minutes until she could leave. Once she did get away, she rushed back to Mrs. Vale's house so she could shower off all the sweat and the grease and put on fresh clothes. And the new lingerie she had picked up because, somewhere along the line, it had slipped her mind that bras and panties didn't have to be utilitarian and, well, bland and church-lady-like, embarrassing really. Actually, she hadn't shopped for lingerie in ages. So there were distressing, anxious moments in the changing room at Nordstrom, which at first she blamed on the bad lighting or the funny angle of the mirror when she craned her neck around to look at her ass. Ultimately she had to face the simple fact that she had put on a few pounds, a combination, Susan figured, of that period of not working and stress. So there were new bulges and pouches in odd places, which prompted her to swear up and down she'd start swimming again or jogging or at least take power walks with Edie's dogs.

Not that she didn't figure this thing with Griffin was just a fling. First of all, there was the age difference to think about and then worry over. She knew she was older, but then she snuck a look inside his wallet one night when he was in the bathroom. She pulled out his driver's license, and there was the evidence. He was fourteen years younger, it turned out, and that sort of stunned her. She was practically Henry's age when he was born. She couldn't stop thinking about that. Also, she couldn't stop trying to figure out exactly where she was at that age. Well, she was in her freshman year of high school is where she was, a nearly fully grown person, and he was just a squirmy little baby.

She tried to put that out of her mind as she headed up the stairs at Mrs. Vale's. The house was dark and hushed as Susan padded down the hall to her room, stopping outside Henry's door. This had become a routine of sorts. She put an ear to the door but could make out nothing. She softly knocked. If there was no response, she'd silently ease the door open, then poke her head in, not closing the door again until she could see the covers moving, which meant Henry was breathing.

She showered quickly, dried her hair with a towel, yanked the tags off the new bra and panties—racy black lace—and slipped into them. She was pleasantly surprised that basically they held everything in place. In the flattering light of Edie's guest bathroom, she felt she could pass for sexy. Although she tried hard not to look too closely at her neck, which was developing that odd sort of wrinkling seen in women of a certain age. Now for something to wear over the lingerie. She stood before the open closet for more than a few minutes. Some of her favorite jeans were just too tight, so they were not just unflattering to be seen in, but it was difficult to move or sit in them or, well, to breathe.

Again, she made a vow to start an exercise routine. Or buy Spanx. Or maybe she could just eat less. Like earlier this evening, at the staff meal, always a high-fat hazard. Did she really need that second helping of the macaroni and cheese Stacy had put out, especially when the first helping was so generous? Did she need that second sliver of the special dark chocolate torte that was on the dessert menu?

After a few minutes of digging and poking through her closet, with discarded items strewn haphazardly on the bed and floor, she settled on a pair of worn and frayed jeans that had always been slightly too big and then a rather loose-fitting short-sleeve black top and finally a well-seasoned brown suede jacket she'd had for years that always felt, when she put it on, like the warm embrace of an old friend. She spritzed on some of the perfume Griffin said made her smell like flowers. Some mascara and lip gloss and she was done.

Downstairs, she grabbed her keys and headed to the kitchen for a bottle of water, and there was Andrew, sitting in the dark at the kitchen table shoveling in spoonfuls from a bowl of Froot Loops.

"Oh!" said a startled Susan. "Hey."

"You coming or going?" Andrew asked.

"Um. Both, actually. I was at work. I came in to change. Now I'm on my way out."

An eyebrow arched. He regarded her coolly.

"What are you doing here?" she asked, because she didn't like what she figured he was thinking. Meanwhile, she dug into the box of Froot Loops for a handful. Like many chefs, Susan, a foodie at heart, also had an affinity for junky things. Her list included Froot Loops, Spam, and at the very top, Cheetos.

"Linda told me to leave, if you must know," said Andrew. "I didn't want to come here, but the house we've been renovating has no plumbing."

Now it was Susan's turn to regard him coolly.

"I didn't cheat," he said, a little too defensively, she thought.

"Well, you must have done something. I mean, didn't she just come back to you? I thought everything was good."

"So did I."

He finished his Froot Loops and took the bowl to the sink. "I thought everything was cool too. But then, you know I went to Chicago that weekend I was supposed to go up north with Henry?"

"Yeah. A client died, right?"

"Mrs. Bindle. She was ninety-four years old and completely gaga, but I've known her since forever. In fact, it was my father who brought her in as a client. She outlived her kids. Then, she's barely cold, and this niece and nephew are already fighting over who gets what because the estate was pretty large."

"That's sad."

"Yeah. Anyway, I got sort of drunk in the bar of the Drake that night. There was this . . . um . . . lady at some conference. I ended up in her room."

"So you did cheat. Why can't you men just keep it in your pants?"

"No, that's the thing. I *almost* did. I mean, she was in the bathroom and I'm sitting on the bed in my boxer shorts when it suddenly dawned on me that I love Linda and I don't want to jeopardize my marriage. So I ran out of there before anything happened."

"So what's the problem then?" She was getting impatient. Even with no traffic, it would take a good twenty minutes to get to Echo Park from Pasadena, and that's when Griffin's band was going to start its set.

Then she lost her train of thought, because Andrew pulled off his shirt. He turned around and pointed at his shoulder. There was a fresh, brightly colored tattoo. Susan leaned in for a closer look. It was a heart, and inside, in a tiny but delicate script, were the initials of his children, Henry first, then Serenity and Alexander.

"Nice. Did it hurt?"

"Yeah. Sort of. I was pretty well lubricated at that point, though."

"Right. So was I when I got mine."

"Let me see yours again?"

Susan lifted her pant leg to show him the tiny place setting at her ankle, then wriggled out of her jacket and lowered her top to show him the jaunty chef's hat on her shoulder. Andrew smiled at that. Suddenly there was the flick of a switch, they were bathed in light from overhead, and she and Andrew nearly jumped out of their skin, like teenagers again, it felt like to Susan, caught in the act. She turned to see Henry standing at the entrance to the kitchen. He wore a rumpled T-shirt and sweats. He had that heavy-lidded look, where she could never quite tell whether he was sleepy or just plain bored. He eyeballed them both for a long beat. He loped over to the refrigerator, pulled out a carton of orange juice, and took a few almost comically noisy gulps.

Then Henry said, "So nobody will scream like a maniac at me if I decide to get a tat?"

"Well," Andrew said, "actually I'm fairly certain in the state of California you need parental consent, right, Susan?"

"I . . . hmmmm. I'm not sure, actually."

Henry gave them each another long look, then headed back out of the kitchen, of course neglecting to switch off the light he had turned on. Susan turned back to Andrew while pulling her top back into place to cover her shoulder back up.

"Do you wonder," she asked, "if we will ever figure out what he's thinking?"

"Most likely we won't," Andrew answered.

"Well, anyway, so you got inked. It's kind of sweet. A little nuts, maybe. I mean, for a trusts and estates lawyer."

"That's exactly what Linda said when I finally let her see it. At first I wasn't sure how she was going to react, so I kept it hidden for a few days. But that only made her more suspicious because I wouldn't take my clothes off in front of her, so I finally had to get naked to prove I didn't have an STD. Now she thinks I'm going through some sort of life crisis. That's why I did something so out of character, and now I should take some time to figure out what I want to do with my future."

"Well, are you in crisis?"

"I don't know. Honestly, after I left that hotel room, I sort of just wandered around. Maybe this was some kind of act of rebellion. I'm not sure. I am almost the same age as my father was when he had his breakdown and left my mom, though."

He sank back into his seat across from her. It struck her that they sat in this very same room as they decided to end their own marriage, but that felt like a lifetime ago. Then a thought popped into her head, where she wondered how old Griffin was when she was leaving Andrew. Had he hit puberty yet?

"We're quite the pair, aren't we?" Susan finally said.

"What do you mean by that?"

"I don't know. Here I am off to meet up with a pothead fourteen years younger than me and you're in the middle of screwing up another marriage. I'm just saying . . ." Susan stood. "I have to go. Try not to fuck things up too badly."

"Yeah. You too!"

She smiled. And to her surprise, he smiled back.

***

It was one of those underground clubs, Susan figured, because there was no sign out front. So she drove up and down the dark, somewhat menacing streets of this unfamiliar neighborhood until she saw people congregating, huddled around the glowing orange ends of cigarettes or, more likely, joints. She parked as close as she could, then hurried up the street, one hand in her purse, feeling for the little canister of pepper spray she knew she had somewhere, just in case.

Inside, the first thing that hit her was the noise. The band—four guys just like Griffin, skinny and long-limbed, with shaggy hair and tattoos that made Andrew's look like an Eagle Scout's—was in the middle of the song that had recently gotten them a deal with a small label, something about being in love but with a tinge of melancholy that seemed Beach Boys–like to Susan, until the scruffy lead singer went up into his falsetto and was somewhat shaky, although there was also something endearing about that, and all the girls around her seemed to swoon in what felt almost like a wave tilting the room from one side to the other, so she started to feel a little dizzy. The audience was, indeed, mostly female. Once Susan realized that, the next thing to hit her was she was clearly older than all of them or, worse, she could have been the mother of some. Not one looked to be over twenty-one or twenty-two; in fact, they were about the age that Susan was before her life took a detour after meeting Andrew. Now she wondered how different things might have turned out had they never met. And for the next few minutes, mashed in below the stage with all these kids, singing along with them at the top of her lungs, trading what she was sure were meaningful glances with Griffin as he banged away at his drums, it was as if she was that young again too, and if she tried really hard, she could pretend that she too didn't have a care in the world.

XVI.

Edith Vale's mother, Lois Lee, was one of the first customers lined up at the door when the beauty parlor opened on Fair Oaks Avenue in 1955. The proprietor was a French man known all through Pasadena and San Marino as Monsieur Pierre, and at the time, little seemed as delightfully exotic. Edie could still remember the day her mother came home looking like a Southern California version of an Italian movie queen. Pierre had dyed her hair jet-black and given her a poodle cut. When she walked in the front door, Edie's father nearly had a heart attack and demanded that she get rid of it. Mrs. Lee ignored him and went on with her business, steadfastly sticking with a head full of tight, rigid black curls until the day she died.

Pierre fast became the local hairdresser of choice, and the salon grew into a baroquely ornate homage to the ladies of the city, all red silk and Louis IV knock-off furniture, a cozy, comforting oasis where tea was served with little sandwiches cut into triangles or madeleines and cocktails were offered during afternoon appointments, including a killer Sazerac that monsieur perfected during a stint in New Orleans. He was a gentleman, fastidious in his appearance, and he had the knack for truly knowing his customers, when to fuss over this one or send a compliment that one's way. Soon he expanded the services offered so a lady could have her nails done or a facial too. Business really took off with the arrival of the bouffant, a style few were brave enough to attempt on their own, and that was when Edie, Tish, Evelyn, and Oatsie O'Shea became customers, all of them setting Saturday morning appointments at the same time, and loyal customers they still were all these years later—through turbulent times of war and social unrest, through recessions and gas lines, through impeachments and then the boom eras, with all their gaudy excess—the bouffants survived.

The ladies would descend on the shop en masse, their hair-dos more than a little disheveled and sometimes, you might even say, lopsided, or at least slightly off-center, after six days and six nights of wear and tear, showing up even though Pierre had died in the late 1980s of that new disease called AIDS, they later learned. Indeed, they had all watched Pierre grow more and more emaciated without understanding why, and then he passed and they learned he had a whole other life behind the suave and sophisticated facade he presented to them week after week, year after year. So the shop's future seemed in jeopardy. In fact, one Saturday soon after Pierre's death, the ladies tried out a new place on the other side of town, but it was all loud music, hard, shiny surfaces, and young girls snapping gum, and not one of them really knew how to blow out, tease, back-comb, and shellac their hair into place, so they hightailed it back to Pierre's and put their hair into the hands of the boys who would inherit the shop, Marco, a fiery Cuban, and Bruce, who had worked at the studios in Hollywood for years and gos-siped like an old hen. Which was where they were this Saturday morning, at the beauty parlor.

But Edith Vale, who had her hair washed, set, blown out, back-combed, and then shellacked for as long as anybody could remember, had experienced a rare change of heart when she had returned from that weekend up north all those weeks back. Not about the color of her hair, of course. She had no intention of letting herself go grey. Oh, sure, Tish stopped dying her hair years earlier and looked elegant and refined. No, Edith Vale was firmly committed to remaining a blond. But because of the hair emergency, when she had unexpectedly shown up at the beauty parlor on a *Tuesday*—it was closed on Mondays, mind you—something clicked in her brain, like a switch somebody had flicked: she was sick to death of spending all this time on her hair, exhausted from all the primping and spraying and constant care and attention it seemed to need. So she had it cut to shoulder length, colored, and then pulled back and secured with a pretty bow.

Later, at the Alta Arroyo Women's Club monthly meeting, Edie arrived, somewhat tentative, with her new, more casual and easy look, no more stiff dome hovering overhead like a lampshade, as Henry used to always say. She felt somehow lighter, but she worried what the others might think, not that they would actually say anything too mean, she figured.

But Oatsie exclaimed, "I love it!"

Evelyn Brookby practically shrieked, "You look seventeen again!"

And Tish said, "The best part, you'll see, is you can roll over onto your side when you sleep."

So this Saturday Edie was getting just a color and cut, Tish a cut as well, while Evelyn Brookby and Oatsie O'Shea were having their bouffants redone.

"According to Cis," Oatsie was saying as all four were lined up at the sinks, robes around their Saturday morning clothes, heads back, getting shampooed, "the fact that we still call it a beauty parlor is an indication of our old age and decrepitude."

"Well, what are we supposed to call it?" said a suddenly fretful looking Evelyn Brookby.

"Good Lord, I don't know," said Oatsie. "I long ago stopped trying to understand Cis. It's like she speaks a whole different language."

"Speaking of Cis," said Edie, "are you still refusing to acknowledge that baby?"

"I don't have a problem with the baby," said Oatsie. "But marriage? Two women? Why do they have to call it marriage?"

"Because if you call it something different," said Tish, "maybe that's what it remains. And they want equal. Not separate but equal."

"I talked to Father Flannigan about it. He says if I sanction the union, if I give my blessing to the baby, well, then soon people will marry their pets and we're all heading to hell in a handbasket."

"Nice," Tish said. "And where was he when all those priests were molesting all those children?"

"By the way," said Edith, because this thought had been on her mind, "just who is the father of Cis and her . . . er . . . wife's . . . uh . . . Who fathered this child?"

"Well, apparently," Oatsie said, "a sperm bank. They sat and leafed through a book, as I understand it, and picked the fellow they liked. Now they tell me it was all about his education level and artistic streak and what have you, but if you ask me, it's as if they were buying a sweater out of a catalogue."

All the ladies clucked and tsked over that until Oatsie, seemingly eager to change the subject, said, "Have you spoken to Frank, Edie, since you slept with him?"

Evelyn's head popped up out of the sink, sending soap bubbles flying. "She what?"

Tish just stared at Edie.

"Oh, for goodness' sake, Odette. I told you that in the strictest confidence."

Oatsie gave Edith a tight smile. Edie turned to the others. "It was a one-time deal. There was alcohol involved. It won't happen again, I assure you."

"Well," said Tish, "at least one of us is seeing some action." This was said with a wink and more than a hint of sarcasm.

"You have a husband. What are you complaining about?" asked Evelyn, who, since joining the ranks of the widowed, had, like Edie, seemed to give up on men altogether. There simply was too much competition for the few available prospects who were ambulatory, financially stable, and not looking for thirty-year-olds, and Evelyn found she just couldn't even work up the energy to try to compete.

"Oh, please," said Tish. "Sure, I have a husband, but you know Bertie has two single-malt scotches every night and falls asleep in his chair after shouting expletives at the evening news, which as you can imagine doesn't do me a whole lot of good."

Evelyn nodded, turned back to Edie. "Did you remember where all the parts go?" she asked and then she started to blush.

"Yes, you didn't give any details," said Oatsie. "Did he smell? Had he brushed his teeth?"

The truth was Edie hadn't yet begun to sort out all the feelings that had been aroused over what happened, some that had lain dormant for what seemed like centuries, growing all dank and musty, like the objects she'd sometimes come across in cartons stored in the attic; occasionally she'd find herself up there, and she'd pry open one of these boxes, and then gasp in delight at the sight of some long-forgotten photograph of some person she could barely remember or a keepsake that once was fraught with meaning. She had similar feelings when she thought about what happened in Sonoma, a sort of awe that it could possibly have happened at all and she didn't imagine the whole thing, that she had the nerve to go through with it—actually letting him see her naked, for instance, even though she had insisted he not dare go near any light switch lest he found her revolting, which, in truth, was her biggest fear—mixed with a sense of delight that was as fleeting as a puff of air, with some consternation and annoyance thrown in. In the end, like most things vexing or unpleasant, she tried to just put the whole thing out of her mind. But the girls pressed on in their quest for particulars.

"How long did it last?" Evelyn whispered, and Edie decided it was none of their business, though it lasted long enough. (She assumed Frank took Viagra or some such thing to help him along.)

Anyway, the questions kept coming, but Edie could take no more, and she sat up, grabbed a handful of suds from the sink behind her, and threw them right into Evelyn's face. Evelyn scooped up some facial mud from the open jar on the counter and launched it back toward Edie, but she managed to duck, and it hit the mirror behind her. Soon suds and mud were flying in every direction, until Bruce, who, since a minor stroke a while back, had to move around with the aid of a walker, came toddling toward them with a stern look on his face, and each lady went back to her best behavior.

***

But Edie had spoken to Frank since that night. Many times, in fact. She just had kept this to herself. People were far too nosy, if you asked Edie, always prying and asking irritating questions. Why was it, she often thought, that people these days felt the need to tell everybody—perfect strangers, even—their business. It was just tacky and uncalled for, really. Plus, she rather enjoyed having and keeping a secret, something she hadn't done in ages. She had forgotten how much of a charge one could get from withholding information, how it felt almost tantalizingly mischievous.

The phone calls began shortly after she had returned from up north. She had just run through her bedtime routine—the dogs were let out one final time, Edie walking with them through the backyard, gently encouraging them to "come now and pee-pee for Mummy." After checking the lock on the front door, she'd invariably have to undo some of the damage Blanca had done during the day, scooting a picture frame in the living room, say, a few inches to the left or that Ming-style vase on the mantel, the gorgeous one from Gump's, just a hair to the right. She had tried to stop letting these little things make her crazy, but then she'd lie in bed grinding her teeth together; she'd sleep better if she knew everything was in its proper place. She had poked her head into Evangeline's room, but she wasn't in there that night. Edie found her downstairs, safely ensconced with Blanca, both of them eating Dove Bars in front of some TV drama where all the characters were chattering in Spanish, Evangeline nodding right along as if she suddenly understood a language that was foreign to her.

Back upstairs, she had paused momentarily at Henry's door, moving on, reassured, when she heard him tapping away at his laptop. She had methodically removed her makeup. She hung up her clothes. She wriggled into a nightgown, a favorite cotton one, soft and cozy from many washings. Finally, she climbed into bed with her Parliaments, a stack of the latest magazines, and some knitting, slipping under the cover of her freshly ironed sheets, arranging her pillows just so. The dogs turned little circles, then settled in at her feet, and the truth was she was perfectly content. Oh, Edie knew that in so many ways—in every way really—she was a terribly lucky woman, had won some sort of cosmic lottery. She'd always had a roof over her head. This very roof. There was always food in her cupboards and money in her pocketbook. Yes, there were some lean years after the divorce, even though her mother would step in and soften the blow financially, but then she married Mr. Vale, who was, to put it bluntly, loaded. When he died, he left her well set. She knew there were women all over the world who struggled every day, struggled for the simplest things, and for her good fortune she said a silent prayer of thanks, as she did every night.

So at first when the phone rang at such a late hour—it was just past eleven—there was a combination of mild panic (Who's dead now?) and annoyance (Who's bugging me?). Then she heard Frank's voice and she nearly slammed the phone down.

But an "Aw, don't hang up, Edith Lee" kept her on the line.

"What is it that you want?" she had said tartly.

"I just wanted to say it was really great seeing you. In fact, in a strange way I was sort of sad when you left."

"Oh, poor you," Edie said, and then added, "If you're so lonely, why don't you call your friend the cheese maker in Petaluma?"

"That's nothing serious. Plus, she's way too young for me anyway."

"Is that supposed to make me feel better?"

"Yes."

She thought about hanging up.

But Frank continued. "I mean, it's like you and me can relate to each other, on a deeper level, you know?"

She had to admit, at least to herself for now, that she did. They had a shared history that went back nearly fifty years. They had a son together. There were now grandchildren.

Although in the early years after the divorce and during her subsequent marriage to Mr. Vale, Edie had tended to view her first marriage as all bad. All she could recall, it seemed, were the things she had grown to loathe about Frank, many of them small and petty but irritating just the same. Like the way his ears stuck out, at first an endearing trait, but as time passed somewhat annoying. Or how he'd fail to notice or tweeze the stray hairs in his nose. Or the way he'd guzzle a beer after a game of tennis and then belch loudly more than once, with not even a "beg pardon" or an "excuse me." Or how when he'd urinate, he'd splash the toilet seat or the floor. Or he'd pass gas while they were driving somewhere, and he and Andrew, a child at the time, just laughed and laughed, while Edie thought it was disgusting.

Not that there weren't annoying things about Mr. Vale as well. Like how he often pretended he didn't hear her when she knew perfectly well he was just tuning her out. Or he'd cup a hand over an ear and shout "Hah?" like an old coot. How annoying was that? Or how he'd sometimes make that horrid choking sound while coughing up phlegm in the morning, and on a couple of occasions, she found herself secretly wishing he'd just choke to death already. Or how slowly he ate his food, methodically cutting each bite and then chewing each little piece to smithereens, and if he didn't, she'd hear about the digestion problems.

Anyway, the more years that passed, the more she remembered there were good times with Frank. In fact, shortly after that weekend, she had come across some old photographs. Well, actually, she had dug them out of the back of her closet, where there was a whole stack of albums of the early years of her first marriage marked by subject and year. She had plopped herself down on the closet floor and started to leaf through them. One album in particular fascinated her because it was like she could chart the course of their relationship. Somewhere they had gotten the idea to take a picture of themselves in an amusing pose to use as an annual holiday card, so there they were on one page, 1963, in midair—genuine smiles in place, eyes on each other in an almost adoring way, it seemed—as they leapt, fully clothed, into the sparkling blue water of the pool in the backyard, Frank in a narrow-lapel seersucker suit, Edie in a crisp hot pink A-line shift and pearls. She flipped a few pages. Nineteen-sixty-five found them in shagadelic hippie garb, a prank, of course, the outfits picked up at the costume store downtown. The picture had them in the rose garden out back, Edie plucking petals from a stem held by Frank, a halo of flower petals in her hair. They didn't look quite so happy in this picture, though not so unhappy either, Edie thought, as she tapped a fingernail against it. A few pages later, it was the 1970s, just before they divorced. They sat in club chairs in the library, a roaring fire between them but obviously no actual warmth. Frank, with mutton chop sideburns, a rather loud blazer, and a scotch rocks in hand, sat rigidly, perched on the edge of the chair, Edie noticed now, as if he was planning on bolting any second. Edith, her blond helmet firmly in place, was wearing a Bill Blass pantsuit in a rather large and unfortunate plaid, and her smile was so tightly clenched, it seemed as if her jaw might shatter.

"We look like statues," Edie told Frank when he called at precisely the same time the following night.

"That was a great old camera, though," Frank said, "a Zeiss Ikon."

"Yes," Edie said. "I remember how you'd mount it on the tripod and fiddle with it forever until you were sure it would take just the right picture."

"Remember where we picked it up?"

"I do," said Edie.

They had gone abroad early in their marriage, because Frank had business, a client who needed an estate plan and lived in Switzerland. So they had flown to Geneva, where they spent a few days at the Beau-Rivage. While Frank took care of the legal work he needed to take care of, Edie toured the galleries, gardens, and museums. She sent boxes of chocolates back to Oatsie, Evelyn, and Tish, and then she and Frank took a train to Zermatt for a few days of skiing and après-ski—lots of mulled wine fireside, followed by pots of rich fondue and then cozying up under a thick down comforter in the rented chalet—in the shadows of the Matterhorn, an idyllic vacation, she realized now, of crisp air and electric blue skies against jagged snow-capped peaks, all documented fully by the little Zeiss they purchased in town, the camera fitted neatly in a brown leather case lined with soft red felt.

When they got back to Pasadena, Frank turned into something of a shutterbug. He claimed a portion of the basement and set up a darkroom. Sometimes Edie would join him. She could still conjure up that acrid chemical smell that tickled her nose as she stood next to him to watch as a blank sheet of photo paper would move from one solution to the next and a picture would slowly take shape in the eerie red glow of the safety bulb overhead, first just shadows and outlines, then the fully formed photograph. She never really encouraged this hobby, and for a time, she regretted that, thinking maybe he needed something more creative than redlining contracts, drawing up wills, and mediating nasty disputes between greedy heirs.

"Where is the Zeiss now?" Frank wondered on that same call.

"I thought you must have taken it," Edie said.

"No, I don't have it."

Which prompted Edie to head down into the basement the following day. When Frank bailed on the marriage, there were things he left behind, and for a while, they stayed where they were, until Edie married Mr. Vale and she decided it was best to expunge all traces of her first husband, just as all traces of Bunny Vale had been erased. So she had rummaged through closets and desk drawers. She had grabbed pictures and books they had bought together and all the little knickknacks picked up on travels. She packed them up and moved the boxes down to a little-used crawl space next to the furnace in the basement. The boxes were still there, covered in layers of dust so thick it made her sneeze. When she ripped the tape off one and dug into it she found, among other long-forgotten objects, the Zeiss, still in its brown leather case, only the leather now had spiderwebs of fine little cracks and the red felt lining smelled dank and musty.

When Frank called next, at the same hour, when she was cozy in bed, he suggested she give the camera to Henry, and when she did, Henry looked it over and said, "You know, there's film in it, Mrs. Vale."

This sent Edie into town. Somewhere along the line, how-ever, all those little one-hour photo kiosks she remembered had vanished into thin air, more victims of the digital age, she fig-ured. Finally, she found an old-time camera shop off Colorado, where the stooped ancient man behind the counter first mar-veled at what a gem the Zeiss was, then promised he'd do the best he could. The pictures that came back were something of a shock to Edie. There were a few snaps of the King Charles spaniels she had at the time, chasing their tails in one, posed regally next to a Christmas tree in another. There was a photo of Edie in her gardening clothes, smoking and deadheading roses. Most of the pictures, though, were of the little-boy ver-sion of Andrew. Indeed, at first she thought it was Henry. She had forgotten how much they looked alike. But what struck Edie most as she sat in the Mercedes gazing at the images was how sad and lonely and miserable her son looked. These must have been taken just before Frank left. Edie, way back then, had convinced herself that the separation and subsequent divorce would have no effect on Andrew, that in fact he might be better off not having to live with two people who clearly couldn't stand the sight of each other. Here was evidence that she was mistaken. So right there in the parking lot, she pulled her cell phone from her pocketbook, put on her reading glasses, and punched the speed dial for Andrew's office.

"I'm sorry for everything," she blurted out when Andrew finally picked up.

"What, Mother?" he said.

"I mean," Edie said, "did we damage you?"

"Okay, what are you talking about?"

"When your father and I divorced. Was it awful? Did you hate us?"

"Well, frankly, Mother . . ."

Suddenly, Edie didn't want to know the answer. In fact, she didn't know what had gotten into her. She was sorry she brought the whole thing up. "You know what?" she said, interrupting. "We'll chat about this later. Toodles, darling."

She ended the call and headed home.

Still, she looked forward to telling Frank about the pictures. Maybe he'd want one of Freddie and Min, the first incarnation of the spaniels, posed by the Christmas tree. The truth was that somehow, without her realizing it, she looked forward to telling Frank things on these nightly calls, that it was, in fact, the highlight of her day. She'd hang up, and the sound of his voice, still very present, helped lull her to sleep. That night, Henry was off somewhere, and Susan was at work, so it was just Edie and Evangeline at the table. Not even one of her favorite dinners, an extremely tame version of enchiladas Blanca had been fixing for years, could take her mind off just getting to the right time so she could get into bed.

But when she finally was in bed, in a new nightgown, mind you, something frilly she'd found at Nordstrom, the hour came and then went. For the first time since the calls began, there was just a silence that seemed loud enough to hurt her ears. At first Edie simply stared at the phone. She wondered whether or not it was actually working. She picked it up. The flat hum of the dial tone felt like a stern rebuke. Still, just to be sure, she dialed her home number from her cell phone. The home phone rang. It was like a second rebuke. Then she got mad. She marched downstairs and poured a nightcap. Back in her room, she lit a Parliament and sucked on it furiously, in between scolding herself for acting like an idiot schoolgirl at an age when she should certainly know better with the very person she thought was out of her life for good. She reached for the phone and dialed Frank's number. When his voice mail picked up, she left a very nasty message, in no uncertain terms telling him never to bother her again. She stubbed out the cigarette, finished the nightcap, and downed a couple of Ambien. She shut off the lights and waited for the good, long sleep she knew was about to come.

XVII.

The first time Henry gave Luz a swimming lesson, it was in the backyard at Mrs. Vale's. It was a blazing hot day in late August under a glaringly harsh sun, the air so dry it parched his lips and made his eyes burn. They probably should have called the whole thing off, Henry figured, because everybody was around, wanting to cool off in the pool, and that sort of spoiled the atmosphere he had hoped to create. The scenario he had concocted in his mind and thought about ninety percent of his waking hours went something like this: Luz would emerge from the house in a slinky robe, which he'd have to coax her out of. When she did let the robe drop to the ground, she'd reveal the kind of thong he'd seen on the covers of the *Sports Illustrated* Swimsuit Issue, or even better, the Pirelli Calendar. Of course, she'd insist that Henry practically carry her into the water. They'd start in the shallow end, and he'd demonstrate how to float on her belly, but naturally he'd have to keep a hand just beneath her to prevent sinking. Of course, it would be a total accident if somehow his hand brushed up against her breasts. That would somehow lead to a kiss, and they wouldn't be able to keep their hands off each other.

They'd wind up back in Henry's room. So of course that morning he surveyed his room in order to remove anything that might prove embarrassing. Suddenly, there were potential embarrassments everywhere. Like the dopey trophy he won in the third grade spelling bee, the fake gold leaf all flaked off to reveal the plastic underneath, or the fraying and faded 4-H club ribbons from summer camp because he was good at shoveling up horse dung. There were framed pictures where suddenly he looked even dorkier than usual, he thought. There was a stack of comic books he hadn't looked at in years. He removed these and other items from the shelves and hid them in the closet.

Then it was time to pick something to wear. In the scenario he concocted in his mind, he looked different too. During chemo, Henry had learned to do everything possible to avoid seeing himself without clothes because, in early stages especially, he had lost so much weight that bones protruded at his hips and he could count his ribs. He felt like a freakish walking skeleton. Though much of the weight had come back, he still took a long time picking just the right trunks.

Of course, even with all the planning, the reality of the day turned out to be nothing like the fantasy. First of all, it wasn't supposed to be this hot, and it wasn't, in his mind, an irritating dry heat but one of those rare sultry humid days. In the real version of events, Luz emerged from the house fully dressed, protesting that she wasn't sure this was a good idea after all. Even worse, she had her long black hair up in a bun, like a librarian. Also, she was wearing her glasses, as the idea of getting her contacts wet was a worry. Plus, she was getting a zit and it was in a really prominent place on her face, making it impossible not to stare at. Finally, Henry convinced Luz to put on a swimsuit. But it turned out to be a one-piece deal that barely revealed a thing.

Then there was the running commentary from his grandmother perched on a lounge chair under an umbrella in her big straw hat and the giant sunglasses that made her look like a bug. "Just jump in, dear. That's the ticket," Mrs. Vale kept urging, and then a few minutes later, clearly getting impatient, teeth a bit too clenched, "It's just water, dear. It doesn't bite."

Henry half expected Mrs. Vale to pluck Luz up and toss her in as she had once done to him. His mother, asleep on another lounge chair, was roused and started throwing in her two cents. Meanwhile, Linda and the twins were splashing around the shallow end and offering Luz their floaties, and every time he looked up at the house, Blanca was framed in a window, wringing her hands, her face a mask of worry that Luz would instantly drown. By the time his mother and grandmother wound up in the pool determined to help, Henry had pretty much given up.

Except that Luz did learn some of the basics, and at least she began to overcome her fear of the water. A few days later when she had clocked out of her job with Evangeline, they met in the pool again. This time they were alone, and Henry taught her to dog-paddle from one end to the other. Luz considered that such an accomplishment she threw her arms around him for a hug. Henry seized the moment and tried to plant one on her. Of course he missed. Their foreheads knocked together with an audible thump.

Luz drew back, apparently alarmed.

"I'm sorry, I'm sorry," Henry blurted out, mortified, and also annoyed that every time he tried to put the moves on, something went terribly wrong, as if the fates were against him in this instance too.

But Luz was smiling when she said, "You don't have to apologize."

"Oh. Okay. I don't? Really?"

"It's not like I don't want you to," she added.

They were facing each other, not in the shallow end, but not in the deep, treading water somewhere in the middle as he had demonstrated so they wouldn't sink.

"So what's the problem?"

"I don't know," Luz said. "Maybe that God will punish me?"

This gave Henry pause. "God would punish you for kissing?"

"Well, not for kissing. I could see getting a pass on that."

"Okay. For what then?"

"Well, for what might come after."

"Something might come after? Really? Seriously?"

"Oh, Henry, there are plenty of ways to sin. You know that."

He did. He also knew her grandmother was staunch and devout in her beliefs. Blanca regularly attended Mass. The church was central to her life, it always seemed to Henry. She carried a rosary and a prayer book in her purse. A picture of the pope was the sole decoration in her little white square of a room off the kitchen. Maybe it skipped a generation, though, because from what he could tell, Luz's mother never seemed all that into religion. But Luz always had that little gold cross around her neck, and often she went with Blanca to church.

"What ways did you have in mind? To sin?" he finally asked.

This made Luz blush.

They came close to kissing again, but Blanca suddenly emerged from the kitchen and noisily started whacking her broom against the side of the house, pretending she hadn't noticed them and then telling Luz it was time to get home. So Henry didn't see her again until a few days later. His phone rang, and when he saw Luz's name on the caller ID, he could swear he felt a flutter in his heart. She said she had a favor to ask, that she was curious to try dipping her toes in the ocean, something Henry was shocked to learn she had never done, even though she grew up barely ten miles from the Pacific. She had walked on the sand, but that was it. Henry hadn't surfed in ages—doctors were still against the idea, but he was tired of listening to them—so they pulled one of his dad's old boards, a dinged-up Becker Malibu Super Sport, out of Edie's garage, hosed it down, strapped it to the roof of the Catalina wagon, left a note for Mrs. Vale, and headed west.

Henry, still somewhat terrified of saying something lame, texted back and forth with Zach Julian, until Luz said, "Is this a bromance? You two are just buddies, right?"

Henry grinned and set down the phone. "Yes. We're buds."

"You're going to miss him, I bet."

"How do you mean?"

"You start your new school next week, no?"

"Yeah."

"Well, he won't be there, right?"

"Right. They let him back in to our old school. The only person I know at Pasadena Prep is Edgar Brookby."

"Who's that?"

"The grandson of one of Mrs. Vale's friends. We've known each other forever. He's a total dweeb. Plus, he's a real downer. All doom and gloom twenty-four seven. So I will avoid him at all costs."

Luz nodded.

They drove up to the cottage. Nobody was home when they entered the house, so they headed down to the sand.

They were nearly at the water when Luz said, "Promise you won't let me drown?"

"We'll just get our feet wet today. But, if you want, I guess you could, um, you know, take my hand."

He tentatively extended his toward her, hoping she wouldn't notice that it was trembling slightly. She gripped it hard as a wave swept in around their ankles. The foamy surf at the height of this summer heat still felt bracing and icy; Luz screamed and darted back to the sand.

"Come on," Henry said, "give it a second. When you get used to it, the water feels good."

Again, she took his hand, and when another wave crashed around them, a slightly bigger one this time, with water surging up over their knees, she screamed but didn't try to bolt.

"There's one thing you need to remember," Henry said, as water now moved up higher, around their waists.

"What?"

"It's about riptides. Remember, we talked about them?"

"Yeah," Luz said. "What do I need to know?"

"If you're out and the tide's high, and the water's over your head, you may find the current pulling you further out to sea."

"Oh, I don't like the sound of that."

"Just remember one thing," Henry said. "Do not panic. Swim parallel to the shore. What will happen is you'll eventually get past the rip and can work your way out of it. You got that?"

"I'll try to keep it in mind."

She tried to sound serious, but she was smiling as she said that. It made Henry all nervous and queasy again. He dunked his head under the water and hoped she couldn't tell. When he came up he shook like a dog to get the water out of his hair.

Luz laughed as she got sprayed and licked her lips. "Oh! Salty!"

Suddenly the waves were getting bigger. Henry led Luz back to dry land. They sat on a towel and scrunched their toes through sand warmed under a strong midday sun. They watched boats and surfers off in the distance. Somewhere a radio was playing top-forty pop, one of those girls with thin voices singing about a boy.

"So," said Luz, breaking a somewhat awkward stretch of silence, "I've been wondering about something."

"Yeah? What's that?"

"My grandma says that when they cut your head open, there was a tumor the size of a grapefruit. That's just her exaggerating, right?"

"Yep," said Henry, "it was the size of a walnut, if you really want to know. Does that gross you out?"

"Not particularly," said Luz, and Henry remembered she was always into scientific things. "Was it scary?" she asked. "The operation, I mean."

"Nah. I mean, everybody gets all serious, but they're super super nice to you, like they're afraid you'll go all mental or some such thing, and then they wheel you into the operating room, but before that, they give you some good drugs so you're feeling no pain. Then, you get into the OR, and the anesthesia lady says, 'Start counting back from one hundred,' but you only get to, say, ninety-seven, and then it's all blank until you wake up, and you're all, 'Dude, did you do anything?' And they go, 'It's over.' And honestly, I didn't really believe them until I reached up to touch my head and all I could feel was this big mess of gauze. Oh, and my head felt sort of numb too. You know, like when your arm falls asleep?"

"Were you afraid?"

"Of what?"

"I don't know. Dying? Did you pray? Because I think if it was me, I'd be on my knees. I'd be praying."

"I didn't really. No. Not that I have anything against it. My grandmother's been dragging me to church since I was a kid, and she was always nagging at me to say my prayers and all that, but I don't know. I don't think it took the way it was supposed to. I guess it did with you, though."

Luz was quiet a moment. "There are things I love about the church," she said. "Especially the music and the ritual aspect of it all."

"But the big guy with the beard and the robes watching over us? You having trouble with that?"

"Why does it have to be a dude? Can't it be a girl up there?"

"You know what I mean."

"Yeah. Also, sometimes I get bogged down in the whole idea of religion versus science. I mean, like, say this guy gets run down by a car. Couldn't you argue that it was God's will? But they rush him to the hospital and the doctors fix him. Is that going against God's will? If I become a doctor like I want to, will I be going against God's will if I decide to treat patients? I talked to our priest once about it. He told me not to overthink this stuff. But I guess I can't help it. And all I do is get more conflicted. It was so much easier when I was little, when I was a candy striper, and that's all I wanted to be."

"Yeah, I remember your uniform," Henry said.

"I loved it. Red and white stripes. All starchy and crisp, my grandma used to make it. I loved those afternoons at the hospital, even though my sisters and my mom were all like, 'How can you work and not get paid?' Nobody understood that in my family. But I was happy just pushing my little cart with all the magazines and the books. And just my being there seemed to brighten up a patient's day."

"Is that when you realized you wanted to be a doctor?"

"Actually there was this nurse. She took me under her wing. She was one of the first people who told me I could be whatever I wanted, even though at first I didn't believe her."

"She was right. You can."

Luz smiled. She took a closer look at him.

"What?" he said, because the scrutiny was suddenly making him uneasy.

"Can I see the scar?" Luz asked.

Henry bent his head and pointed to the spot. Luz leaned in to inspect it. She ran a finger along the line where the surgeon made the cut. A shiver went up and down his spine. Then they were face-to-face. Henry tried to kiss her, but Luz suddenly turned away.

"No," she said.

"I'm sorry. I get it. I'm like a freak. Damaged goods."

"Oh, Henry. No. That's stupid."

"What is it then?"

"C'mon. You don't know?"

"No."

"You're a rich white kid, and I'm not. Isn't that a good enough reason for you? Don't you think we'd just be asking for a whole mess of heartache?"

"I can't help how I feel," Henry said. "Can you?"

Luz turned back to look right at him, seemed to be studying his face. He couldn't tell what she was thinking. Then she pulled him in for a proper kiss.

***

Later, Luz asked Henry, "Didn't you want to go?" She was pointing at a group of surfers heading into the sea.

"Well, kind of," Henry said. "It's been a while. The doctors are still against it, I think, but I wouldn't mind."

"So why don't you?"

"Honestly, I'm not so hot to begin with. Plus, now I'm rusty too. I don't want to look like a kook."

"A kook?"

"In surf-speak, a lame ass. It's actually derived from a Hawaiian word for shit, kook is."

"Ah. Okay. What if I promise not to laugh?"

Henry sprinted to the storage room on the lower level of Mrs. Vale's house, where wet suits and other beach paraphernalia were stored. He slipped into a wet suit and grabbed the board from the roof of the Catalina. Back at the beach, he splashed noisily into the surf. He paddled out, past where smaller waves were breaking, to a calmer section of sea where he joined other surfers in the lineup waiting to catch something bigger. In the lull between sets, he floated on his back, looking up at a vast and cloudless sky. Then, there must have been a wind shift somewhere in the distance, because he could sense waves start to pick up in mass and speed, passing beneath his board in their inexorable hurtling toward shore. It dawned on him that the surf had been doing this for an eternity and would do it for an eternity to come. He turned and saw a wave approaching he thought he could tackle. He found all the moves seemed to be at his disposal, as if stored in some hidden crevice of his somewhat damaged brain. He started paddling in long, deep strokes, felt the wave propel the board, and managed to get to his feet, first in a wobbly crouch, throwing his arms out awkwardly for balance, but then standing taller and letting his arms drop to his side. He attempted and nearly ripped an aerial before wiping out closer to shore in the short but exhilarating ride. He noticed Luz on the beach, looking concerned. He gave her a thumbs-up and paddled out for more, until he ate foam one too many times and his muscles started to ache.

In the house, they dug up provisions. Luz grilled cheeseburgers out on the deck while Henry stood under the shower and let steaming hot water run all over his tired limbs. As he dried himself off, the smell of grilling meat mingled with mesquite from hardwood chips on the grill, and suddenly he was starving. He pulled aside the curtain and looked out the window. He breathed in the salty scent of the sea, and then Luz crossed into his line of sight, her black hair glistening in the sun, her smooth skin even browner against the blue of the Pacific, her almond-shaped eyes almost sparkling, it seemed, when she turned and held his gaze. No matter how hard he tried, he found it impossible to look away.

XVIII.

Of course, Susan should have known she wasn't the only one, that Griffin had other girlfriends. Maybe deep down, she did know, but she never asked because she didn't want to hear the answer, and of course, she wasn't supposed to really care, the way a steady significant other would. She did know the facts: He was an edgy surf dude. He played drums in a band. He was twenty-six and had some money in his pocket. If all of that wasn't catnip to women, she wasn't sure what would be anymore. And it's not that Griffin lied or even implied in any way that they were exclusive. Still, it was something of a shock to find there were at least two others he was juggling. She knew this because she stumbled upon two of the girls making out in Griffin's trailer up in Malibu when she had arrived early for a date. Apparently, these girls were dating him *and* each other. Or they were just hooking up, or whatever the kids were calling it these days. Plus, it looked like one of them might be pregnant. Anyway, the scene she interrupted was discombobulating enough that Susan rushed out of there, surprisingly flustered and flushed.

Later, at the restaurant, in the chaos of dinner service as she expedited, shouting out orders and checking plates before they went out, Griffin appeared and tried to make things right, but Susan had finally come to her senses and broke things off for good. She thought about letting Mike Finley know. She figured he'd be happy to hear it. But he had completed his FAA training and moved back to Boston. Which was fine, really, Susan figured. Oh sure, two men competing for her attention was fun for a while, but in reality, it was exhausting and she just wanted some space.

Actually she felt as if she had arrived at an okay place in her life. The restaurant was humming, even though it was far from a challenge. She knew she could do this executive chef gig in her sleep. Henry was settling in at his new school. She had managed to save some money. She was scanning online ads for a place to live because she knew it was time to get out of Edie's hair. She had even begun to make a mental wish list for her new apartment: two bedrooms so Henry could stay over. Hardwood floors. A fireplace would be cool. In fact, she was looking forward to the move. Which was when the news arrived that threw everything back into chaos, which she should have known would happen, because isn't that how it was when you became too complacent or had the temerity to start making future plans?

It started when Henry decided he wanted to drive up north to Palo Alto. It was parents' weekend, but nobody from Luz's family could make it, and he wanted to be there, he said. He brought up the subject on a Sunday morning, which in Edie's house meant a man did the cooking. Indeed, these Sunday breakfasts were a tradition going back seemingly forever, Susan understood. When Edith and Evangeline were children, they'd all gather at the big table in the dining room after church, their mother dressed in her Sunday finest, while their father donned an apron and rattled around the kitchen, producing what Edie often remembered were surprisingly delicious platters of buttermilk pancakes and sausages, or eggs softly scrambled over a double boiler with tons of cream and crisp bacon.

When Edie was married to Frank, the tradition continued, Frank experimenting with quiches and frittatas, and mimosas or Bloody Marys were added to the mix, depending on the mood. Evangeline and her husband would bring Gigi, and if the weather was nice, Gigi and Andrew would splash around in the pool after breakfast and well into the afternoon when, Andrew once told her, the adults would haul out the gin and tonics and drink until dinner. When Frank left Edie, the tradition was temporarily put on hold until Edith married Anderson Vale. He took over the duties and was still at it when Susan first joined the household. She recalled pancakes that were heavy as lead and sunny-side up eggs that were both rubbery and burnt to a crisp at the edges.

When Anderson died, Andrew stepped into the void, and while he was in the kitchen on that particular Sunday with Linda and the twins, Henry pulled Susan aside and said he had something important to discuss. He looked so serious and solemn that Susan almost laughed. Also, something else struck her. Somewhere in the last few months, he had one of those sudden growth spurts, so he was taller than she was for the first time and seemed almost, well, adult. Even his hands looked like a man's. She wasn't sure if she was imagining it, but his voice seemed to have dropped an octave as well. It was shocking, actually, to realize that a young man seemed to have replaced her little boy.

"I'll leave Friday afternoon," Henry was saying, "and I'll come back sometime Sunday night."

"I don't know," Susan said. "You haven't had your license that long even. It's a long drive all by yourself."

"You drove me all the way here from Boston by yourself. That was way longer."

"I wasn't alone. I had you."

"But I was barely speaking to you then, and you did all the driving."

That was true. So much had happened since they had left the East Coast that the road trip seemed like something Susan might have dreamed. Right now she decided to take the easy route and pass the buck.

"Go ask your father," she told Henry.

Later, Susan learned that Andrew wouldn't make the decision either. He hemmed and hawed and told Henry to ask his grandmother. This occurred when they were all around the table, gobbling down the huevos rancheros and chorizo Andrew had cooked up.

"You most certainly will not. You young people are far too distracted in your cars with your phones and all your gadgets and gizmos," Edith said before Henry had even finished the question, and that seemed to be that, as Henry rarely defied his grandmother.

But he did defy Mrs. Vale. He swiped the keys to the Catalina from Edie's pocketbook that Friday and headed north. Nobody had realized anything was amiss until late in the afternoon when Henry hadn't come home and Edie made a frantic call to Evelyn Brookby, who called her grandson Edgar, who told Edie that Henry never showed up at school. After numerous calls and texts and e-mails, Henry finally responded, basically begging them all to leave him the hell alone. In the end, the adults all caved but insisted he be home by dinner Sunday.

So Susan tried to put her worries out of her mind. She worked late into the night on Friday, but when the kitchen crew was heading out to carouse after closing, she headed back to Mrs. Vale's and fell into a deep slumber. In the morning, she found that Min, one of Edie's spaniels, had jumped into bed with her during the night and was nestled in the crook of her arm. She didn't move for almost an hour, not wanting to disturb the dog and the gentle little puffs of warm breath that caressed her neck. Then, when she did finally climb out of bed, there was a twinge in her back she hadn't felt before, and that, combined with that still new fact that Henry had outgrown her, made Susan feel like she was getting old, a subject that had come up the other morning with Andrew, when she had joined him in the kitchen while he was fixing Sunday breakfast.

"You feel old?" Andrew said. "How about this: I find myself forgetting the dumbest things. Like Linda's cell number. I've only called it about three thousand times, but the other day, I was using somebody else's phone, and because it wasn't on speed dial there was just this blank space in my head."

"How about the fact that the only music I seem to listen to is from twenty years ago?" Susan added.

"That must go over well with your new boyfriend. Was he even born yet?"

"Oh, that's all over with," Susan said, letting the dig slip but silently filing away the thought that Linda was, in fact, several years younger than Andrew.

"Or like these quote-unquote celebrities," Andrew went on, pointing at the cover of the flashy magazine Linda was leafing through at the table. "I mean, who are these people and what exactly are they famous for?"

"Oh, for heaven's sake," Linda had said, rolling her eyes in Susan's direction, "even the twins know who they are."

"Serenity and Alexander should not be reading that junk. Why, when I was their age . . ." But Andrew didn't finish that thought because Susan and Linda were staring at him as if he had indeed turned into an old man.

Susan put that image out of her head as she padded down-stairs for coffee. The instant she entered Edie's kitchen, she knew something was wrong; it was one of those moments, she figured, that would be with her until the end. "When I saw the expression on Edie's face . . ." She looked—Susan at first groped for just the right word, but later it came to her—stricken. That was it, a word that denoted something terrible had gone wrong, and the world would never be the same.

A frantic Luz was on the other end of the line, calling from the emergency room. The weekend was going great, appar-ently, and then Henry had a seizure. Deep down somewhere, Susan had known this moment would come, almost expected it, despite the good news they were given earlier. Chalk it up to mothers' intuition, she thought, that mothers just know these things, even though she also knew many would consider her a lousy mother. By the time Andrew, Susan, and Edie arrived at the hospital after a race north up Interstate 5, Henry had undergone another MRI, this one revealing a troublesome shadow. After a race back down the freeway, more tests, and consultations with doctors, they were told the mass that had been removed had returned, more aggressive this time, now coiling itself in and around other parts of Henry's brain, and all Susan could picture were the tentacles of an octopus with its prey in its clutches.

"Well, that kind of bites" was Henry's reaction, while everybody else tried to smile and put on brave faces and tell each other everything was going to be fine.

Henry began an intense round of radiation. When side effects began to appear, Susan plotted an escape. Well, it wasn't much of a plot. She bought herself a plane ticket, drove to the airport, and just like that, she was gone. She flew across the country in something of a trance, her mind oddly focused on getting back to her old place in Boston without being detected, either by anybody in California or by Mike Finley. Because somehow, in her head, she had decided nothing worse would happen if she stayed hidden, if nobody could find her to tell her about it. So she took pains to slip into her apartment unnoticed, and she holed herself up, for the first day or so not even turning on her phone or even bothering to charge it. She spent hours either staring blankly at the TV or curled up in bed with the blinds closed and a pillow over her head, or she'd stare up at cracks in the ceiling and the cobwebs that had taken over the corners of the room. Every now and then she'd hear a baby crying overhead, and she recalled the upstairs neighbor who had told her about finding out she was pregnant. It seemed like it happened in another lifetime. Or she'd hear the old lady who lived downstairs shouting at her callers to speak up already. She heard Mike leave for work one morning and then, through the peephole in her front door, watched as he returned home drunk, it seemed, because he fumbled with his keys as he tried to unlock the door. She ate whatever canned items she had left behind—strange combinations like sardines and French-cut green beans or dry tuna and baby peas. Nothing seemed to have any taste.

One night, she couldn't sleep and stood at the open window, wondering what would happen if she jumped. Then she contemplated swallowing the whole bottle of sleeping pills she found in a bathroom drawer. Also, she drank. She drank a lot, and that helped numb things, first what was left of liquor bottles dug from the back of cabinets. She found two bottles of Cabernet in the bedroom closet. She couldn't recall where they came from, but through the course of the night, she polished off both.

In the morning came a pounding on the front door almost as fierce as the pounding between her ears. Susan found herself all tangled up in a blanket on the living room couch and made no move to untangle herself, figuring whoever it was would give up and go away. But then there was the rattle of a key in the lock. The front door flew open, and there stood the building manager, a tentative look on his face, as if he expected to find a dead body. Behind him was Edith Vale. The manager, always rather slovenly, looked even more wretched next to Edie, who was impeccably turned out in beige slacks with a crease that could slice meat, a blue sweater set, sensible flats, and a handsome Chanel jacket she'd been wearing ever since Susan knew her. Clutched before her was that big, sturdy Hermès pocketbook that always seemed to say, "Get out of my way, I know what I'm doing, and I'm prepared for any emergency."

Susan considered dashing into the bathroom and locking the door. Instead, she shouted, "Who said you could just barge in here?!"

"She told me she was family," said the building manager, already shrinking, it seemed to Susan, under Mrs. Vale's steely gaze.

"She is my former mother-in-law. We are not even related by blood."

"Thank you, sir. You may now leave," Edie said to the manager with such authority he quickly backed away, almost bowing, and then retreated.

"Okay. Pack up and come with me," Edie said once he had shut the door behind him.

"Oh, screw yourself, Edie. You've been ordering me around since the second I met you."

"First of all, there is no need for that sort of language."

"We're in my house now. I can say what I want."

Edie took a quick survey of the room, and Susan felt herself flush with embarrassment. The place, a wreck before she left for California, had deteriorated even further. She'd done nothing since she arrived to clean it up. But all Edie said was "Second of all, I have not ordered you around."

"Oh no? Really? You practically ordered me to marry your son."

"For God's sake, Susan, you were pregnant."

"It was going to be your way or no way, and you took advantage—you knew I was too weak to fight you." These words came flowing out, a torrent. She sounded like she'd gone mad. Maybe she had. She wasn't sure of anything anymore.

Edith was silent for what seemed like forever. Finally, she said, "If you want to abandon your son again, that's fine, Susan. But at least have the decency to tell him." She turned and walked out of the apartment.

Susan wanted to follow. But as much as she tried, she couldn't seem to make her limbs move.

***

Later, Susan was able to track Edie down, which didn't turn out to be all that difficult. She picked the one hotel that had been around since forever, the Parker House, called it, and asked to be connected to Mrs. Vale's room. When they started to put her through, she hung up the phone. For the first time in days, she stripped down and stood under the shower. She threw on clean clothes, brushed her hair, then pulled it back in a ponytail.

She found Edie in the bar at the Parker House, intermittently sipping from a Manhattan and taking bites from a hefty slice of Boston cream pie.

"Yes, yes, I know it's an odd combination," Edie said when she noticed Susan had arrived and was staring. "But I wanted to see if it was still as scrumptious as it was years ago when Evangeline and I came to Boston with our father."

"Is it?" Susan asked.

"Indeed it is," Edie said, without hesitation. "Not that much else is as good as it used to be. Like air travel. Oh my God. What a nightmare flying here. Mind you, I can recall the days when one was served a hot meal on real china and then was tucked in for a nap with blankets and big fluffy pillows on long flights. In fact, I decided on this horrid flight that if I never leave California again, I'll be just fine, thank you. You can have air travel. I am just all done with it."

Edie said that with such finality Susan knew she'd stick to it. Indeed, she had trouble imagining Edith Vale among the hordes she had encountered at the airport, too many people toting too much stuff and the bewildering slog through security.

"Anyway," Susan said, "can I sit?"

"Suit yourself," said Edie tartly.

Susan took a seat. "I'm sorry for what I said. I'm just a mess."

"Apology accepted." Edie nudged the dessert plate just slightly in Susan's direction and handed her the fork. Susan took a bite. It was good, layers of moist white cake and dense, eggy pastry cream, all covered in rich, dark ganache. Not just good, it was comforting, like a warm embrace. She ate more, knowing Edie would only allow herself a few bites anyway.

"How did you find me anyway?"

"Oh, for Heaven's sake, Susan, you used Henry's laptop to buy your plane ticket. It took him all of five seconds."

"Does he hate me?"

"Of course he doesn't. Sons may often dislike their mothers. Sometimes intensely, I would imagine. Lord knows I can drive Andrew absolutely mad at times. But you've run away from him before. I won't let you do it now."

"Well, at least you still hate me, I guess."

"What makes you say a thing like that?"

"You've never cared for me, Edith. Why don't you just admit it?"

"That's not true."

"It's not? You never wanted me to be part of Andrew's life. You made it clear from the time he first brought me home."

"It wasn't that I didn't like you."

"Well, what was it? Because you criticized everything I did. You made me feel dumb and foolish and really inept."

"Because you were, dear."

Susan just stared at Edie.

"Oh, come on," Edith said. "You were young. Everybody is foolish and inept at that stage of the game. My son included. Neither of you were ready for marriage or a child. I was wrong if I made you feel bad. But in some ways I was right."

Susan rubbed at her temples. She looked around at the crowd in the Parker House bar. Everybody was so swank, smiling and laughing and dressed just right, like they didn't have a care in the world, and Susan silently wished she could trade places with any of them. Edith paid her bill, grabbed her pocketbook, and stood.

"I need some air. Come along, dear." It was more of an order than a request.

Susan followed Edie toward the exit.

Outside, Edie pulled her pack of Parliaments from her bag. Susan grabbed one too. She leaned toward Edie, and their foreheads almost knocked as Edie ignited the flame of her little gold lighter. They made their way to Beacon Street, smoking in silence for a few minutes before Edie said, "You asked if I hated you? But you couldn't have been further from the truth, Susan. The truth is I've always sort of admired you."

"Oh, please. What for?"

"I don't know. You had more opportunities than I had. Or maybe it's just you took advantage of the opportunities more.

You went places. You have a career you can be proud of. You're just so, well, free. To do almost anything. The truth is that women like me—like Oatsie and Evelyn and Tish and me—women like us—we were raised to be a certain way. We never really adapted to all the changes that sprang up all around us. Or maybe we just didn't want to or we were afraid of change because—let's be honest—change is scary. The truth is I struggle sometimes now because I feel sort of irrelevant really. Like my life hasn't meant much."

"I love women like you," said Susan.

"Oh, stop."

"No, it's true. You have manners. You have great taste. In everything. There are things you can do like nobody else."

"Like what?"

"Well, your garden, for one. I've watched you work back there. You know how to make stuff grow. It all seems effortless, but it's not. Or, like writing a proper thank-you note? On pretty blue stationery. With just the right words to make a person feel special. Or a fun little sketch to make somebody smile. That's a talent, if you ask me. Nobody knows how to do things like that anymore. Maybe some would say that doesn't matter. But maybe it does."

"Well, you might have a point there. Honestly, I don't really know if I understand the world as it is now. And don't get me started on Henry's. But once us girls are gone, I'm not sure anybody will notice or even care about the things we cared about. I don't know if anybody will really miss us."

"I will," Susan said, and Edie smiled.

They had reached the gates to the Common. Inside the park, trees had shed their leaves. They now stood all naked, spindly, and frail-looking in air that was taking on the crisp chill of autumn. Joggers were bundled up, as were mothers pushing strollers, as was one elderly couple walking slowly, arm in arm, their breath rising in small wispy clouds.

"Should we go into the park?" Susan asked Edie.

"I think you should go and get your things. We'll fly home to California together."

"I'm afraid to go back," Susan said.

"Well, maybe we're more alike than we think."

"How?"

"Because," Edie said, "that makes two of us. But we'll go as a team, and all will be well."

She turned and started toward the hotel. Susan had no choice but to follow.

***

Back in Pasadena, Susan became determined to be the best mother ever. She cut back her hours at the restaurant. She ferried Henry to and from his doctor's appointments. She cooked all his favorite foods. She peppered him with questions: Are you too hot? Do you need a sweater? Are you dehydrated? Is the house too cold? Should we try to see a movie?

"Mom, you have to chill," Henry finally said one morning when he mentioned that his eggs were a little runny and she tossed them to Edie's dogs and started to make a new batch before he could say he was kidding.

She just stared at him for a long moment.

"What?" Henry finally asked.

"You called me Mom. You haven't done that in ages."

"Oops. What the hell was I thinking? Sorry, Susan."

"I just want you to be happy, sweetheart."

"In the time I have left?"

"That's not funny, Henry."

But Henry was smiling at Luz, who had flown down for the weekend and was sitting across from him at the breakfast table next to Evangeline and Blanca. He seemed to like needling Susan. He'd pretend his hearing was failing or that all he could see was shadow, just to test her reaction. Or she'd find him sprawled on the floor as if he'd fallen. Once he pretended she had run over his foot while bringing the car around and she nearly had a heart attack. He certainly seemed to enjoy being the center of attention in her life. Still, she was running herself ragged trying to do it all, until one day a few weeks later, Henry was having a good day after a couple of difficult ones, when all he wanted to do was sleep, and Edith Vale, along with the other members of the Alta Arroyo Women's Club Beautification Team, decided to make Susan their next project.

"Get dressed. You're coming with us" was issued as an order from Edie as Susan was coming out of her room in dirty sweats, her hair unwashed.

Susan could see Evelyn Brookby, Oatsie O'Shea, and Tish Van Buren, each impeccably turned out, with the right purses and the right shoes, waiting in the front hall. "Where are you taking me?"

"You'll see," said Edie.

Before they left, Susan made sure Henry was comfortably situated out back by the pool. She hesitated, not wanting to leave, but Henry insisted. So she kissed the top of his head, and she whispered into his ear that she loved him.

"Yeah, yeah, I love you too. Now go," Henry said.

Susan followed as the ladies piled into Edie's Mercedes for the ride into Old Town. The first stop was the beauty parlor, where there was much animated discussion about what to do about Susan's hair, which apparently Susan had damaged beyond repair after years of neglect, exposing it to the constant heat and steam and grease of all those restaurant kitchens.

Susan dug in her heels and wouldn't allow Bruce to cut off more than an inch. She agreed to some deep conditioning, and okay, a little color to cover up the grey, but that's where she drew the line. So she joined the other ladies at the washing stations, and as she leaned back so her hair could be properly cleaned, she listened to the chatter of Edie and her friends, submitted to a massage of her neck and scalp, and nearly fell into a blissful sleep. When Bruce finished with her hair, it was cleaner and darker but pulled back and secured at the nape of her neck in a ponytail. Also, it had an almost luxurious sheen to it, which she had to admit she liked. All the ladies had their hair just so—Evelyn and Oatsie in freshened bouffants, and Tish and Edie in tidy ponytails secured with a bow, like Susan. Slowly, it seemed, she was turning into one of them, like in some strange alternate-universe horror movie where victims turned more beautiful and elegant.

Next came manicures and pedicures for all, after which they all piled back into Edie's Mercedes and drove to the mall. There, the ladies picked out a tasteful suit and insisted Susan try it on. It was a wool blend in charcoal grey with a skirt that fell just below the knee and a fitted jacket with big brass buttons.

When she emerged from the dressing room, Evelyn Brookby said, breathlessly, "Oh, darling, it's just stunning."

"Marvelous!" said Oatsie O'Shea. "If I could only get Cis to put something like that on, but all she seems to favor are blue jeans and plaid flannel."

Tish smiled broadly, nodding her approval.

"Now you look like a proper lady," added Edith Vale.

Susan stepped before a three-way mirror and at first wasn't sure who it was looking back. "Here's the thing. I'd never wear it," she protested to the ladies, who wanted her to buy not only that one but another in a flattering shade of pink. Susan assuaged them all by purchasing some new jeans and a couple of rather conservative tops.

They followed the shopping expedition with lunch back in Old Town at some joint Susan didn't even know existed, which appeared to be frozen in a time capsule, a dimly lit space with roomy red leather booths, dark wood paneling, salty waitresses just this side of elderly who wore too much rouge and bright lipstick, and hanging everywhere, the kind of potted ferns nobody had seen in forty years. They all ordered steak sandwiches, the petite cut, it was called—a thick fillet plunked down on a slab of garlic toast—and washed them down with icy martinis, up with olives, each served in its own little shaker with sidecars for the overflow, a touch Susan loved. By the second one, Susan was feeling all flushed, warm, and at least for the moment, at ease with the world. She looked at Edie and her friends as they gossiped and hurled zingers at each other, one of the barbs causing them all to laugh so hard that Evelyn Brookby screamed that she was going to tinkle right there in the booth, and that made them all laugh even harder, which sent Evelyn racing to the ladies' room.

Some people, Susan thought, would probably think these women were shallow or silly. All they seemed to do was eat, shop, and drink like sailors. But Susan could tell they loved each other deeply, had bonds that went back decades, and for the first time, she was envious; nobody had friendships like this anymore, it seemed. It took too much time, was too much work. Anyway, the outing was exactly what Susan needed, a totally restorative day. She felt better than she had in weeks. She promised, when Tish Van Buren asked, that one day she would join them again.

***

And while they were gone, Henry died. He was by Edie's pool, bathed in the warmth of the midday sun, the dogs on either side curled up beside him, Luz sunning herself in a chaise just a foot or so away. He had told Luz he might take a short nap. He never woke up. All Susan knew was that when she and Edie arrived back at the house, there was a police cruiser, an ambulance, and there was Andrew, his face ashen. Blanca was wringing her hands, her eyes swollen and red. Luz wouldn't dare look at Susan. Out of the corner of her eye, Susan could see a ghostlike Evangeline peering out from a second-floor window.

Andrew opened his mouth. He wanted to say something, she could tell, but he struggled for words. What came out was some strange, strangled sound, like you might hear from a wounded animal.

She didn't need to be told anyway. Because mothers just knew these things. From out of nowhere came the urge to run.

She turned and sprinted back down the driveway. She ran nearly as far as the next town of Altadena. She was aware of people staring and dogs barking, of traffic all around her, of a bus filled with passengers passing in a haze of exhaust, of all the people going about their business as if nothing was wrong. She kept running until she finally had to stop because it felt as if her heart was going to burst right through her chest.

***

Later, of course, Susan had to know every detail. "Did he say anything?" she asked Luz about those last minutes.

"Just that he was sleepy and was going to take a nap," Luz answered.

"He didn't wake up at all. You're absolutely sure?"

"No."

"Didn't ask for anything? Scream out in pain?"

Luz shook her head.

The doctors wanted to look inside and see what happened too, and Susan and Andrew, exhausted already from all the details and questions, gave their okay, and secretly Susan wanted to know too, needed to be told it wasn't her fault and that she wasn't to blame. They discovered the tumor had pressed on one of the vessels that supplied blood to the brain. The blood vessel burst. So, a stroke. Which struck Susan as odd, like Henry was an old man. It couldn't be. Did they make a mistake, she wondered? Would it make a difference? And even though they said nothing could have been done, Susan just couldn't let go of the fact that she wasn't there, that she had let him down again, one final time, and now there was no chance to atone for it.

Until Edie said, "Well, you know, Susan, maybe he wanted you to go off with me and the girls."

"What? Why?"

"Because these last few weeks, you were hovering. You barely left his side. He knew what was coming, and he wanted to spare you."

"Do you really believe that?"

"It was an act of charity," said Edie. "Yes."

Edie said it so firmly, with such conviction, that Susan decided she must be right.

***

There followed a day or so of trying to figure out what to do. Should they bury Henry? Edie's grandfather had long ago bought a plot in a cemetery that, all those years ago, was quite the place to be, apparently, if you had the good luck to expire in the still mostly raw, wild Southern California, but over the years, it had been under siege by surrounding development and, quite frankly, not the sort of neighbors one would truly desire for eternity, Edie admitted now.

"I mean, I don't even want to be buried there," she said as they sat around her kitchen table the next morning debating the matter.

"I would like to be shot into outer space," said Evangeline.

"Of course you would, dear," said Edie, humoring her sister, who had yet to grasp that Henry was gone and kept asking when he'd be coming back.

Then Susan found a sort of journal on Henry's laptop. At first she wasn't sure she should be reading what were surely private thoughts. Then she came upon a section that startled her.

"Okay, what do you suppose this means?" she asked Andrew and Edie, who were with her in Henry's room as they searched for something to bring to the funeral home for Henry to wear. "Here's a file that says 'Open When I'm Toast.'"

"Well, open it," said Andrew.

Inside was evidence that Henry was the son of a trusts and estates lawyer. He had thought things through. He didn't want to be buried but cremated. He had seen at the beach a paddle out, a sort of memorial to lost surfers. He wanted something like that. Or they could scatter his ashes in the sea.

They decided on a brief service at the Episcopal church in town. There were the appropriate hymns, chosen by Mrs. Vale, and a reading from Anne Steele's "Psalm 147," which Edie insisted Henry loved, but Susan suspected it was actually one of Edie's favorites.

The thick descending flakes of snow
O'er earth a fleecy mantle throw;
And glittering frost o'er all the plains

Binds nature fast in icy chains.
He speaks: the ice and snow obey,
And nature's fetters melt away;
Softly the vernal breezes blow,
And murm'ring waters freely flow.

Zach Julian, who flew in from the East Coast, all natty in his blue blazer and chinos, stammered through a short speech about losing not just his best friend but, well, his only friend. He turned beet red and stared at his loafers when those words elicited laughter. Frank said a few words and so did Andrew. Susan sat quietly and just listened, silently praying that Henry had forgiven her for all the mistakes she had made.

Later, they all gathered on a boat that belonged to a friend of Andrew's. They cruised to a spot not far off the coast from Trancas, a place Henry always loved. They huddled at the boat's stern and tossed the ashes into the sea. Susan watched as, at first, they seemed to coalesce into a form that looked oddly wraithlike, like a whole human again, and then, as the tide bobbed up and down, they slowly dispersed. She watched until she could see them no more.

Afterward, everybody returned to Edie's house by the beach—there was food and lots to drink—but Susan headed outside and planted herself on the sand. Soon she was joined by Edie. They both watched waves tumbling in.

"You know, it occurs to me," Susan said, "that there was a time he was afraid of the water."

"Yes," said Edie. "I remember that."

"You threw him into your pool."

"Of course I did. And after that, he was no longer afraid. In fact, he adored it."

Susan nodded. It was true. "You always knew just the right thing to do."

"Well," Edie said, "not always. But if I didn't, I pretended."

"You know what I'm afraid of?" Susan asked. "I'm afraid I'll forget him. I'm afraid that the more time passes, the more my memory of him will fade away too, and I won't be able to stop it."

Edith regarded Susan for a long moment. "That won't happen. But you know, for me anyway, there is something positive."

"Is there?"

"When my time comes, I'll be ready. Because I'll see him again."

"Do you really believe that, Edie?"

"It's a consolation."

Susan nodded. It wasn't a complete answer, but it worked for now.

Edie stood, brushing sand off her slacks. "Are you coming in?"

"In a bit."

Susan continued to sit on the beach, even though people kept showing up to check on her.

"Can I make you a cup of tea?" asked Linda.

"How about a jacket?" This came from Andrew, the twins hovering and hiding behind his legs.

Susan told them all she was fine. There was something soothing, in fact, about being out here. She watched a woman in a sarong jog behind two galloping golden retrievers. She watched lanky guys in wet suits, longboards tucked under their arms, lope toward the shimmering surf. Gulls circled overhead in search of stray crumbs. Way out in the distance, a sailboat passed lazily this way and then that. But then the sun started to set, and Susan felt a chill. She stood and started toward the house, but something caught her eye, an incongruous sight on the beach, a tall man, chunky, in a blue suit and black shoes. A cop, or some government agent of some kind, she figured. Why was he walking with such a sense of purpose, though?

She wondered if she had left her car in that no-parking zone or had accidentally dropped a piece of litter. Then, he got closer and she saw it was Mike Finley, that he had that look on his face that people had the last few days, as if they weren't sure if it was okay to smile.

"Sorry, babe," he said when he was right in front of her. "I hoped to make it for the service. But there were storms over the Midwest. Tornados too. Planes have been backed up all the way to O'Hare."

"It's nice that you tried," said Susan.

"Actually, I pulled a few strings. It helps to have an air traffic controller on the plane. Most people don't know that. I did manage to get us bumped up a few slots. Just not enough."

Susan pictured airliners reconfiguring themselves in the sky so Mike's could pass on by. She found it somehow reassuring.

"I knew you had come back to town," he said.

"Why didn't you knock on my door?"

"I wanted to. By the time I got up the nerve, you were gone."

Susan looked back at Edie's little house, hunkered down between the two giant ones on either side, both of which were dark. But people filled the cottage. Lights had come on. She could smell a fire burning in the hearth.

"You want me to make you something to eat?" she asked.

"Yeah," said Mike. "That would be good."

She reached for his hand, and together they headed for the house.

XIX.

The weary travelers were just looking for a quick bite to eat. After all, there were two cranky children in the backseat under the age of five. Any old fast food would do, said the mother to the father, who was behind the wheel. What they didn't know is that this town in Sonoma County had long ago banned chain restaurants of any kind, even the ones with overpriced cups of specialty coffee.

"How about there?" said the father when he spotted the one neon sign that said simply "Eat Here."

"It's attached to a gas station," said his wife, almost instinctively reaching for her sanitizing gel before he even slowed the rental.

"Yeah, well, I read somewhere that's where you find some of the best joints in the country."

His wife looked dubious. But if those kids didn't get some food soon, it would be meltdown time in a very big way. So they parked in the small gravel lot of what appeared to be an old-time roadhouse and trooped inside. Surely a positive sign, the husband silently reasoned, was that the place was jammed. Just off the entrance was a cozy little bar. The restaurant itself was long and narrow, like an old railroad car. There was a counter set before an open kitchen, a woodburning oven taking up one corner. But every stool at the counter was taken. Booths lined the other side of the space, but each one was filled. A back wall was all perfectly cut firewood, simply stacked floor to ceiling. There was a happy buzz to the place, thick with the aroma of sizzling bacon and of burgers and steaks cooking over fragrant red oak. A woman was pulling something from the woodburning oven, a fresh loaf of bread. She looked cool and efficient in her crisp whites, her dark hair pulled back tight in a ponytail, an apron precisely cinched at her waist.

Susan Jones sometimes looked in the mirror and could read the last two years like a book, in the little creases that were forming around her eyes, in the more copious amount of grey creeping into her hair.

"There's a booth about to open up in the corner," she said to the waiting family, pointing with her spatula, annoyed, because where had that greeter gotten off to again?

Well, she wasn't the regular one. She was filling in for the woman who was sick. But still. Susan set her spatula down, asked her sous to take over at the grill, and headed for the screen door in back.

"You're supposed to be greeting and seating," Susan said, because there was Edith Vale, perched on the trunk of her Mercedes, smoking a Parliament, one leg crossed over the other, that leg swinging back and forth like a schoolgirl's as Frank Entrekin was unloading the week's order of cheese from the back of his truck.

"She is a total boss from hell," said Edie to Frank. "It's no wonder people keep quitting on you."

Susan had been the first one to move north.

For once, she wasn't running away. This time she was running toward something. Mike Finley had finally gotten his promotion to supervisor and was transferred to an FAA command center outside Oakland.

"Yes. Let's do it," she answered when he said he loved her and they should get married, surprising even herself, because rarely before did she know so quickly what she wanted.

Meanwhile, Edie mentioned to Oatsie O'Shea that Susan was moving north, and Oatsie said, "Make sure she calls Cis. She and that . . . wife . . . just bought some run-down old restaurant in Sonoma. They don't have a clue."

It was indeed run-down, a rambling old greasy spoon that Cis and her partner bought when they grew bored of the antique shop in Sebastopol. The building began its life, according to local legend, as a whorehouse, and Susan found that amusing. She was hired to get the kitchen up and running. She wrote a menu, deciding to keep things simple, drawing heavily on local ingredients, on the bounty of produce and meats, seafood and dairy that were right at her doorstep, and the less she did to them, she decided, the better. She added some favorite recipes she'd been honing over the years, a rich, creamy macaroni and cheese, and collard greens she'd learned to make during a stint in the South. She created a bar menu of little plates and snacks—crisp arancini, sliders, deviled eggs, and just-shucked oysters fresh from Tomales Bay. She added fries cooked in duck fat and then house-made charcuterie.

Then there was the old file box from Edie's kitchen, which Susan had begun raiding earlier in Pasadena and which yielded more unexpected treasures the more she looked, including a recipe for croquettes that customers went mad over, the old-fashioned sort rarely seen on menus anymore that began with a thick béchamel and then included folding in minced-up chicken or ham or fish. The mixture would cool, then be shaped into small, torpedo-like ovals that would be dusted with flour, dipped in an egg wash, and coated with bread crumbs. After a quick dunk in the deep fryer, the croquettes came out crunchy on the outside and creamy on the inside. Sometimes Susan would tuck special treats in the middle, like a hunk of aged cheddar inside the ham croquettes that would get all melty. Of course, in the old wooden box, the croquettes were filed, Susan could never figure out why, under H, and just behind that recipe, again for some unfathomable reason, she found one for a fried chicken that was marinated for twenty-four hours in a zesty brine, and chile rellenos from some long-forgotten source, this one most likely filed under H because Edie had scribbled "Hot as blazes!" across the top. Susan started turning the file box recipes into weekly specials, and a fast-growing stable of regulars would line up early.

When Cis and her partner grew tired of the restaurant business, Susan went to the bank, filled out reams of paperwork, secured a somewhat scary loan, and bought the place. When it was actually hers, she decided to turn the weedy yard in back into a garden, so when she needed herbs or whatever vegetables she was raising, all she had to do is step out the back door.

Then Edie appeared at the little Craftsman that Susan and Mike Finley were renting in Healdsburg, her King Charles spaniels in tow. She had gone through a rough patch. First, Evelyn Brookby climbed into her huge Lincoln Continental one morning after they all had their appointment at the beauty parlor, waved gaily goodbye, made one bad turn—she wasn't paying attention or that growing sense of being slightly befuddled all the time had finally taken root—and she wound up driving in the wrong direction on the Pasadena Freeway, dodging oncoming high-speed traffic for almost a whole mile, the CHP said, until she finally careened off the road and smashed into the support pillar of an overpass. Shortly after her funeral, a newly widowed Tish Van Buren was on the golf course when she took a tumble and threw out a hand to break her fall. She fractured her wrist was all, but the doctors wanted to keep her overnight in the hospital because her blood pressure was fluctuating, and while she was there, she picked up a nasty infection. Rapidly, her condition deteriorated. Edie went to visit, a box of See's Candies in hand, along with a spray of wildflowers from Tish's garden casually arranged in a little basket, and was confronted not with her friend, all put-together and made-up and elegant, but a shrunken, very frightened old woman who beseeched her to get her out of there, to get her home.

"Don't be silly, you'll be up and about in no time," Edie trilled, but Tish died two days later in the middle of the night, all alone in unfamiliar surroundings.

Edie remained composed until she went to Tish's house and saw the evidence of how quickly it could all go wrong; there on the kitchen counter was Tish's somewhat mundane to-do list for later in the day after golf: "Pick up cleaning. Defrost chicken. Gutters? Cash for maid." Oh, it wasn't the list that set Edie off. It was when she opened the refrigerator. Tish had also set aside a postgame treat, one small cupcake that sat waiting to be devoured, such a simple little anticipated pleasure, now shriveling and starting to form a crust of fuzzy green mold. She burst into tears, slammed the refrigerator shut, and got on with picking an outfit for Tish to wear in the casket.

At the funeral, she and Oatsie O'Shea huddled close to each other, hands clutched together, but deep down they both knew that even if they put up a united front, they couldn't ward off the inevitable forever. So shortly thereafter, Edie got in her car and drove north, claiming she needed a change of scenery, but she was really scared out of her wits that something awful would happen to her too if she stayed in Pasadena. Susan and Mike gave her the spare room, but Edie decided to stay for a while up north—she found she actually relished the change. It popped into her mind, she later said, that, at well into her seventies now, it was time to finally leave the only house she had really known. She turned it over to the care of Andrew and Linda, who had repaired what was broken between them and moved in with the twins. She knew they'd make changes, but it didn't seem to matter. She had asked Blanca if she'd like to come, and when she said she would, Edith Vale made another decision: She decided that Blanca was done with work, just all through with it. She would remain a sort of companion to Evangeline in the small house Edie rented, but Edie hired somebody new to look after them all, and sometimes, like today, Edie would help out Susan at the restaurant. If she wasn't needed, she'd survey Susan's garden. She'd point out all she was doing wrong and then set about trying to make it right. Or she'd pop by to pick up the filtered vegetable oil for her Mercedes.

"You want what?" Susan had asked when Edie first mentioned she'd take the used oil off her hands.

"I let Frank convert my diesel to run on used veggie oil. Now not only do I never have to buy gas, but I'm doing something for the planet." She said this, all smiles, wearing her new green label like a badge of honor, blithely forgetting a lifetime spent being wasteful.

Susan told Edie she could help herself to all the oil she wanted. Meanwhile, she was curious about all the time Edie seemed to be spending with her ex-husband. She often could be found at Frank's, helping out with the goats or doing other chores. One time, after loads of coaxing, she even went up with Frank in his old Piper Saratoga. Edie later told Susan how thrilling it was to fly over the valley, swooping down past vineyards and farms, circling lush green hills where happy cows grazed, and then zipping over toward the coast, bursting through a cloud over the blustery bay, Frank so dashing at the controls.

Finally, Susan asked, "What's really going on with you two? Because the last I heard you never wanted his name mentioned in your presence again or something like that."

"Oh, well, that was just a dumb misunderstanding," Edie said. "I was irritated because he didn't call me one particular night, but when I learned he was in the emergency room because of his angina, I forgave him."

"I see," said Susan.

"You know, it was just indigestion. These things happen to people our age. One little piece of raw onion and you're certain you're dying. Anyway, we're not really dating formally, mind you. We're just F-buds."

"What?" said Susan.

"You know, friends with benefits."

"Edith, do you know what that even means?"

"I'm not an idiot, Susan. It means sometimes, if we can summon up the energy, we sleep together." And then, off Susan's look, she added, "And when I say sleep, I do mean mostly sleep. Because some might say, 'Oh, you know, sex gets better with age,' but honestly, they're just lying. Do not believe one word those people say. Sex is for young people, if you ask me."

Susan's mouth opened but nothing came out.

Edie continued, "Listen, dear, my advice is get it while you can. Young, supple bodies. That's the ticket. It's not pretty when people get wrinkled and saggy in all the wrong places."

"Okay. Right," said Susan, when she regained her equilibrium after a near outburst of laughter.

For the longest time, she thought she'd never laugh again. Eventually, the ability to do so returned, although always there would be a lingering sense of sadness, she supposed, just beneath the surface, even though she could hardly cry over

Henry, no matter how hard she tried, not when she last saw his face at the funeral home, not at the service at the church, and not when they scattered the ashes into the sea. Later, tears came, always at odd times, when she wasn't prepared. Like the day she was still in Southern California. She had been approached by producers to audition for a pilot for some competition cooking show. She was halfway through her portion of the pilot when she caught sight of some kid in the audience. He had shaggy hair, glasses, and big ears, and before Susan knew it, she was sobbing, big heaving sobs, so that the producers looked at her with alarm. She fled from the studio and never looked back, which she figured was the beginning and the end of any career she might have on television. These days, when she looked around her restaurant or out at the garden or thought about how she was considering a chicken coop or how it felt to have Mike snoring away next to her, it didn't seem important.

"By the way, F-buds?" Susan said to Edie now. "Where do you hear this stuff?"

"It may appear like I'm ancient, dear, like I'm just some silly old lady. But that doesn't mean I don't know any young people."

"Okay," Susan said and figured she was picking up new bits of lingo from Luz.

Within a year of Henry's death, Luz had given birth.

For the first few hours of the life of Henry Andrew Guttierez-Entrekin, nobody knew about him. Luz hadn't told a soul about the pregnancy. At first this was because she was mostly just stunned. They had been careful, had taken precautions, she and Henry. She wasn't stupid. The last thing she wanted was a baby. Once the initial shock wore off, she went to church. She confessed her sins. The priest assured Luz that God loved her, that the future was in his hands, and that all would work out for the best. He suggested Scripture for her to study, and asked for three Hail Marys. Luz had more pressing concerns. She had turned nineteen, but just barely. She had the end of her freshman year in sight and had decided on summer classes to prepare her for declaring premed as her major. Although she had a scholarship, she was working part time as well. So she set God, penance, and contrition aside, at least temporarily, and considered her options. She could terminate the pregnancy. There was adoption. She wavered back and forth between the two, but there was also a part of her that wanted to keep this baby, because even though Henry was gone, he had been a part of her life since forever. She found she missed him more than she could have imagined, and she wondered about what kind of God would take him away so young.

So as she thickened at the middle, eating everything in sight, gaining weight by the day, she managed to keep her condition hidden—from her roommate, a sullen girl from back east who spent most of her time in the library anyway, from the few friends she had made so far—at least, she figured, until she made a decision about what to do. This continued almost until the first pangs of labor, and then Luz broke down and confided to her sister Elena back in Los Angeles, who told their mother, who told Blanca, who told Mrs. Vale, who got the news as she was about to take the first sip of the evening's first Manhattan and, realizing this would make her a *great*-grand-mother, dropped the drink to the floor and passed out cold. A few minutes later, after shooing Blanca away and tidying up the mess herself, fresh drink in hand, Edie called Andrew and Susan.

Soon the whole lot of them converged on the hospital, and though there was consternation and tears and a little bit of anguish, they all marveled at the perfect little boy, all swaddled up and sleeping soundly in the crib, the boy Luz had already nicknamed Hank. Luz adored this tiny creature, with his hair like hers the color of ink, but with what seemed to be Henry's eyes and somewhat large ears, marveled at his little toes and his fingers and his perfect little nose, but she was smart enough to know she couldn't handle things alone. She wasn't even remotely ready to be a full-time mother, nor was she ready to give up the goals she had long ago set for herself.

"What if we brought him here?" Susan had said to Mike Finley that next morning as she stirred eggs in a skillet and poked at sausages on the grill.

"Who where, kid?"

"Hank. To live. Luz and I talked about it. She will stay in school. She's going to be a doctor, you know. She'll come out every weekend. Plus whatever weeknights she can manage."

Mike finally looked up from the game he had recorded. "Who will be the baby's mother?"

Susan rolled her eyes. Sometimes Mike could be so clueless, and it occasionally got on her nerves. Still, she was learning to be more tolerant of these things. "Luz is his mother. That will never change. We all know that. I'm his . . ." She broke off abruptly, feeling as if she might have to suppress a scream. It was a second before she could continue. "I'm his grandmother. Anyway, I'm just saying somehow we'll all pitch in and make it work, but I guess some of it we'll figure out as we go along."

"Well, whatever you want, babe. I told you. I dig rug rats."

In fact, Mike went on to become a favorite napping spot, Hank sprawled on his belly as both snored away. So their house became the baby's primary home, at least for the time being. When Edie moved north with Evangeline and Blanca, they began pitching in too. Soon, this baby had at least three women competing for his attention, some of them determined to right past wrongs, feeling renewed, as if a second chance was truly within reach.

Now, Susan and Edie stood in the parking lot of Susan's restaurant with Frank and watched as Luz's car made the turn off the road. They spotted Hank strapped into his car seat in back. Susan got a head start toward the car, smiling wide, arms outstretched, but Edith Vale was coming up fast, a determined glint in her eyes, and she looked like she just might elbow Susan out of the way. As they got closer, Luz's first thought was that these women were just out of their minds. But when she looked back at Hank, he was smiling and laughing, and she was almost one hundred percent certain that this time he wasn't just trying to pass a little gas.

ABOUT THE AUTHOR

Photo © 2016 Steven Murashige

Jason Pomerance was born in New York City, grew up in Westchester County, and graduated from Middlebury College. He lives in Los Angeles with his partner and their beagles. He has written film and television projects for numerous studios and production companies, including Warner Bros., Columbia Pictures, FremantleMedia, and Gold Circle Films. *Women Like Us* is his first novel.

LIST OF PATRONS

This book was made possible in part by the following grand patrons who preordered the book on inkshares.com. Thank you.

Amanda Orneck
Catherine S. Funk
Charles Dickinson
David Podber
Don and Joanna Harlan
Elaine Haney
Joe Destro
Kathy S. Pomerantz
Lisa Bramante
Marcia Pomerance
Mark Gunsky
Matthew Isaac Sobin
Nina Tullett
Paula Diamond
Sal Ladestro
Sidney Sherman

Quill

Quill is an imprint of Inkshares, a crowdfunded book publisher. We democratize publishing by having readers select the books we publish—we edit, design, print, distribute, and market any book that meets a pre-order threshold.

Interested in making a book idea come to life? Visit inkshares.com to find new book projects or to start your own.